To Sheila & Rex

Thanks for the many, many years of friendship & support.

My imagination's come a long way since 7th grade — or has it.

Best wishes,
Rick

6-24-06

The Conflicted Liberal

Richard A. Schwartz

Copyright © 2006 by Richard A. Schwartz

All rights reserved. No part of this book shall be reproduced or transmitted in any form or by any means, electronic, mechanical, magnetic, photographic including photocopying, recording or by any information storage and retrieval system, without prior written permission of the publisher. No patent liability is assumed with respect to the use of the information contained herein. Although every precaution has been taken in the preparation of this book, the publisher and author assume no responsibility for errors or omissions. Neither is any liability assumed for damages resulting from the use of the information contained herein.

This is a work of fiction. Names, characters, places, and incidents either are the product of the author's imagination or are used fictitiously. Any resemblance to actual events or locales or persons, living or dead, is entirely coincidental.

ISBN 0-7414-3196-3

Cover art: *The Pie-throwers* by Richard A. Schwartz

Published by:

1094 New DeHaven Street, Suite 100
West Conshohocken, PA 19428-2713
Info@buybooksontheweb.com
www.buybooksontheweb.com
Toll-free (877) BUY BOOK
Local Phone (610) 941-9999
Fax (610) 941-9959

Printed in the United States of America
Printed on Recycled Paper
Published June 2006

Disclaimer

With the exception of Thomas Pynchon, who is a greatly accomplished and much respected novelist, all of the characters in this novel are fictional and bear no resemblance to actual persons, living or dead. The actions and statements of the character Thomas Pynchon in this novel are fictional, made up for the purposes of the story, and do not necessarily reflect the actual sentiments or activities of the real Thomas Pynchon, whose imagination and energetic writing were an inspiration.

Dedication

To my still-flourishing teachers, Professors Sara Deats, John Cawelti, and William Veeder, to the memories of Professors Joseph Bentley, John Camp, Arthur Heiserman, Sheldon Sacks, and Hamlin Hill

And to the memory of my dear friend and colleague, Professor Peggy Endel

Chapter 1

I remember the first time like a dream: walking out of Sharon's apartment with Mighty Mouse and Pocahontas, putting on the homemade cape and then the black trench coat, Pocahontas driving us to campus in an old, gray Toyota Corolla. We enter the room where the speech is already underway and carefully make our way toward the front row. As the crowd cheers the orator, we slip on our masks and slide the trench coats silently from our shoulders. I nod at Mighty Mouse and he nods back. Then we race up to the podium.

    A pair of eyes engages mine. Wide open and suddenly alert, they show stark, uncomprehending terror. A split second later my cream custard explodes against his beefy right cheek, and an instant after that Mighty Mouse's pie pummels his chin.

    Light bulbs flash and people shout as we run past them across the stage and back out to the street, into the waiting car. As Pocahontas roars off across Chicago's south side, Mighty Mouse and I hug each other in the back seat and laugh uproariously. Pocahontas turns onto Lake Shore Drive, and we disappear among the speeding headlights.

    A year and a quarter later now, I lie before the ocean, soaking up the sun in preparation for my incarceration. I am awed by life's utter unpredictability and its incredible, unsuspected powers of rejuvenation. Back then, I felt weary, stale, flat, and unprofitable, lacking in purpose and direction. Divorced by my wife and estranged from my daughter, I made myself unhappy by seeking love from women who had none to give. Now as I prepare for prison, I feel vibrant, yet serene. Whoever would have imagined?

    Back then I watched history from the wings, taking notes

and teaching students. Now, I have made history--no small achievement for a history professor. Not that I'll get much credit in the textbooks, which mostly address large scale conflicts instead of isolated, individual acts by the little people of history, as Burnt Umber calls us. But that's OK. I'll settle for the sense of purpose and loss of fear that Burnt Umber, Tom Pynchon, and Belkis taught me. But I get ahead of myself. No doubt, from this introduction you hardly recognize me.

They call me Killer. They call me Gentle Ben. They say I'm a terrorist, a pacifist, a revolutionary, a martyr, and a saint. That I died in Kuwait, Korea, Kosovo, Bosnia, Mexico, Iraq, and Iran. I'm Benny to my friends. My ex-wife Diane and my daughter Sharon know me as Benjamin Branch. But to the downtrodden masses and the oppressed workers who labor under the boot heel of cutthroat capitalism, the tyranny of communism, or the repression of religious regimes--to these people I am simply the Pie-thrower.

To my knowledge I did not die in Damascus, Chiapas, Beijing, Belgrade, Havana, or Kabul, although I have been spotted in each, along with thirty or forty other trouble spots across the globe. A contemporary Kilroy, I seem to have been everywhere, dying for everyone's sins.

No, not for their sins. I am not Jesus, nor was meant to be. I'm just a poor attendant fool who has been born again in cyberspace, transformed into some postmodern savior who promised the illusion of salvation. And then, much to my amazement, in my own small way I delivered on my promise.

In cyberspace I am indeed like a god: everywhere and nowhere at the same time. Otherwise, I am right here, on 14th Street, in Miami's South Beach, savoring the calm before the storm. How I got here is the thrust of my story.

Where to begin? I suppose I should start with Martina.

At first glance, Martina seemed too good to be true. I suppose she was. I met her at a Fourth of July party last year at the home of a friend who teaches courses like Psychopathic Fiction, Literature of Evil and Redemption, and Narrations Displaced in Time and Space. When I arrived around 7:00, the party was already in full swing. At first glance, it was surprisingly traditional. In fact, it was excruciatingly traditional, right down to the miniature American flags that adorned every fence post surrounding the capacious half-acre lot, every white wooden Corinthian column supporting the second-floor veranda, and the armrest of every lawn chair in Brian Mulligan's back yard. Brian had arranged these folding vinyl chairs in a perfect semi-circle to afford each guest an equally spectacular view of the private fireworks display he planned for later in the evening. He'd wheeled his portable barbeque upwind so everyone would smell the burning hickory chips and hear the hot dogs sizzle as they got soused and waited for the sun to set. Afterward, he intended to raffle off six seats of honor in the "Presidential Box" on the veranda, where the view would be even more exciting. The seats were draped with red, white, and blue bunting, and American flags hung down from the guard rails.

"Privately, I think of it as the Abraham Lincoln box," Brain confided as he pointed to the upstairs seating.

I looked upward. "Who's playing John Wilkes Booth?"

"That's the question, isn't it?" He paused. "Perhaps no one. Perhaps this is a different night, a different play, an entirely different cast. Perhaps they're performing *Uncle Tom's Cabin*, instead of whatever they acted when Booth killed him."

"Perhaps," I agreed.

"Or perhaps not," Brian shrugged. Then he added, "Do you know why I always raffle off something at every party I give?"

"No, I never really thought about it."

"It's because raffles remind us of the fundamental randomness of existence and the subsequent, ever-present possibilities for unexpected and undeserved good fortune."

He ushered me across the yard to a massive oak tree. An ice-filled tub stocked with beverages sat beside it. We each grabbed a Budweiser. As we sipped our beers, Brian made a sweeping gesture that encompassed the entire yard. "This year's theme is Ronald Reagan's *Morning in America.*"

Sitting in a tree swing beside us, Brian's twelve-year-old son Roger and his little girlfriend Natasha were whispering and holding hands. Brian winked encouragingly at the boy, who turned crimson in embarrassment. Natasha, however, winked back. I liked Natasha. Beyond them, half in shade and half out, was a volleyball court with about five students playing on either side. Glenn Miller, a World War II casualty, played his big band swing from a portable CD player as the college students giggled and flirted and cajoled one another.

It was a hot, humid Miami summer afternoon, and they all wore shorts or bathing suits. The girls wore halter tops. Athletic and well built, the young people would try to punch the ball or spike it with one hand, while holding a can of Pepsi or Budweiser in the other. Sometimes they'd even dive for the ball, tumbling onto the thick St. Augustine grass. Laughing as they stood, they would triumphantly raise their drink high into the air to prove it had not spilled. A group of swimmers cheered them on from the pool behind.

"What?" I asked.

"My party theme is Reagan's *Morning in America* election campaign. It's the perfect postmodern Fourth of July. The icons of a wholesome, pre-industrial America. Just like Main Street, Disneyland. I've got it all here, the whole shebang: hearty laughter, hot dogs, the good clean fun and games, and wholesome *pre-electronic* music–not that decadent rock-and-roll, hip-hop, or rap that liberals' kids listen to.

"Believe me, it set me back a bit, this reconstruction," Brian continued in an artificially serious tone. "But I think Independence Day is worth it, don't you? I had to hire actors for the volleyball players and swimmers. Even this lad here"– pointing at the swing beside us–"he isn't my real son."

"Dad!" Roger whined.

"Well, OK. I'll own him. He's my boy alright. But Natasha beside him. She charged me a pretty penny just to sit with him."

"DAD!"

"OK, OK," Brian raised his hands in self-defense. "I see my work here is done. I'll leave you love birds alone now." Then he turned to me. "Mingle. Make yourself at home. Remember the theme and be perky. The fire needs tending, so if you need me I'll be at my barbeque roasting flesh."

Brian ambled off to char meat. I sipped my beer a while longer and then headed for the lounge chairs by the pool, where a group of graduate students caught my attention. They were engaged in animated conversation, and as I approached, I heard a young woman ask in a distinctive eastern European accent, "If a medium contains no message, can it still be said to be a medium?"

"Take that, Marshall McLuhan!" replied a handsome, young black man whose voice suggested Jamaican or perhaps Trinidadian origins. "Martina says the message is the medium."

I sat in an empty chair and listened to the academic leaders of tomorrow debate whether any message can ever finally be distinguished from the medium that carries it, or vice-versa. Visions of medieval scholastics arguing over how many angels can dance atop the head of a pin pranced through my head like sugar plum fairies.

I kept my thoughts discreetly to myself, but my expression must have revealed what Martina calls my "devilish smirk," because she turned suddenly, walked toward me, and demanded, "So, you are amused by our prattle. Do you think you know everything? O.K. Where does the message stop and the medium begin?"

At first I was startled to by her challenge. But after a short pause I answered, "Maybe it's just a problem of language. "If we had a single word that meant *a message expressed through a medium*, we wouldn't be having this discussion. It's all just postmodern Zen. What's the sound of one poststructuralist deconstructing?"

Now don't ask me where that babble came from. It just flowed through my mouth like a lyric from a poet divinely inspired. Or the incoherent shrieks of Apollo's sibyl. Perhaps because of my unusual parentage, I've always had a passion for literature and have read my share of *avant garde* writers–Beckett, Pirandello, Ionesco, Nabokov, Barth, Coover, DeLillo, and, of course, Thomas Pynchon. And I've suffered through some literary theory, or at least accounts of it in the *New York Review of Books*. Plus, I've had some passionate intellectual exchanges with Brian and a few other members of the humanities faculty. But quite frankly, I have no idea from which dark recesses of my mind came that glib quip about poststructuralism. But I liked it.

It certainly caught Martina's attention. She looked surprised by the directness of my response and, I think, intrigued by my sentiments. "You don't like postmodernism?" she interrogated in her charming Czech accent.

"It beats neo-fascism by a long shot."

Suddenly, a roman candle whizzed overhead and streams

of colored light showered down upon us. Brian's neighbors across the fence had begun their celebration early. After two or three more exploded, the Jamaican fellow and his friends sauntered over to a nearby cooler to grab a drink and watch the show. I remained seated and enjoyed the spectacle, but the air burst seemingly transported Martina to another place and time. Still enthralled as the last embers faded from view above her, she whispered, "A screaming comes across the sky."

These were not words I was expecting to hear. Still, I answered in a reassuring tone, "It has happened before, but there is nothing to compare it to now."

"It is too late," she insisted. But her voice was now questioning, and her intense blue eyes bore into me with eager anticipation.

When I told her, "It's all theater," Martina's jaw dropped.

"Who are you?" she demanded.

"I'm Benjamin Branch. A professor in the history department."

"So, why has a history professor memorized the opening lines to *Gravity's Rainbow*?"

"Well, my reasons are personal," I equivocated.

"Oh, you're just trying to be mysterious," she announced and then turned her back and walked away.

I felt a churning in my stomach, and my spirits plummeted as I watched her march back to her chums. But then Martina suddenly spun around again and returned to confront me. I stood as she approached.

"Why won't you tell me," she insisted.

"Why do you care so much?"

"I'm writing my dissertation on Thomas Pynchon. *Gravity's Rainbow* is my favorite novel."

"Really? You like him that much?"

Martina leaned over and whispered confidentially, "Thomas Pynchon is my obsession." She gestured back to the other graduate students who had resumed conversing among themselves. "None of them, no one around here, not even Dr. Mulligan, has read *Gravity's Rainbow* more than once. Most of them not at all. How many times have you read it?"

Martina's breath felt warm against my cheek. As she spoke, I inhaled the sweet scent of her perfume, and a wisp of her fine, long, blond hair brushed across my wrist, tickling me lightly.

"Seven or eight," I confessed.

Martina's face brightened at my response. She smiled for the first time since we'd spoken, and her eyes sparkled. Then she became serious once more. Her eyes were still bright, but her expression again turned intense.

"Do you know what it's like to have a passion and no one to share it with?"

"Yes, I do."

"Well, I have a passion for Pynchon. It would seem you do too. So, what gives?"

The sun had just begun to set, and the sky was a soft mix of purple, red, magenta, and blue. Green-leafed, orange-flowered poinciana trees swayed back and forth on a light breeze that carried the sweet scent of gardenia, and a puffy white cloud drifted overhead, reflecting the pastel colors of the sunset.

"What if I tell you, and you don't believe me?"

"That's the chance you'll have to take." Her tone was provocative.

"OK. But remember, in Pynchon's world you must always expect the unexpected."

"Always."

I took a deep breath. "Thomas Pynchon's my dad. I'm his illegitimate son."

In an instant a look of disgust replaced the fascination on Martina's face. She pulled her body back and stiffened. She was angry, nearly in tears. Like she was disappointed as well as furious.

"Of all the cheap tricks. You know, I thought maybe you were serious. I thought maybe I'd found someone Pynchon speaks to like he speaks to me. But for God's sake!"

"Don't you think it's possible that somebody is his kid?"

"Not you?"

"Why not."

"You're too old."

I had nothing to say to that, so I just turned and walked away. But although I remained at the party through dinner and the fireworks, *Morning in America* had lost its charm for me, and I excused myself shortly thereafter.

I returned alone to the spartan studio apartment I'd rented

after my family moved away, fed Pandora, my calico cat, and took down a copy of *The Crying of Lot 49*, my father's second novel. I turned to my favorite part, where Oedipa confronts Driblette in the shower, and Driblette, speaking behind a mist of steam, denounces the inability of words to capture reality. Flipping a few pages further I noticed a line I'd underlined perhaps twenty years earlier, one that Oedipa too had underscored: *"Shall I project a world?"*

Chapter 2

A week later, I was in my office. I'd finished my teaching in April but came in most every day to do research and catch up on university matters. I was sitting in my leather chair with my feet propped up on an open desk drawer, reading a book manuscript I'd been asked to evaluate for publication. *Eugenics and YOU: Winners and Losers In Utopia* doesn't really seem like material for a university press, but I like the concept. The author has identified about fifteen distinct visions of master races and genetically improved societies that have been advocated over the past two hundred years. She enumerates all of the qualities that constitute the ideal man, woman, and child in each vision and concludes each chapter with a questionnaire so we can rate ourselves within that particular utopia. That way each reader can see whether he or she would be included among the genetically chosen or "relegated to the backwaters of human evolution." The visions are sufficiently different so that no one is likely to make the master race in all of them. I like that. There's something about failing one of those questionnaires that brings home the threatening aspect of eugenics, utopias, and master race philosophies.

I was going through the manuscript when a firm rapping on my door diverted my attention. I looked up, and to my surprise Martina stood in the doorway.

"May I enter?" she asked, and I gestured for her to come in and sit. As she did, I was aware of her poise and self-possession. Naturally, I was curious about why she had come. But I remained silent and left my expression neutral. The ball was in her court.

"I've come to apologize," she said without preamble. She

appeared sincere, but not overcome with remorse. "I spoke with Dr. Mulligan, and he informed me that as far as he knows, you really are Thomas Pynchon's illegitimate son. I was rude to you, and I shouldn't have acted like that, especially after I practically begged you to tell me. I'm sorry. Please forgive me."

"Apology accepted." What else could I say? Her remark had touched a nerve, but I wasn't interested in holding a grudge. "Most people don't believe me. That's why I rarely mention it. Next time, though, try not to be so quick to judge. Or humiliate."

Until then, Martina had seemed more businesslike than penitent, as though she'd made the apology because it was the right thing to do, but not especially to make me feel better. However, my reminder about her statement about my age made her blush.

"I'm sorry about calling you old too. That was very rude. She looked down, shook her head, and blushed some more. Then she raised her chin and look directly into my eyes.

"It's just that in my mind Thomas Pynchon is always about thirty-five or thirty-six, his age when he published *Gravity's Rainbow*, and I guess that's about your age, and I couldn't admit to myself that my idol must already be twice that old. I'm only twenty-seven. It was a shock."

I was surprised to notice my spirits leap at her words. I'd gone from an old man to a thirty-five year-old in one move. However, I merely replied, "I don't think he's quite twice my age."

"Well, let's see. He was born in 1937. So, he's about 63 now. Not quite double, I guess."

"No, not quite." I smiled inwardly.

"Well, tell me. What's it like being Thomas Pynchon's bastard? It all sounds so romantic."

"Pynchonesque would be more accurate."

"Tell me, how so?"

"Well," I said, paying closer attention now to the exotic blonde before me, "I get to meet people like you."

Martina shooed away my last remark to show that she didn't take it seriously. "If *only* I were like a character from Pynchon. I've always wanted my life to be Pynchonesque. But it's so *ordinary*. Tell me, do you know him? Have you met him? Does he communicate with you?"

"No, I don't think my father knows I exist. Such is the lot of a bastard."

Martina blushed again. "I'm sorry. My choice of words was once again rude. I meant the term only for its denotative meaning. I grew up under communism, and legitimacy or illegitimacy mean nothing to me."

"Apology accepted."

"So how do you know you are his son?"

"That's what my mother's told me ever since I was old enough to ask. To my knowledge, she's never lied to me yet. She says she and Pynchon had an affair in Greenwich Village in 1959, while Pynchon was working on *V* and she was making wild, action paintings in the loft upstairs. They met one day when she and one of her friends were playing loud rock 'n' roll, hurling paint onto a canvas they'd spread out on the floor and then stomping on it and rolling around nude in the colors. According to Mom, Pynchon marched up the stairs ready to vent his anger, but when two, naked, twenty-year-old girls answered the door, each a rainbow of pigments, it was love at first sight, even if it wasn't destined to last. 'It so rarely does,' she would say.

"Pynchon left for Oregon to work at Boeing on the Minuteman program before Mom knew she was pregnant, and she was never able to track him down to tell him. She could have filed a paternity suit and traced him through his publisher, but Mom was too proud."

Martina listened with her head slightly cocked to the side, a strand of blond hair drifting across her face. He blue eyes were open wide; her mouth was agape. *I've never had anyone cling to my every word like that, or look at me with such sudden adoration. This attention from such an attractive young woman was an unexpected but satisfying development.*

"Have you ever tried to find him?"

"Yes. After my wife left me and took my daughter with her, I felt I needed family. Mom by then had been committed to a mental institution--she always felt she was misunderstood, but the bottom line is that we all have to function in the world, and she couldn't anymore. Anyway, Diane and Sharon were the only other relatives I knew. Now they were gone too. So that summer I set out to find Thomas Pynchon."

Martina squirmed in her seat. "Oh, tell me more. Tell me

more." Then she pointed at a brightly colored action painting I'd hung above my desk. "Did your mother paint that? It's so full of passion and energy."

I looked up at the canvas. The colors had literally flown off the surface. It was one of my favorites. "Yes, she made it after Chinese invaders chased the Dali Lama from Tibet."

"She must be an extraordinary woman."

"She is certainly that," I agreed. Then I glanced at the clock on my desk. It was nearly 3:00. I had an important meeting on the other side of campus, so I regretfully answered, "Thanks for coming by. I appreciate the apology. But I have another appointment soon. So I guess I need to get going." I began to collect some papers on my desk and put them into my briefcase, along with the book on eugenics.

"Oh, but this is so interesting. Your mother, Thomas Pynchon, Tibet...."

"Perhaps another time."

"When?" Martina demanded. Once again, I was surprised by the intensity of her response. And flattered as well.

"I don't know...."

"Why don't I make dinner for us tonight. What do you like to eat?"

"Anything's fine." I answered before I had a chance to consider whether pursuing an acquaintance with Martina was really a prudent idea. "Chicken, steak...."

"Chicken Parmesan. And artichoke salad."

"I'll bring some red wine," I offered. "What time?"

When I arrived at Martina's apartment a little after 7:00, she surprised me by kissing me on both cheeks.

"A Czech greeting," she said as she accepted my bottle of Burgundy. Her lips felt warm and moist on my face, and when she pressed her cheek lightly against mine, I couldn't help notice how soft it felt. She wore a sweet perfume that I recognized as *Obsession*. However, these pleasing sensations were quickly jarred by a kettle drum pounding in angry dialogue with its orchestra across the room. I later learned the music on the stereo was from Leos Janacek's *Sinfonietta*.

Both Martina's Czech heritage and her postmodern tastes were immediately evident in her livingroom decor. Framed posters calling for and celebrating the departure of the Soviet army from eastern Europe hung on mauve and purple-colored walls. Her sofa and chairs were framed in shiny chrome and upholstered in black leather. They were bent in sharp, irregular angles that I later learned were not quite as uncomfortable as they looked. A chrome-framed, glass-top coffee table sat before the sofa. The room was illuminated solely by the light of perhaps fifteen or twenty votive candles she had purchased from a Greek Orthodox church and scattered across the apartment. I inferred that their origins were intended as some kind of ironic statement, as Martina later reminded me that, having been raised under communism, she naturally was an atheist. She had standard wall-to-wall shag carpeting but had strategically placed throw rugs with bright orange and black geometric designs around the living room to create a sort of hypnotic labyrinthine effect. Pleasant smells of oregano and garlic issuing from the kitchen mixed with the heavy fragrance of jasmine incense.

Martina served the meal in a little dining area adjacent to the livingroom. "Have a seat while I serve." Martina smiled as she pointed to my chair at her table. The rectangular glass-top table was predictably sleek and sparse. Her plastic plates were octagonal and rainbow colored. Stainless steal forks and knives with orange plastic handles rested beside them on black paper napkins. Hanging on the wall across from me was a large abstract painting rendered in bright acrylics. The fire-engine reds, lemon yellows, and ultramarine blues all swirled in on themselves, and whenever I moved my head they seemed to undulate. The effect was mesmerizing. On the CD player Janacek's *Sinfonietta* ended and his *Cunning Little Vixen* began.

Chapter 3

When Martina reappeared from the kitchen she was carrying two salad bowls brimming with marinated artichokes. I don't know what else was in the marinate, but I could tell it included a generous helping of dill, both by the smell and the disorientation that suddenly overcame me. I always react that way to dill. My mother claims that I once overdosed on kosher pickles at a Jewish delicatessen when I was about five or six, and that dill has made me woozy ever since. In any event, the combined effect of the dill, the psychedelic painting on the wall, and Martina's *Obsession* was to leave me a little dazed.

"So tell me about your quest," she demanded as soon as she seated herself.

"Quest?"

"For your father. It's so archetypal and so Pynchonesque. How did you begin your search?"

"The Internet. It was still pretty slow and undeveloped back then. It's strange to think that was just five years ago. But it was already a meeting ground for people with shared interests."

"1995," Martina recollected. "We were just getting online then in the Czech Republic. I remember those early days on the Internet. Everything was so slow, but so wide open." She smiled for instant, as though my reference had stirred a secret memory that delighted her. But then she frowned. "Go on," she commanded. "You pioneered the Internet."

"Well, not exactly. But as a historian, I was finding it increasingly useful, so it seemed like a natural place to search for Dad."

"You're an armchair researcher?" Martina suddenly accused. "You like to do your research in books and online, not in

the field."
"Well, I'm a historian. It's a little hard to travel back in time, except through the documents that have been left behind."
"So you searched for your father through books and Internet accounts?" Martina's furled brow showed her disapproval.
"I did my share of field work too. But I prepared myself as well as possible before I plunged headlong into the field."
Martina shrugged. "If you say so. I would have just surrendered to the search and let it take me to him."
"Exactly how would you do that?"
"I'd drive places and talk to people. I'd visit the settings from his novels." She paused a moment to think. "I'd place myself physically in his world instead of holing up in an office or a library. To find Thomas Pynchon a person must dive deep into life, not tiptoe around it. That's what Oedipa Maas learned when she went after the Tristero."
"And what did she find in the end?" I countered. "Just madness. The world's, or her own, or both."
"Or the Tristero," Martina reminded me of the fourth possibility.
I held up my hands and surrendered the point. "Anyway, I did drive places and talk to people. But first I wanted at least some leads to get me started. So I ran a keyword search, and sure enough, I found enough kooks and support groups to supply any Pynchon addict for months."
As I described some of the more bizarre characters I'd run across, Martina's resistance to my methodology evaporated, and she listened with rapt attention--her elbows propped on the table, and her chin cradled in the palms of her hands, pointed directly at me. Her blue eyes were wide open, her eyebrows raised, and her mouth formed a tight little O.
"Inevitably, I ran across accounts of Pynchon sightings: in Mexico, California, Oregon, Switzerland, New Zealand....You name the place, and Dad's been spotted there. And yes, I was able to debunk most of these leads from the air-conditioned comfort of my studio apartment. But there were a few reports that I couldn't dismiss outright. So I used my summer vacations and other school breaks to track them down, driving in my car, talking to people, and visiting sites. In the long run, they didn't lead anywhere."
"So maybe there is some Oedipa Maas in you after all."

"Well, I don't know." I smiled. "I didn't find any vast underground postal conspiracy among the downtrodden and dispossessed, or anything like that. I suppose it might have been...what, challenging, frustrating, thrilling...if I'd suspected that somehow Dad was manipulating my search, like Pierce Inverarity posthumously planting clues for Oedipa to find."

"Oh, I bet he is. I'm sure he must be!" Martina was sitting up straight now. In her enthusiasm, she grasped the table's edge. "I'll bet he has a master control room where he can monitor all the Internet traffic in the world. Maybe he's transformed himself, and he *is* the World Wide Web. Maybe he died and that's how he was reincarnated: as a vast electronic communications network that has acquired a consciousness of its own and directs the lives of everyone who's wired in. Wouldn't that be wonderful?"

My mouth dropped in amazement. Martina became increasingly excited as she ascribed more and more godlike powers to my father. I'd never seen anything like it. She reached out, grabbed my wrist, and looked into my eyes. "He's behind your quest. I know he must be. Maybe he caused your divorce just to compel you to look for him."

The pressure from her grip was beginning to hurt, so I placed my other hand on top of hers and caressed it gently to calm her down some. Her skin felt alive beneath my fingertips, and I felt stirrings within myself I hadn't known for years. She relaxed her hold, but her hand remained on my forearm, and mine remained atop hers.

"Maybe," I said.

"Oh, it's true. I'll bet anything it's true."

"I wish I could believe it." With my free hand, I took a sip of wine. The taste lingered a moment on my tongue. "It would be nice to think there's been *some* kind of sense to my life in the past five years, no matter how perverse."

Martina released her grip, sat up again in her chair, and then slid it towards me. "Tell me about your quest. What have your learned?"

I didn't often talk about my efforts to track down Thomas Pynchon. They were both too weird and too personal. But Martina's perfume was intoxicating, and under her spell I found myself compelled to begin.

"Well, to quote Hamlet, the greatest lesson I've learned is that there are more things on Heaven and Earth than your philosophy dreams of, Horatio. Or at least than mine ever imagined."

"Oh, I love Hamlet. He's so dark and disturbed." Again, she stared directly into my eyes.

"You'll get no argument there." I held her gaze until she finally glanced down at her wine glass. Then she looked back up at me.

"So what have you discovered from your search that you didn't know before?"

I looked over at the wall and watched the colors in the painting turn in on themselves. Then I faced her once more. "Overall, the effect has been humbling, I'd say. It's easy for professors to fall into the traps set by intellectual pride, and I think my experiences looking for Dad have helped me avoid some of those. I can see more clearly how much about humanity, about life, about the universe itself that I don't know...that no one knows, or will ever know. I guess I owe Dad something for showing me that, however indirectly."

"Oh, I love indirection," Martina swooned. "It's so subtle and nuanced. So European."

"Yeah, well I met a few Europeans too on my quest. But they weren't exactly subtle. One almost ripped my throat out."

"No!" Martina declared.

"Yes. I'm not kidding. I still have the scar." I turned my head to reveal a faint mark that ran down the side of my neck from my larynx to my collar bone.

Martina reached out and touched it lightly, and a shiver passed down my spine. "Amazing," she said. "What kind of European did this? Where was he from?"

"*She*. The European was a woman. She claimed she was a gypsy from the Spanish Pyrenees. But I met her on an island off the Texas coast, so who knows if she was telling the truth."

Martina pulled suddenly erect. "I've met many gypsies in my home town. You must be very careful with them. They have strange powers." She thrust her finger at me. "Never look at them directly," she insisted, "or they will curse you with their evil eye."

"I'll remember that. This gypsy called herself Natalia."

"And you tracked her down on the Internet? I didn't think gypsies were so hi-tech." Martina reclined back into her chair and then offered, "More wine?"

She filled her goblet, and I nodded for her to replenish mine too. I hadn't thought of Natalia for several months, and I drank deeply before continuing.

"What can I say, Natalia was a gypsy of the '90s. She had a laptop back when laptops weren't cheap, and she spent a good three or four hours a day in chat rooms. That's where I first met her. In cyberspace. She claimed to have remedies for all kinds of ailments and to be willing to share them for a price. A friend of mine with arthritis found her. Traditional medicines weren't doing him any good and he was seeking alternative cures. Natalia sent him some special home-made balm that she sold for an exorbitant price. It actually did him some good. It came with a xeroxed advertisement with her picture and a paragraph describing her credentials. Among her boasts was that several celebrities had sought out her expertise, including Thomas Pynchon. Bob passed the ad on to me, and I contacted her. Eventually, I went to meet her.'"

"Oh this is too fascinating," Martina exclaimed. "Tell me everything." She leaned forward, then took another sip of wine. Her eyes never strayed from mine as I told her about the gypsy.

"Natalia lived in a little wooden house on San Padre Island, off the Texas coast. No matter what time of day or night I came by, and as it turned out I came by often, I could hear the waves crashing against the rocks across the road. She was maybe fifty yards from the ocean, and the sea was louder even than the air conditioner that protruded from her side window and ran noisily throughout the day. At night she'd turn it off and open the windows to admit the sea breezes and smell the salt air, but she always kept the curtains drawn, day and night. The house had electricity—she used it for her computer and appliances, but Natalia never lit the place with electric lights, only candles. So the rooms were always dim. Now that I think of it, I don't believe I ever saw Natalia when she wasn't illuminated by candles or by the sticks of incense she burned incessantly. She had a wooden porch that overlooked the Gulf of Mexico, but she never stepped out on it during the day, only at dusk or in the dark of night. I guess like Blanche DuBois she looked better, or more mysterious, in soft lighting.

"Gypsies never want you to get a good look at their face," Martina interjected. "So you can't give *them* the evil eye. When I was visiting in Prague last summer, an old gypsy man screamed at me in Romanian because he thought I was looking at him too closely. Actually, I was staring at the fashion display in the storefront behind him. But go on. Tell me more about the gypsy who tried to rip out your throat by candlelight."

"I met Natalia last spring," I answered, wincing at the scene Martina resurrected. "For the past few years, I've dedicated the final two weeks of May to tracking down leads. Last year, I also met with a waitress in Galveston. She claimed she'd spent a weekend chewing peyote buttons with my father in the desert. I guess she was in her mid-forties. On the Internet Gert mentioned some vision Dad had. God was supposed to be synonymous with the Big Bang, which he maintained created not only all of the matter and energy in the universe but also a sort of universal consciousness that infuses the Void. According to him, each person's own consciousness is just an infinitesimal sliver of the original, cosmic consciousness. All matter and energy possess a part of it."

"So animals have consciousness too," Martina asserted, as though I had vindicated some belief of hers.

"Not only animals, but plants and rocks, even planets and stars, which, presumably, would have greater consciousness than people, because they contain more matter and energy."

"That makes sense," Martina insisted. "Oh, your father is so brilliant."

"Well, he may be brilliant, but later Gert concluded that it had all been a big seduction ploy. Between the peyote and all his references to the Big Bang and vibrating pulsars and exploding stars, she'd gotten really horny. Apparently they'd followed their philosophical speculations with some pretty wild sex out there among the sage brush."

"Cosmic consciousness and wild sex," Martina's face lit up. "What *I* wouldn't give to spend a weekend sharing peyote in the desert with your father."

Martina squirmed as she spoke, clearly tuned on by the thought. I didn't quite know what to make of *that*, so I just continued. "The idea seemed enough far out there to be worthy of

Dad, which is why I went to talk to her in the first place. But Gert gave herself away when she told me she'd met him when his band came to town to give a blues concert. When I probed deeper, it became apparent that an aging, honky tonk pianist with the gift of gab and a glint in his eye had given his name as Thomas Pynchon, either as a joke or an alias. He'd somehow convinced her to run away with him to his next gig in El Paso, and they'd passed through the desert along the way. So all the talk about the Big Bang was actually just a way for some drug-crazed musician to get into her pants. They split up not long after, and she returned to Galveston, where she learned she was pregnant."

Martina seemed even more disappointed than I had been to learn that Gert's tale had been a false lead, but she recovered her equilibrium soon enough. "Well, what about the gypsy?" she demanded.

"There were more names on my list than I had time to visit that spring, so I'd mapped out a route that took me along the coast, since, for some reason, a higher concentration of prospects lived close to the Gulf of Mexico. Natalia was the last stop on my tour.

"I met two more women whose claims to wild sexual adventures with my father also disintegrated under my questioning. It seems that honky tonk pianist really got around."

"Did he get them pregnant too?" Martina sounded suddenly indignant.

"Yes, as a matter of fact he did."

"And how do you know he wasn't really your father. Maybe he plays the piano too?"

"Well, nothing about his description matched what we do know about how the real Thomas Pynchon looks." Martina seemed satisfied with my explanation, so I continued. "An author in Corpus Christi told me that my father had twice appeared unsolicited at her doorstep while she was bogged down in her writing. According to Mina, both times Dad just thrust a handful of typewritten pages into her hands, turned, and disappeared into the night. And both times my father's notes and revisions crystallized core issues for her and energized her stalled projects."

"Oh," Martina gushed. "Do you think Thomas Pynchon... your father...might appear at my apartment some stormy night when I am struggling to find just the right words to express myself? Wouldn't it be wonderful if he would come to rescue me from my cluttered mind and stagnant imagination? We could take psychedelic drugs together and have incredible sex in the desert. Do you think it's possible?"

Maybe it was the wine; maybe it was all the attention she was paying me, but I was becoming turned on by Martina. She was beautiful, no doubt about it, and her Czech accent and European manners excited me. So did her openness. Her apparent lack of self-censorship was a refreshing contrast to my own more guarded personality. But Martina's unconcealed lust for my father was disarming and not a little confusing. In fact, I found myself feeling a little bit jealous. At first I took her question to be rhetorical, the expression of her desire. So I didn't say anything. But then she insisted, "Well, do you? Do you think it could happen to me?"

"Well, it happened to my mother," I finally replied. "I suppose that if Dad's writing teaches us anything, it's that anything is possible. But I wouldn't give up any dates so you can stay home and wait for him."

"Well, as long as there is hope," she sighed. Then she reached out and squeezed my hand again. "At least I have his son. That's a miracle in itself."

There was another silence and then Martina silently drew closer. Her perfume enveloped me, and the suddenly haunting melodies from *The Cunning Little Vixen*, still flowing from the CD player, began to wash over me in waves. To break the spell, I looked up at the painting across the room. But the colors kept spinning in on themselves. As they carried me with them, I felt myself drawn into the vortex of Martina's *Obsession*. Then softly, silently, almost absent-mindedly, she passed her fingertips back and forth along my forearm, and I felt a charge pass through my body. We fell into a silent, all-consuming gaze, neither of us willing or able to look away. With every breath I took, Martina's rich aroma literally filled me with her being–like the divine song the muse breathes into the lungs of the poet. Suddenly, a bolt of white light leaped from her eyes to mine. Or perhaps it sparked between and exploded out at each of us. The jolt was electric.

The next morning over breakfast I finished my tale about Natalia, and two days later Pandora and I moved in.

Chapter 4

The day Martina and I began our cohabitation, Sharon contacted me for the first time all summer. She sent me an e-mail saying that she'd read one of my articles for a class. It really impressed her, and she wrote to tell me how much respect she'd gained for me and my work. "The article was assigned reading," her email read, "and I felt really proud when I told everyone that you're my father." Then she invited me to her 21st birthday party in Chicago in two weeks, at the end of July.

Sharon's e-mail brought me more joy than anything I'd experienced since she moved away. Out of nowhere an opening appeared in the brick wall she'd erected after the divorce. Best of all, it was her appreciation for my research that breached the barrier. My work is so much a part of who I am, and now, at last, my daughter respects me for it. She's proud of me because of it. I can't begin to describe how gratifying that is.

I told Martina, and she was excited for me. Martina knew first hand about the outcomes of social engineering, and she opposed it vehemently in any form. For that reason, she shared my aversion to eugenics. It was one of the things that united us, and she was pleased that Sharon had now joined the fold.

However, I didn't know how my new lover would feel about meeting my college-age daughter so soon in our relationship. I know those things can be sticky. But when I told her that Sharon had invited her to the party as well, Martina accepted at once, with enthusiasm. On the one hand, this was a relief. On the other hand, I hadn't actually told Sharon about Martina yet. I'd wanted to see how things worked out between us first. So Sharon hadn't actually extended an invitation to Martina, because she didn't know Martina existed. I'd been afraid that if Sharon invited Martina, and Martina turned her down, the damage would be greater than if Sharon were to snub Martina. Either way, I could see that this joyous occasion held some potentially dangerous pitfalls.

That night I called Sharon in Chicago. We communicated mostly via e-mail back then, but I felt I should tell her in a real-time conversation, in spoken words, that I wanted to bring to her party a woman only about six years older than she. Fortunately, Sharon didn't mind at all.

In the intervening fortnight, Martina and I worked out our living arrangements more firmly and came to know one another a little better, although, as I later learned, there were many other sides to her I had yet to see. In those first two weeks she was enthralled to be living with Thomas Pynchon's son, and I was the beneficiary of her passion for my dad. I still found her unconcealed lust for him weird and a little off-putting, but I elected simply to go with the flow, as a Pynchon character might. This attitude represented a change for me, but I thought perhaps I was ready for a change. In Thomas Pynchon's world, after all, the ability to embrace change is the name of the game. Moreover, I assured myself that, as we came to know each other better, Martina would come to love me fully for myself and her passion for my father would take a more appropriate form. Thomas Pynchon, in my mind, was just the vehicle that brought us together. Maybe that was just a convenient belief that enabled me to indulge my long-suppressed passions, but that's what I told myself at the time.

As the first week passed into the second I did notice that Martina would sometimes criticize something I said or did, or lash out against my more moderate political sensibilities; but don't all relationships involve reconciling differences in points of view? In any case, these disruptions were quickly glossed over, and I paid them little attention. I was happy again, for the first time in years, and I didn't want to burst my bubble. I guess I was just a willing partner in my own self-deception–an all-too-human phenomenon. But as we boarded the plane for O'Hare, I was looking forward to an exciting future. And it *has* been exciting, although not in the ways I imagined.

Martina loved Chicago. She loved the Impressionist collection at the Art Institute, the open-air Picasso sculpture downtown, the outdoor concerts in Grant Park, the Greek restaurants that served retsina wine, and the Polish sausage stands on the corners of busy streets. But most of all she loved the University and Hyde Park, the south-side neighborhood that houses it. We flew up two days before Sharon's Friday night party and left the following Sunday. Little did any of us expect that this visit would be the turning point in our lives.

Sharon and her roommate, Helena, greeted us at the airport. I hadn't seen my daughter in over six months, and I loved how vibrant and enthusiastic she looked. She'd broken off with her latest boyfriend right after Thanksgiving and was still feeling low when I last saw her during winter break. Then, Sharon had vowed that she was giving up on men. "They're all selfish and manipulative," she complained. "Everything always has to be done *their* way. And whenever I stand up for myself, they either break up or try to force some guilt trip on me."

I explained that I'd known several women who behaved in exactly the same fashion--I didn't mention her mother specifically. But Sharon was too angry and broken-hearted to hear me. She didn't communicate much that winter or spring; so her good spirits now were especially gratifying.

Her friend Helena seemed nice enough. She was a graduate student in political science with a slightly repressed smile and intense black eyes. A few years older than Sharon, Helena was tall, dark, and slender with straight, long, raven-colored hair. She dressed plainly, unlike Sharon who has always shown a flair for style. Standing side by side, they presented a study in contrasts. Although not tiny, Sharon is on the short side and more curvaceous and ample breasted. In those respects she takes after her mother. She has my wavy light brown hair, but it looks better on her, flowing down below her shoulders. Her big, bright, brown eyes come from her maternal grandmother, who also passed them down to Diane. Sharon doesn't have any of my mother's features, but she inherited her creativity and some of her impulsiveness. Fortunately, my daughter is more stable than my mother, more firmly rooted in reality. Diane and I both felt it was important for her to think for herself and form her own opinions, and in that regard, at least, we were successful parents. Perhaps too successful; Sharon is easily outraged, a little strident, a little quick to judge, and impatient to see justice administered.

We left the airport in Helena's car and drove south to the exit for the Museum of Science and Industry. Helena and Sharon shared an apartment in Hyde Park not far from there, near the Illinois Central Railway stop on 57th Street. It's a choice location for University of Chicago students. The main library is only about half a mile away. A Henry Moore statue in front commemorates the world's first self-sustaining atomic chain reaction that Enrico Fermi orchestrated at the site in 1942, when the property was the university's football stadium, then called Stagg Field. The achievement ushered in the nuclear age, with all its blessings and curses.

Helena graciously offered to let Martina and me use her room. She'd share Sharon's. I had already reserved a hotel room, but the girls insisted that we stay with them. Delighted that Sharon was so eager for my company, I consulted Martina. She was up for it, so we agreed.

We dropped our bags off and then headed out again for a walking tour of Hyde Park and the campus that boasts the most Nobel Prize winners per square mile of any in the world. Despite the August heat and humidity, the exercise felt good after the plane and car rides. My favorite stop was an old, used-book store where a fluffy gray cat lay curled atop a pile of nineteenth-century hardback novels in the picture window. This store was an academic's delight. The shelves brimmed with volumes on every conceivable subject. There were arcane texts in medieval Latin; political treatises, religious tracts, and artistic manifestos; memoirs of travelers and explorers from Marco Polo to Walter Raleigh and Mary McCarthy; books filled with maps, tables, charts, demographics, diagrams, and raw data of all kinds; and studies of everything from exile literature, to the engravings on ancient Greek gem stones, to the Peloponnesian, Napoleonic and Persian Gulf wars, to mutant caterpillars, to the politics, arts, and letters of the Cold War, to the novels of Eudora Welty, and the films of Woody Allen. I hadn't lingered in a bookstore like this one since my college days in Berkeley.

Martina naturally gravitated to the section on contemporary literature, and Sharon, who was majoring in English with a creative writing emphasis, joined her. Helena went off to pet the cat. Maybe it was my imagination, but she suddenly seemed out of sorts. I briefly checked out the history selections and then looked over some books by a couple of emerging fiction writers I'd been reading about. I liked to keep an eye on Dad's competition; plus I've always had a soft spot for literature. I had contemplated majoring in English as an undergraduate, but the over-emphasis on literary theory turned me off. It showed too little love for the artistic brilliance and profound insight of the writers who so excited me and engaged my imagination. So I stuck with history and explored independently how my father's fiction questioned our ability ever to accurately apprehend it, let alone know history's meaning. Maybe my reasons for becoming an historian were Oedipal, and, unconsciously, I wanted to repudiate my father. His writing demonstrates very convincingly that history is ultimately unknowable--that it's just an artificial narrative constructed by people trying to impose order on the inherent chaos of human existence. My ambition as a scholar had always been to negate his position, not by repudiating it--I couldn't do that--but by showing how we nonetheless can acquire insight and give value and direction to our lives by imposing coherent narratives onto past events. Now it occurs to me that perhaps I studied history instead of literature just to get back at Thomas Pynchon for never being there for me. One more replay of the eternal human narrative of the son proving himself by rebelling against his dad.

In any case, Martina and Sharon were hitting it off famously. Standing two aisles over, I didn't overhear the particulars of their conversation, but I could tell they liked each other. Each was pulling down books from the shelves to show the other, and their voices were strong and animated as they spewed out the names of authors and titles they were sure the other would enjoy. Helena joined them after a while and started to point out some things as well. Soon she seemed more engaged too, and she and Martina had a lot to say to one another. Three quarters of an hour later the trio strolled out of the store together, arm in arm like European women do, Martina in the middle. I stayed behind to pay for the stack of books that the four of us had accumulated. The dent in my Visa account was sizeable, but it was priceless to see my daughter and my girlfriend becoming pals.

When we arrived back at the apartment Sharon put out tea and cookies for everyone, and Helena opened up a little more about herself. She's close to Martina's age; perhaps two years younger. And it turned out that she and Martina share a heightened political awareness. It was apparently under Helena's influence that Sharon's longstanding aversion to social injustice morphed over the past year into political activism. Helena's father is a Greek national from Cyprus, her mother the child of Romanian Holocaust survivors who emigrated to the States after World War II. Her parents met as students at Hunter College in New York, and Helena grew up in Queens. She did her undergraduate work at City College and then came to the University of Chicago to earn a doctorate in political science.

Actually, Helena's research overlaps considerably with mine. Motivated by her family history, she was planning to write her dissertation on how hate groups use the Internet to promote their agendas. It was she who steered Sharon into the class that assigned my article, and I could tell Helena was pleased to meet its author. Over the next few days we had several interesting conversations about our shared interests.

Martina was even more taken by Helena. I'd always believed I could make my greatest contribution to humanity by doing what I have real passion for. That's why I take my research so seriously. It's my contribution to my species, something I hope can make a difference and be used for greater understanding that might improve the human condition.

I know that in a postmodern milieu such an attitude is hopelessly outdated, a throwback to the Enlightenment, for God's sake. "Can't you see that the entire twentieth-century experience proves that knowledge and reason can never achieve secular salvation?" Martina had demanded of me a few days earlier on one of the increasing occasions when our world views conflicted. "Don't you know that your beloved Western intellectual tradition offers only the illusion of truth? Its very foundation is erected on shifting sands?" She stressed *beloved*, prolonging it to mock me.

"Don't you know that there is neither absolute truth, nor objective reality?" she went on. "Or that nothing exists apart from the contexts in which it appears. That truth, beauty, and goodness never brought people closer to the divine, if there is a divinity at all, which I doubt."

"Well that doesn't mean they are worth aspiring to anyway," I argued.

But Martina just dismissed my words. "Those ideals were never even really intended for achieving such lofty goals anyway. Plato was just spouting propaganda for the oligarches. People preoccupied with seeking truth, creating beauty, and being good don't overthrow tyrants; they accommodate them. The so-called verities that Shakespeare and the others are supposed to be so full of–well, I can tell you what they are full of! Their *truths*," again she stressed the word, "were just tools for subjugating women and the non-propertied masses. And for enslaving non-Europeans and robbing nature of its spirit, its *anima*. For squeezing the very life out of existence."

"Oh, come on," I objected. "Don't you think that's a little heavy-handed?"

"Heavy handed," Martina rejoined. "Don't you know that Faust's passion for knowledge, which was really a passion for control, is the only true original sin, that it culminated in Auschwitz and Hiroshima? Where have you been these past thirty years?" she finally concluded, her voice filled with exasperation and disdain.

Well, that's the difference between Martina and me. We both know all about postmodern uncertainty, how reality reduces down to spin control, as they say in the media. Martina accepts this and lives accordingly. I think its partly a generational difference and partly cultural--after all, she grew up under a communist regime that deliberately instituted revisionist history as a matter of social policy. And then some of it's just a difference in personalities. Martina expects neither certainty, nor completion, nor consistency. She lives in the moment, not in the long run. She believes that if truth and morality exist at all, we can apprehend them only as an unknowable hodgepodge. We may think they represent a higher calling, a divine impulse, an ideal human aspiration. But in fact they subtly, stealthily, insidiously reinforce the prejudices of our cultures. So, if truth and morality have been exposed as mere tools of social and economic oppression, then the best thing is to by-pass them altogether. Let instinct and passion guide us, since reason will inevitably entrap and destroy us. DADA DADA DADA DADA.

My response is different. I can't live in an amoral universe where basic notions like acting in good faith are purely matters of interpretation, where cold blooded, unprovoked murder might be acceptable depending on how you look at it or feel about it. Martina can. I don't reject instinct and intuition--I rely on them often. But I think we can salvage knowledge and reason if we become aware of their limitations and remain vigilant of their capacity for abuse. We can use them for good purposes as well as ill. If they should not be valued more than our passions, neither should they be rated less. So that's why I practiced my politics through my intellectual pursuits, and that's why Martina practiced hers on the street.

And that's why Martina and Helena hit it off so well. Helena belonged to a group on campus that worked against the work of hate groups. She'd picketed her share of right-wing speakers on campus and was once even arrested when she and her cohorts tried to block a road leading to the lecture hall where an official from the Nation of Islam known for provoking violence against Jews was scheduled to speak.

So that evening at dinner in a downtown Greek restaurant Helena and Martina swapped stories of street protest over glasses of ouzo, while Sharon and I sipped retsina and listened in wonder. My courtship of Martina had indeed been brief, and each day revealed a new aspect of the woman I was living with. For her part, Sharon seemed to regard both women with awe and a certain amount of reverence. I, too, admired them for their readiness to live according to their convictions.

The next night, Friday, was Sharon's party. Martina and I helped decorate. I set out the booze and finger foods, and together Martina and I hung computer-generated banners from the walls and arched brightly colored crepe paper from the ceiling.

"A streaming comes across the sky." she joked from her stepladder as she tossed a roll of orange crepe to me on the far side of the room.

I laughed at the playful reference and answered, as I had before, "It has happened before, but there is nothing to compare to it now."

"It is too late," Martina countered.

Guests began arriving around 8:00; by 9:00 about twenty-five had gathered, all between the ages of twenty and thirty, except me. The Americans mostly wore shorts, tank tops, and other attire appropriate to the steamy summer heat. The guests from Europe, Asia, Africa, and the Middle East either wore colorful garb from their native countries or dressed in Western clothes, but more elegantly than we gringos. Sharon, however, had bought a tight-fitting, sexy black gown for the occasion, and, after consulting my daughter by e-mail prior to flying up, Martina had packed a bright red, yellow, and blue peasant outfit from the Czech Republic that I found fetching. Even Helena, who typically wore jeans and a T shirt, had put on a dress and fixed her hair in an alluring half twist. I wore my usual navy blue Dockers and a new pair of white tennis shoes. My pale blue shirt, open at the collar, sported a pattern of red, purple, and yellow hibiscus.

Exotic odors wafted over and around the buffet that overflowed with finger foods as culturally diverse as the guests: miniature hot dogs and meatballs on toothpicks, tempura vegetables, humus dip with pita bread, stuffed grape leaves, falafel, Indian mango chutney, potato pancakes, and a Cuban dish of black beans, white rice, and fried plantains whose ingredients I'd brought up from Miami. The bar was similarly international. I passed up the ouzo and tequila and settled for Scotch and soda. Ever daring, Martina poured herself a shot of moonshine that a friend of Helena's had brought back in a clear mason jar from a backwoods still in Appalachia, where he was gathering data for his doctoral dissertation.

After we helped ourselves to some guacamole and a Nigerian delicacy whose name I never learned, Martina and I drifted over to a corner where two graduate students were passionately discussing how U.S. anti-drug policies in South America were undermining civilian efforts to free the democracies from dependence on their armies. In the background, conversations buzzed in English, French, and Spanish, as well as a few other tongues I couldn't identify.

Sharon forbade smoking inside, but throughout the evening several young men and women passed into the glass-enclosed sun room that was closed off from the apartment. Sharon and Helena had converted it into a patio, with chairs and a couch, outdoor carpeting, and numerous potted plants. In the summer Sharon and Helena opened the windows and read there or worked on their laptops while enjoying the cooling breezes that rolled off Lake Michigan. Now, partygoers came to light up cigarettes, cigars, and even some reefer. I noticed the Europeans were among the heaviest smokers. To my surprise, Martina excused herself to have a smoke with Helena. I hadn't known Martina to smoke before.

"I used to be a heavy smoker back home. I quit when I came to the States," she said in reply to the puzzled look on my face. "But, there's something Old World about Helena that makes me want to light up a Lucky Strike." She smiled and waved happily as they walked outside.

I doubted the wisdom of a reformed smoker starting again, but Martina was an adult, and it wasn't my place to tell her what to do. Besides, I was just glad she was having a good time. So I waved back and wandered across the living room, where I found a vacant chair close to where Carlos, Sharon's saxophonist friend, was jamming to a CD. Carlos is about twenty-two and a back-up for the Chicago Symphony. When one of the regulars is out, or a score calls for an extra sax or two, he fills in. But now he was wailing to some hot and heavy jazz.

Sharon walked up to me, grabbed my arm excitedly, and stooped over to speak into my ear.

"Isn't he terrific?" she beamed.

I nodded in agreement. Indeed, Carlos *was* terrific. She'd mentioned him on several previous occasions, and I wondered if she had a crush on him. For that matter, perhaps they were already an item, and for her own reasons she had concealed it from me. Probably to get a sense of how I'd react first. Or perhaps she was embarrassed to contradict herself after having so recently sworn off men. On the other hand, maybe there was nothing between them at all. Sharon had always been reticent to discuss her personal life, and nothing about that had altered during my visit so far. But I'd noticed a change in her demeanor since I first arrived: she seemed like a woman in love. And I thought quietly to myself that she could do worse than fall for someone whose music conveyed such passion, sensuality, and vitality.

Sharon pulled up a chair and sat with me through a couple more numbers. Then she rose and patted my hand.

"Gotta mingle."

I listened a while longer, then decided to track down Martina. I made my way to the sun room, where I found her and Helena together on the couch that faced outward to the city. They were in animated discussion with one other. Nearby were two young couples who were dressed in outlandish Halloween costumes. The blond man and blond girl occupying the love seat beside Helena were ostensibly attired as Batman and Batgirl. They had made their outfits themselves, and what the costumes lacked in authenticity, they made up for in gaudiness. Each wore black tights and a bright yellow cape with a large, black B. However, someone had spilled yellow paint on Batman's cape, erasing the bottom portion of his B and making it a P, instead. A tall, dark-haired fellow dressed as Mighty Mouse stood on the other side of the couch, beside Martina, speaking passionately; his date, a slim, Asian girl with long braided hair and a headband, listened attentively from a folding chair beside him. She was Pocahontas. As I stepped inside, Batgirl was passing a joint to Helena on the couch, who took a deep drag and passed it on to Martina. Martina took a hit and offered it Mighty Mouse, who declaimed, "I never smoke that shit!" Pocahontas also declined, but silently. Then Mighty Mouse returned to the discourse he was giving, but only Pocahontas was paying attention. Across the room, a young man and woman stood in the corner with their arms around each other, looking out at the skyline and puffing on cigars.

I walked over to Martina and smiled. "Having fun?"

"Ben, here, have some." She exhaled and then giggled as the smoke blew into my face.

I've never smoked grass heavily; my work load and responsibilities have been too great. But I had some fond memories of festive occasions spiced with marijuana. So, taking the joint from my lover, I took a deep hit, figuring it was consistent with my new resolution to go with the flow.

I stopped after the joint came my way two more times, but Batman had provided some good stuff. Soon I was feeling otherworldly. I sat on the armrest of the couch beside Martina and stared out at the skyscrapers silhouetted in the distance. While Martina and Helena joked about Czech and Romanian idioms, I took in the mixed fragrances of tobacco and marijuana smoke, the aromas of curried goat and Swedish meatballs, and the big city air pollution from Chicago's south side. As I sat watching and smelling, the sounds around me faded into the background. After a while, though, I noticed undulations in the noise from the three conversations transpiring beside me and the general din from the party inside. The noise never lapsed into complete silence, but it seemed that there were unintended patterns of a loudness followed by sudden quiet. Perhaps this was one of those cycles that mathematicians described through chaos theory: the inevitable degeneration of order into chaos (entropy), followed by the subsequent degeneration of chaos into order.

Suddenly, I realized how truly Pynchonesque my life had become since I'd met Martina. Hell, here I was at a polyglot party, thinking about the second law of thermodynamics, and sharing illegal drugs furnished by a costumed superhero, while Mighty Mouse ranted on about the dangers of white supremacy.

I leaned over to Martina to point out how we were inhabiting Dad's story, "Entropy," but she was laughing with Helena, and I didn't want to interrupt. Instead, I turned to Mighty Mouse and asked him to elaborate on something he'd said.

My question opened a flood gate, and for the next twenty minutes I sat on that armrest, stoned, watching and listening to an exhortation against neo-Nazis, skinheads, and right-wing extremists. Mighty Mouse described compounds in Montana and Wyoming as armed fortresses where posters of Hitler loom everywhere, and fascists teach racist, anti-Semitic, anti-Catholic propaganda and plot to establish a separate Aryan nation between the Rockies and the Tetons.

"They intimidate everyone within fifty miles, refuse to pay taxes, and pass bad checks. They say they're committing acts of political protest, but they're really just thieves and thugs. Part of their strategy is to flood the Internet with misinformation, on the perceptive assumption that most people don't distinguish between sources of information."

"What does their misinformation say?" As I asked, I thought how strange it was to hear my own sentiments voiced by an overly animated cartoon character.

"For instance, they keep dredging up the Protocols of the Elders of Zion to prove the existence of a vast international Jewish conspiracy. My God, even if the documents were authentic--and they've been shown to be forgeries in a court of law--the idea that a group of Jews in 1897 could actualize a plan for world domination that had been incubating through the ages, and that this plan somehow shaped twentieth-century history, is preposterous."

"Pynchonesque," I thought to myself but said nothing as Mighty Mouse continued.

"That was over one-hundred years ago. Before World Wars I and II, the Cold War, and everything else that has played havoc with world history since. I think most people would agree that, despite the founding of Israel, the twentieth century was not particularly kind to international Jewry. But according to these fanatics, the Jewish conspiracy orchestrated every cataclysmic event for its own purposes.

"I guess the extermination of six million of their own people was supposed to somehow be part of the grand Jewish strategy," Mighty Mouse mocked. "Oh, I forgot. Never mind the documentary film footage of the camps being liberated, never mind Eichmann's diary, never mind the personal testimony of thousands of victims and witnesses, these people think that the Holocaust was just a lie perpetrated by Jews to win sympathy. One of their websites calls FDR a Jew, and blames Jews for creating the Great Depression and the Russian revolution. I think *that* will come as a surprise to all the European Jews Roosevelt kept out of the United States when they were trying to escape Hitler, and to the Russian Jews who were killed, imprisoned, or forbidden to practice their faith in the Soviet Union. Little did they guess that Stalin was really one of them."

Mighty Mouse suddenly interrupted his rant to look down at his watch. "Oops. We have a mission!" Then he called over to Batman. "Time to go."

"Batgirl and I are going to pass," Batman answered. He and his date were now necking in the love seat.

"Aw, come on," Mighty Mouse placed his hands on his hips, exasperated. "We had a plan. We were going to make a difference."

"Some other time. Can't you see Sally and I are busy. Besides, I shouldn't have had that grass. I'm too mellow for political theater tonight." Then Batman pointed at me. "Maybe Martina's friend will go with you. He can use my costume."

"How about it?" Mighty Mouse asked.

"How about what?"

"The radical right wing of the Young Republicans has invited Perry Norwich to speak on campus tonight. You know, that militia leader who's been shouting to the press that the government has been spying on his organization. An organization which, incidentally, had ties to the Oklahoma City bombing. Anyway, it starts in ten minutes, and there's probably going to be local television coverage. Our plan was to run in, dressed as cartoon figures, and throw pies in his face. Like those protestors did to Bill Gates and the secretary of agriculture, what's his name? It's a non-violent way to make Norwich look as foolish as he really is. At least that was the plan. But these lovebirds," he pointed to Batman and Batgirl, "have decided to turn on, tune in, and drop out." The last remark was uttered with disgust.

"Give it a break," Batman looked up from Batgirl, with whom he'd resumed necking.

"Yeah, give me a break," Batgirl echoed.

"What makes you so sure you can get away with this?" I asked.

"We've planned it all out. We'll wear trench coats over our costumes until the last minute. Then, while Norwich is up there spewing his venom, we'll drop the coats, reveal ourselves as superheroes, and assault him with custard pies. Before anyone can react, we'll run out the side door to the street, where Pocahontas here will be waiting in the getaway car."

I politely declined, but Martina suddenly sat up in the couch.

"Wait a minute," she announced. She and Helena had been in close conversation during the Mouse's discourse, but now she taunted me. "Don't be such an old fuddy duddy." She looked back at Helena and winked.

"Don't you think it sounds a little crazy?" I defended myself.

"Don't you think we live in a crazy world? You and your cult of rational thought. Here, you're the one who's dedicated your career to exposing the myth of racial superiority. Now fate has handed you an unexpected opportunity to expose it before a television audience, and in a visceral way that can really speak to people. Not in your safe, academic language that's calculated to have no public influence."

"My academic contributions make a difference too. I firmly believe that."

"Well, that's a convenient belief," Martina countered.

Then Helena added more gently, "Regardless, here's a

chance to do something more for your cause. You can have some thrills, enjoy a good laugh on the enemy, and maybe give this situation the media attention it deserves."

"That's right!" Martina interjected. She raised her arms and proclaimed to the group at large, "Absurd times call for absurd actions!"

"Yes," Helena agreed. "Absurd times call for absurd actions." Then Mighty Mouse, Pocahontas, Batman, and Batgirl all picked up the mantra, and they too began chanting, "Absurd times call for absurd actions."

The idea still sounded ridiculous, but I realized that was the point. And the way Martina put it, not to participate would be cowardly. "They're right," I thought. "If I really have the courage of my convictions, how can I refuse to take the chance? There's little to lose, and the act is non-violent. Even if I get caught, it's not the sort of thing I'll go to jail for, or lose my job over." The marijuana made it all too easy to picture the look on Norwich's face when a couple of pie-wielding, rodent superheroes came from out of nowhere and accosted him with baked goods. The image was devilishly delightful.

"I'll do it, if you'll come along too," I told Martina.

She looked quickly at Helena and then turned back to me. "You know I would. I live for this kind of thing. But if they catch us, and I'm even just a passenger in the getaway car, I could be deported. I can't risk that. But for you, what's that worst that could happen? Maybe a suspended sentence and a fine. Do it," she reiterated. "You'll be like Bogart at the end of *Casablanca*, when he finally decides to join the good fight after sitting out on the sidelines, just running his bar and teaching his classes."

I ignored the jibe but acknowledged that it would be foolhardy for her to participate.

"I guess it's you and me, buddy," Mighty Mouse put his arm around my shoulder and began escorting me outside. I don't remember ever actually agreeing to go along, but I was out the door before I could change my mind. As we left, Batman tossed me his cape, mask, and a black trench coat, and Martina blew a farewell kiss. Pocahontas followed silently behind.

Perry Norwich was well into his speech when we arrived. A television news crew was filming him from the back of the auditorium, which was decorated with red, white, and blue bunting. A photographer was crouched over in front, trying to be unobtrusive as she positioned herself close to the speaker. The audience contained thirty or forty young Republicans.

"Fifty years of treason," Norwich was shouting from his podium as we made our way quietly toward him. "More than fifty years! Remember Alger Hiss," he insisted, "and how the Democrats defended that Russian spy even after his conviction, just as they defended Julius and Ethel Rosenberg, the atomic bomb spies. We know for sure now, from the Army's Venona files, that there is no question of their guilt. But still the liberals equivocate. And what about the program of moral turpitude that liberals foisted upon our great country in the 1960s? We suffer from it still."

"That's right!" cried a voice from the audience, and then another and another.

Norwich nodded knowingly before he went on. "'Drugs, sex, and rock 'n' roll,' they demanded while our soldiers were dying in Vietnam, bravely defending us from worldwide communism. Under the inspired Republican leadership of Ronald Reagan, the threat of communism was finally defeated. But drugs, sex, and rock 'n' roll now fill the White House!"

As the crowd burst out in cheers Mighty Mouse and I made our move. We shed our trench coats and sprang into action, two superheroes engaging an enemy who would lead us back to a time of warmongering, racial segregation, and gender discrimination. In an instant we raced to the podium and pummeled Perry with our pies. Hardly missing a step, we continued across the stage and out a side exit before Norwich, or the audience, knew what hit him.

After we did the custardly deed, we drove to Old Town and stopped in a pub for about an hour, to let things settle back down in Hyde Park. I remember how good the beer tasted after our adventure. Somewhere along the line, I learned that Mighty Mouse was named Bernard, and Pocahontas was Kim.

It was close to midnight when we marched back into Sharon's party like conquering heroes. The party was in full swing. Carlos was no longer wailing on his saxophone; instead a rapper friend of Helana was shouting into a microphone, surrounded by a throng of intense onlookers. New, exotic food dishes had appeared on the buffet table, apparently the contributions of late comers who had joined the celebration in our absence. I searched for Martina but didn't see her right away, so I worked my way back to the sun room to look for her there. A mixture of cigar, cigarette, and marijuana aromas filled the air, but Martina was not there. So I returned back to the living room and picked at the food offerings. Finally, Martina and Helena emerged from a back room. Martina spotted me first and ran up to congratulate me.

"Helena and I were watching for you on the all-news station. They just announced the pie-throwing. Details at the top of the hour. We've set up the VCR to tape it!"

So, at 12:00, we extracted Sharon from her ongoing debate with Carlos about the role of art and music in twenty-first century social formation and brought her into the bedroom where Helena, Martina, and the superheroes were already gathered. We closed the door behind us, and swore her to secrecy.

"Now that you're twenty-one, you're old enough to see this," I told her ominously. The others assumed serious expressions and agreed.

Then Helena switched the television back on, just as the anchorman announced a pie-throwing in Hyde Park. He showed complete footage of Mighty Mouse and Batman pummeling Perry Norwich with our pies and then racing through the crowd and out the door. I could see the back of my neck and my Batman cape. But caught on camera, the blotched B looked even more like a P, and the caption under my figure read "Pie-thrower." My career as a mythical entity had begun.

Chapter 5

We returned to a steamy Miami simmering in late July heat and the politics of the 2000 presidential election. Ever since the Elian Gonzalez affair that spring, the city had been fracturing along an ever-growing number of ethnic and political lines, and politicians of all stripes were exploiting the fissures to the hilt. In a region as diverse as ours, we must expect inevitable antagonisms, conflicts of interest, opposing attitudes, and varying beliefs about how society should function. But until those fishermen saved little Elian at sea on Thanksgiving day and set off a chain of events as bizarre as anything Thomas Pynchon has ever written, the various factions had existed if not in harmony, at least in a state of peaceful coexistence. However, when the INS raided Lazaro Gonzalez's house that April and snatched Elian away at gunpoint to reunite him with his father--and, inevitably, to send him back to Cuba--it shattered the bonds of common interest that have held the city together.

From that day forward, South Floridians have increasingly retreated back into a tribal mentality: my group against the rest of the world. I'm reminded of Sarajevo. Before the Balkan wars, Bosnians, Croats, and Serbs lived and worked together side by side. In 1984, while still under communist domination, that city was showcased to the world when it hosted the winter Olympics. Merely eight years later Sarajevo was under military siege, suffering daily bombardments, divided by intense hatreds, the scene of untold atrocities. I prayed that wouldn't happen in my home city.

Our ride back from the airport was detoured by a spontaneous demonstration that had broken out at the intersection of LeJeune Road and Flagler Street. Someone had torched tires and rolled them burning into the street. The wind carried the smoke in our direction, making Martina gag on the stench of burning rubber that penetrated the car, even with our windows closed. A crowd gathered along the corners and spilled onto the street, where people chanted slogans in Spanish and English denouncing Clinton's policy of returning Cuban rafters to the communist island. The police had blocked off the road, and Martina and I watched in horror as officers used billy clubs and tear gas to force the protestors back onto the sidewalk. Stuck about a block away in the resulting traffic jam, unable to reverse direction, we watched helplessly as a cloud of gas wafted toward us. This too penetrated my Honda, and in a matter of seconds tears were streaming from our burning eyes. Finally, I switched off the engine and we fled on foot into the lobby of a nearby office building. The occupants of the other cars trapped beside us followed right behind.

At last we caught our breath and the stinging in our eyes eased. Martina shook her head and wiped aside some tears. Then, to my surprise, a smile spread across her face.

"This reminds me of the good old days," she laughed. "When soldiers would shoot tear gas and pepper spray at us as we marched against the neo-fascists back home. The pigs. You could tell they weren't just enforcing the law. They liked hurting us."

Martina never ceased to amaze. She was *enjoying* this. I was terrified!

"I remember when my mother would come home after protesting all day against the Vietnam War," I told her. "Her hair would be all tangled, her clothes were usually dirty or torn. A lot of times her eyes were swollen from the gas, and she'd be bruised from the cops' clubs or from being shoved down to the pavement. I was only about seven or eight, and thank God she had enough sense not to take me with her, unlike some of her friends who wanted their children to participate in history. It was traumatic enough just to see her beaten up all the time. The late sixties and early seventies terrified me."

"Oh, I thought the protests were exciting. I loved them. They were exhilarating," Martina brushed my hair with her hand. "You're all mussed up." A young Latin couple standing a few feet away, also recovering from the tear gas, gave her a funny look, but we ignored them.

"I think I know what you mean." I liked it when Martina was attentive to my appearance like that. It showed she cared. "I was scared shitless, but Mom seemed to thrive on her righteous indignation. I don't think I'd ever seen her more focused and energetic. She was a little more wild-eyed than usual, but overall I think she was at her sanest during her years of protest."

Martina nodded her head. "Street protest is the perfect act of rebellion. You get to confront the authorities and know that this time you are in the right and they are in the wrong. It feels so *good*," she said, accentuating her Czech accent in a way she knew I found sexy. "It's a tremendous turn on. Then you go home with your lover, all sweaty and bruised and beat up, and fuck all night long."

I didn't enjoy hearing about Martina's past sexual escapades, but from time to time she felt it necessary to work them into our conversations. I never really figured out why. It may just have been a manifestation of her frank, matter-of-fact acceptance of her own sexuality, but perhaps it was a demonstration of independence too, although I was doing my best not to be possessive or controlling.

"The problem is," I offered, "that indignation feels good regardless of how righteous the cause really is. After all, Hitler rose to power on a wave of righteous indignation."

Martina merely shrugged. "What are you going to do? That's people for you."

After about half an hour the demonstrations were contained and we were able to return to the car and drive through the intersection. Someone had ripped the antennas from several of the abandoned cars, and my FM radio no longer worked. So Martina flipped through the AM channels, and we listened to talk show hosts rant and rave in English, Spanish, and Creole. Having just returned from another multiethnic city that was apparently at peace with itself, we were struck by how deeply Miami had already regressed into tribalism. The traffic was generously peppered with cars and SUVs flying Cuban or American flags or--for those seeking a middle ground--both. Weirdly enough, crossing Eighth Street (Calle Ocho), we saw three young black men waiting at a stop light in a beat-up, blue pickup truck with a Confederate flag tied to the antenna. Apparently these boys were deranged and believed that the rednecks displaying Confederate colors around town were their allies. Somehow, in the weeks following the Elian raid the Confederate flag had come to represent for some an anti-Cuban, anti-immigrant, pro-American stance--never mind that the Confederacy wanted to destroy the union that is America. In their anti-Hispanic frenzy, these boys had unbelievably forgotten that the Confederates enslaved their ancestors and instituted a program of white supremacy whose effects they, themselves, still felt. Their awareness of current events wasn't any better. Just a few months earlier the Confederate flag atop South Carolina's capital building had stirred a national furor and become an early test for candidates vying for the Republican presidential nomination. But these boys-- they were teenagers or in their early twenties--were blithely unaware of any of that as they beat time and mouthed the words to the hip-hop booming from their stereo and drove through the heart of Little Havana flaunting their contempt for immigrants.

Billboards we passed promoted a vision of a working multi-ethnic community. A clothing manufacture advertising a rainbow of fabrics showed children of all races and nationalities at play with one another, and several other ads with corporate settings likewise presented people of different ethnicities working happily together. But the graffiti on the walls was anti-black, anti-white, anti-Hispanic, anti-gay, anti-straight, anti-Anglo, anti-Haitian, anti-Nicaraguan, anti-Mexican, anti-Honduran, anti-Costa Rican, anti-Semitic. It was altogether a disconcerting scene to return home to.

Finally, we arrived at the apartment. While I brought in the last of our luggage and my briefcase containing the pie-throwing video, Martina put on Janacek's *Sinfonietta*, and suddenly her room with the revolutionary posters and hypnotic paintings seemed warm and familiar. For the first time since returning to Miami, I felt comfortable and secure.

As July faded into August, Martina and I came to know one another better. It was an exciting time in our partnership, as we learned hidden things about each other's past and explored each other's mind, spirit, and body. But still, some conflicts surfaced between us. I was inclined to work within the system, while Martina was more attracted to radical causes. Fortunately, pasting Perry Norwich with that pie had earned points for me with her, and our relationship remained mostly happy.

I found Martina's childhood experiences of communism fascinating and asked about them often. But the post-communist period shaped her life just as profoundly. She was seventeen when the communist regime in Czechoslovakia collapsed. By the time she was nineteen and a freshman in college, the country had split into Slovakia and the Czech Republic; and when she was twenty-two, she came to study at the universities of the world's sole remaining superpower. Talk about culture shock. The same year she arrived in America, Diane and Sharon left me. So the subsequent five years had been periods of great transition and acclimation for both of us.

Almost as soon as Martina enrolled at the university in Prague she became caught up in politics. The republic was young and groups of all stripes were vying to seize the moment and set the course for the new country. The campus coffee shops and lounges were filled with earnest young men and women haranguing one another about the rights of man and the obligations of the state. Western-style feminism was also in the air, and Martina soon gained a reputation for challenging her schoolmates and professors about the entitlements of women too. Her experience of communism had left her leery of leftist propaganda about a classless society and the solidarity of the workers, but she was even more alarmed by the brutal, chauvinistic slogans that burgeoning neo-Nazis organizations were suddenly able to circulate in the new political environment. Fearful of losing her freshly won personal liberties if the fascists prevailed, in her sophomore year Martina joined an underground cell of activists dedicated to thwarting the fascists.

Most of their work was routine rabble rousing: passing out leaflets, organizing protest marches, even publishing a thin, weekly newspaper. The short, unscheduled newscasts they broadcast from a mobile, pirate radio station were perhaps less squarely within the law, but Martina was convinced that they served a good cause. Moreover, as the Internet made its way into the Czech Republic, she and her friends were among the first to employ it as a tool for political activism.

Martina wasn't quick to volunteer information about her underground activities, but after we'd been together for about a month, she revealed that she'd also participated in a "covert action" to humiliate one the more prominent neo-Nazi organizations. Apparently it involved hacking into their website and replacing the pictures of its leaders with fake images of them cross-dressing and kissing. I wondered about the political correctness of the homosexual allusions but took some pleasure at imagining how ticked off those macho men must have been when they saw themselves like that on their own website. I also marveled that Martina had the guts to do it and wondered if, in the same situation, I'd have dared provoke such vicious madmen.

My concerns proved well founded. The fascists had covert operatives of their own, and they somehow learned who was responsible. One of Martina's cohorts was badly beaten and another brutally raped in retaliation.

"You must have been terribly frightened." I shuddered in second-hand terror as I imagined the fury of the fascist goons.

"Of course, I was concerned," Martina answered in an even voice. "I looked over my shoulder a lot in those days; I'll admit it. But I wasn't so scared, mostly just cautious. I still went to my classes, and I engineered the trap that caught the spy among us--one of my feminist friends who'd been secretly seduced by a good-looking Aryan from Germany." Martina pretended to spit on the ground at the mention of the betrayal.

"What happened to the traitor?"

"You don't want to know." I raised my eyebrow, but Martina dismissed my worst fear with a scornful wave of the hand. "Don't worry, we didn't hurt her physically. We just shaved her beautiful, long, blond hair, like we did to collaborators after World War II, painted her scalp blue, rolled her in donkey dung, and dropped her off at her lover's apartment. I don't think he found her so attractive after that."

I shook my head, amazed. "What happened then?"

"I'd received a scholarship offer to study in America about a week before we were exposed. The year before I'd read *Gravity's Rainbow* in one of my college classes, and I knew from the third chapter that your father had much to tell me and I had to go to America to find him. So I applied for the scholarship. At first, I wasn't sure this was the right time for me, but I took the threat from the fascists as a sign that it was."

Although Martina acted tough, from time to time I could see how her brush with the Nazis had left unhealed wounds and bitter resentment. These sometimes burst forth. One night she returned home late in an ill humor over something that had come up in one of her women's groups. After we got into bed she asked me, "Do you want to know how they fuck under communism?" There was an edge to her voice.

"Sure, how do they fuck under communism?"

"Like the filthy pigs they are." She described how, at each weekly meeting, her Party block leader would tell them that communist doctrine regarded women's orgasms decadent, because, unlike a man's orgasm that procreates the species and provides additional workers for the labor force, women's orgasms serve no practical purpose. "They selfishly indulge the individual," he'd preach over and over again.

"I don't remember ever reading that in Marx or Lenin," I replied.

Martina just shot me a look of disgust. "They didn't give a shit about Marx or Lenin. Almost none of them ever did. Communism was just an excuse to put perverts into positions of power whenever it suited their purposes. That's all they ever really cared about. Power.

"This leader, this so-called paragon of communism, was constantly sneaking up on me and my friends, touching our shoulders and hips and breasts while admonishing us not to play with ourselves and insisting that when girls had orgasms, it was like they were stealing from the soviet. Even with our parents standing right there, he'd feel us up while insisting that we renounce pleasure. They couldn't do anything to stop him because he was in tight with the Party. I was only eleven or twelve at the time, and didn't know what an orgasm was, really. Even so, I could see that the bastard's obsession with our bodies was unnatural.

"A few years later, I heard he'd raped the sister of one of my friends. She said he commanded her to come while he was inside her. When she told him what she thought he wanted to hear--that it would be stealing from the soviet--he slapped her hard. Then, when she confessed that she was frigid and couldn't come, he struck her again, harder. He beat her until she finally faked an orgasm. Then he beat her even more savagely because she'd had one."

"That's horrible," I cringed.

"But the Party protected him. They didn't care, just so long as the sonofabitch carried out their orders. So much for the Workers' Paradise. The Party didn't give a shit about the workers." Martina's disgust showed on her face. Then she leaned over to me and said accusingly, as though I were somehow responsible, "Neither do the fascists or the corporations."

"Why are you blaming me?" I demanded, but Martina just huffed and turned away. I lay silent a while, perplexed. Finally I offered, "Do you want to know how they fuck under capitalism?"

Martina turned around back toward me and eyed me suspiciously. "How?"

"Customers pay women to have orgasms over the phone or on the Internet. That's the fundamental difference between the two systems. The communists suppressed the female orgasm, while the capitalists found a way to market it. Nothing like the profit motive to spark the imagination and invigorate a society. The female orgasm boosted our economy. That's why the capitalists won the Cold War."

"So selling orgasms won the Cold War?"

"What else? Reagan's defense spending?"

Martina's expression said that she knew I was putting her on, but I continued with my banter anyway, and her mood finally lightened. At last she gave me a quick peck on the cheek and then slid beneath the covers. She placed the blanket over her head. A moment later she peered out and smiled coquettishly. "Why don't you check out my private enterprise zones?" Then she ducked back under the sheets.

I lay beside her silent but amused. She stuck her head out again. "I think you'll like my bottom line." Then back beneath she dove.

How quickly her moods could change! That was foreign to me. Diane had never been so mercurial. I still can't altogether comprehend it. But it had its moments.

Martina's head popped out once again. "I think an infusion of new capital would really stimulate my economy."

Sliding in beside her, I pulled the covers over my head too, and we set about to redistribute the wealth.

The summer was rapidly drawing to a close, and I had less than two weeks to prepare for the fall semester, which actually begins in late August. I was slated to teach a sophomore course in historical analysis in which we take two or three separate events and approach them through a variety of methodologies. My other course was a graduate seminar on the history of propaganda that began with the ancient Greeks and Romans and moved forward to the 1991 Persian Gulf War. Naturally, one of the common threads traced how eugenics has been used as a tool for propaganda throughout the ages. After all, even the same Greeks who gave us democracy, trial by jury, and a system of rational inquiry had dismissed all non-Greeks as barbarians. Euripides treats the theme in *Medea*.

Anyway, I spent my time mostly getting ready for my classes and working on my eugenics research. Martina immersed herself in re-reading *Gravity's Rainbow*. Over dinner we would analyze Dad's politics. Sometimes our discussion would become heated, as we each stubbornly defended our own interpretations. But mostly we pushed each other, interrogating each other and offering passages from the texts to support our own points or negate the other's. I enjoyed these sessions immensely; Martina has a sharp mind, and she always kept me on my toes. Our dialogues were good for Martina too. They inspired a few new key points for her dissertation. Our intellectual play during this time was one of the most satisfying aspects of our relationship.

One night I was surfing through some right-wing websites when I came across a virulent denunciation of genetic mutations. Among the so-called deformities that we Jews have allegedly manufactured to infect the Aryan gene pool were Houyhnhnms. According to the author of the diatribe, Houyhnhnms were the products of a highly classified experiment that the CIA conducted in the '50s. (And, of course, we all know that the CIA is secretly run by Jews, right?) Curious, I did a keyword search on "Houyhnhnm," but I mostly just came up with were references to the fourth book of *Gulliver's Travels*. One site, however, featured a beautiful white horse that invited me to follow a series of links that would reveal the next step beyond *homo sapiens* in human evolution.

I called Martina into my study to show her.

"Fascinating," she declared after reviewing the site. "We've gone through *homo habilis* and *homo erectus*; I guess sooner or later something will replace us *homo sapiens*."

Martina's wealth of information always impressed me. I'd forgotten about *homo habilis*. But I did remember seeing something on television a while back showing evidence that *homo erectus* and *homo sapiens* co-existed at some point and may even have mated with one another.

"Is it possible," I asked, "that a new species of human already walks among us?"

"Why just one?" Martina rejoined. "Maybe there are several competing new species, and they don't even know it. How would they? They'd just assume they are human like everyone else, only they're a little different."

I paused to consider what she said. "That takes in just about everyone I know."

"Well, sometimes you're paranoid, and sometimes they really are trying to kill you."

"I'm paranoid?" I was puzzled.

"No, I only mean that most of the people you know are probably just maladjusted, but perhaps some of them really are different."

"Most of the people I know are maladjusted?"

"Well, from what I've seen of your friends and from what you've told me of your family, need I say more? What about your mother, and your daughter? Sharon copes pretty well, but I wouldn't exactly call mainstream someone whose idea of party talk is a debate over twenty-first century social formation."

"Are you suggesting that Sharon and I are Houyhnhnms?"

"I'm just saying that I wouldn't rule anything out."

"I don't know if I should be flattered or insulted."

"Just be open to the quirkiness of life. Someone had to be the first *homo sapiens*; someone will have to be the first *meta-homo sapiens*. Or *post-homo sapiens*."

"Like the first poststructuralist."

"Exactly. It might as well be you. Or me. I could be one too."

Somehow our dialogue over what a *post-homo sapiens* might be like evolved into another delightful free-form exploration of absurd but real occurrences in the universe: the fact that Richard Nixon is the only president whose name appears on the moon, "Or that the governor of Minnesota used to be a professional wrestler," Martina never ceased to sound amazed whenever she made this point, which was often.

"Why not? President Truman was a haberdasher. And not a very successful one, either. And, of course, Ronald Reagan was a movie star. It didn't keep him from making history." I then recalled other bizarre events from the Cold War era. Marilyn Monroe allegedly sleeping with both Kennedy and a Mafia chief; CIA efforts to assassinate Castro with exploding cigars; J. Edgar Hoover's rumored penchant for dressing in women's clothes; Nixon's Keystone Cops, the White House Plumbers who wore cheap disguises and bungled the Watergate break-in; the Bible hidden inside an Israeli-baked cake and delivered to the Iranian ayatollahs during Reagan's Iran-Contra fiasco.

"I read that Saddam Hussein's first grab for power involved a botched attempt to assassinate the dictator then ruling Iraq," Martina laughed. "The plan failed because the driver of the car that was supposed to block a key intersection couldn't find his keys." Then she added, gasping with excitement, "And wait, wait. Yes. Someone once told me Nancy Reagan participated in a drug raid in Los Angeles. That's right. She was right there with the cops when they swarmed into an inner-city crack house and busted a group of addicts lying on the floor, stoned out of their minds."

I'd forgotten about that raid. But now I recalled how surreal it seemed when I saw the First Lady wearing a police uniform on television.

"Can you imagine," I asked, "what those poor strung-out bastards must have thought when they looked up to see her grim face staring down at them with that angry, self-righteous expression of hers. It must have seemed like the hand of God reaching out to get them. The president's wife had come all the way across the continent to their filthy little crack house in the heart of the ghetto just to smite their sorry, strung-out asses."

"Talk about feeling that Whitey's out to get you."

"And there's nowhere he, or she, won't go to catch you."

We swapped bizarre anecdotes for almost half an hour. Then Martina suddenly became serious and declared, "We can use the absurd for good."

"I already have. I'm Pie-thrower, remember?"

"Of course I remember. I've never been more proud of you. But we can do more. We need to reach a wider audience."

"How about the Internet? They don't get much wider than that."

Martina liked the idea, and we considered it for the rest of the evening. At last we decided to create an absurdist website that ridiculed the hate mongers—not altogether unlike what Martina had done in Prague. But we'd be more careful about making sure no one could trace it back to us.

"If we're clever about it and come up with some ingenious ways to promote it," Martina offered, "it might just catch on."

"Ridicule can be a powerful political weapon," I concurred. "What should we call it?"

"You've already acquired an identity as Pie-thrower. Why not *Pie-thrower.com*?"

Over the next few days Martina and I designed our website. She has very good computer skills and a stronger visual sense than I do, and she came up with countless ideas to illustrate the stupidity of the neo-Nazi propaganda. One of my favorites shows a skinhead sitting on a stool in the corner of an elementary school class, wearing a dunce cap. He's thinking, "Six million Jews dead, their culture destroyed throughout Europe. Must have been another conspiracy by Jewish bankers and the Elders of Zion." Another cartoon presents distorted pictures of famous, demented kings and queens. The subtitle reads, "Generations of inbreeding created lunacy and feeble-mindedness among Europe's upper class: another case for genetic purity." After that, she designed an entire series of harmful or ridiculous outcomes from practices promulgated in Aryan Nations publications, all with the banner, "Another case for genetic purity." Our home page featured the video clip of Mighty Mouse and me assaulting that fascist in Chicago with pies. It contained the "Pie-thrower" caption from the news broadcast, which Martina programmed to flash on and off while the video played.

Martina's radical friends back in the Czech Republic specialized in launching untraceable underground websites. I didn't understand the details, but somehow they routed ours through Slovakia, Russia, India, and Israel, figuring that the maze of international hostilities would stymie anyone trying to follow all the threads.

Martina has a real, creative flair for this kind of work, and our time together running the website stands out among my happier memories of our relationship. We would bounce silly ideas off each other, making them sillier and sillier with each new suggestion, before one of us would suddenly stop laughing and blurt out a useable concept. She'd discuss her plans for creating visuals, and I'd throw in my thoughts as well. It was a delightfully spirited collaboration.

However, although our shared love of the absurd and our mutual disgust at neo-fascism created a wonderful, common playground for us, our political and temperamental differences soon began to take a toll. Martina can be a hot-head who is quick to change moods. And she is passionate about her causes. Actually, as I think about it now, I can see that she shares these qualities with my mother. Perhaps, dear Oedipus, that accounts for some of the attraction. Maybe what I wanted all along was a girl just like the girl who slept with dear old dad. Martina just wanted dear old dad.

Tensions within Miami continued to grow as temperatures climbed. An early September hurricane, a deadly category 4 storm, came as close to Miami as it could before turning north to lash out at the good people of North Carolina instead. Although many of us felt fortunate to have been spared, the frightening expectation of sudden disaster stirred the pot even more. Then, the week after classes began, a group of radicals blew-up a Cuban radio studio. The station regularly featured anti-gay clergy who virulently attacked homosexuality, and it had been a frequent target of gay protestors. After the attack in which, fortunately, no one was hurt, the Hysterical Lesbians for Freedom (HLF) sent untraceable e-mails to newspapers and television stations claiming credit. And they promised to wage an aggressive, relentless, "hysterical" war against any group that deprived them of equal rights.

You can imagine how this polarized the community. Still, I never expected it to foment a rift between Martina and me. When we heard about the bombing on the six o'clock news, Martina told me that she recognized the name of the group and knew one of its members.

"In fact," she said matter-of-factly, "we were lovers for a short while." Then she turned her attention to the television and shouted, "Good for you, Linda!"

I don't know if I was more surprised by Martina's announcement of her bi-sexuality or her approval of a terrorist act. I needed some time to process the former, so I addressed the latter instead.

"What do you want to do, start a civil war here? Innocent people could have been killed."

But Martina shooed my complaints aside. "Because of these sanctimonious shits, innocent gays are harassed every day, even tortured and killed. It's about time we fought back."

"We?" I asked in a neutral tone.

"Yes, '*We!*'" Her voice was hard and defiant.

"Well, this isn't the way to go about it. Boycott their businesses and hit them where it hurts. But blowing up buildings will only create a homophobic backlash like you can't imagine. Do you think Timothy McVeigh helped his cause when he pulled off the Oklahoma City bombing? He galvanized his enemies and turned the nation against the militias and separatists. If you think things are bad now, just wait until you give these people a real excuse to fight against you."

"What do *you* know?" she huffed. Then she stood up from the sofa.

"Apparently, not much."

"Apparently not." Martina marched into her room, and I remained behind wondering who was this woman I was living with.

An hour later Martina emerged, dressed for the evening and holding her handbag.

"Aren't you ready?" she demanded.

"Ready?"

"We're supposed to go to dinner at Dr. Mulligan's house, don't you remember? Or are you ashamed to be with me?"

"Why would I be ashamed of you?"

"I don't know. You tell me."

"I'm not ashamed of you because you're apparently bi-sexual. But I find it a little strange to find out only after we've been lovers for two months."

"The topic never came up."

"I guess not. It never occurred to me to ask."

Martina shrugged. Then she asked if I was ashamed of

her because she supported a group of radicals.

"Frankly, that troubles me, yes."

"I don't know why. My stand is consistent with everything I've ever said or done since you've known me."

"Maybe that's true. I just took it for granted that you'd seen enough political violence for a lifetime and that you'd find acts of terror morally repugnant."

"You're so bourgeois," the disdain dripped from her voice. "You're a historian. You know that social change is messy and that violence has its place. Look at your Boston Tea Party and John Brown's raid on Harper's Ferry. They played their roles in making America what it is today. Well, my friends are prepared to play theirs."

I had no reply for that. I just shrugged and asked if she still wanted to go to Brian's.

"Of course. He's my major professor. You don't think I'm going to stand him up at the last minute?"

I found it odd that someone who promulgated violent protest was so hung up on the social niceties, but I said nothing. Instead, I changed my clothes, put on a pair of real shoes instead of the sandals I was wearing, and we went out for the evening.

Brian is always a gracious, good-humored host, and we had lots of laughs. He divorced several years earlier and wasn't involved with anyone special now. I'd never met this evening's date before, a thirty-something stockbroker named Valerie. She was tall and slender with auburn, shoulder-length hair, and she smiled easily. She seemed like a good fit for Brian, but of course I had no idea how they got along when they were alone. I didn't even know for sure if she was straight, gay, or bi-sexual. I was learning to take nothing for granted anymore.

Brian had custody of Roger, who joined us at the table with his girlfriend Natasha. I remembered her from Independence Day as a spunky kid, and she solidified that impression during the course of the evening. One of the new English professors also came with his wife, and Brian, who is an excellent cook, prepared an amazing stuffed zucchini. The other English professor brought a bottle of a very satisfactory Chianti, and we all had a pretty nice evening. Martina was clever and witty and seemed to put our quarrel behind her. But during the ride home in the car afterward she responded to my attempts at a friendly conversation with single word answers, grunts, and silences. She went to bed before I finished checking my e-mail and feeding Pandora.

Chapter 6

The next morning Martina acted as though nothing had happened between us. She rose before me and went to check the Pie-thrower website. She liked to report the number of hits on the site over breakfast. We hadn't been getting much action--not surprising for a new site with no advertising--but Martina rushed into the kitchen brimming with excitement. Overnight, we'd jumped from about twenty hits a day to about two hundred. We were delighted but couldn't figure out the cause of our good fortune. Finally, Martina did searches on "Nazi," "neo-Nazi," "skinheads," "white supremacy," "Elders of Zion," and a few other key words. Our site came up among the first ten listings each time. The best we could figure was that some geek at Google stumbled across it, liked what he saw, and did his bit for the cause by giving us prominent exposure.

Later, I checked my e-mail and found a note from Sharon. When Martina and I left Chicago, Sharon promised to visit before beginning her fall semester, which started about a month later than mine. Her message confirmed her plan to stay with us the following week. She asked if it would be alright if Helena came along. Helena had never been to Miami and was anxious to see this classic American "melting pot" first hand. Sharon concluded by stating how people were still talking about my pie-throwing and that new episodes of political theater were breaking out all around the campus. After all my years as a scholar, I was gratified to see that I had finally made my mark on an institution of higher learning as venerable as the University of Chicago.

Given Martina's recent mood swings, I wasn't sure what kind of answer I'd receive when I asked if she'd mind having Helena stay with us too. But to my relief she seemed cheered by the prospect. So I e-mailed Sharon and firmed up our plans.

I spent the rest of the day working at the university; Martina stayed at the apartment reading and surfing the Net. Since returning from Chicago, she'd intensified her efforts to track down my father. A few promising leads had fizzled, but when I returned home that evening, she was ecstatic. Literally jumping up and down with joy, like a kid, she announced, "He's in North Carolina!"

"Who?"

"Who else, silly?"

"Dad?"

"Of course. Your father. He's living in a cabin on a large, secluded piece of property outside of Blowing Rock, North Carolina. It's in the Appalachians."

"How do you know?"

"From a graduate student at Appalachian State University who's on one of my listserves. She works at a coffee shop in Boone, where he comes in almost every morning for breakfast. The owner is a friend of his from way back; they were in the Navy together. Your dad has been living there for the past year or so, working on a new novel."

For the first time in my life, the prospect of finally meeting my father seemed plausible. I was stunned.

"Every day he orders a toasted, buttered pumpernickel bagel and then smothers it with low fat cream cheese."

Suddenly, I remembered my experience with the gypsy on San Padre Island. "Shortly before Natalia tried to kill me, I had a vision of an older man in a coonskin cap pointing to bear tracks around a boulder. He was holding onto his cap so the wind wouldn't blow it away."

"I remember. You told me about it."

"I'd thought of Davy Crockett and Tennessee. But it must been Daniel Boone and Blowing Rock."

"This is freaky," Martina's eyes glistened with excitement.

"So what do we do now?" I asked.

Martina wanted to catch the next plane for Boone and then camp out at the coffee shop. Actually, it wasn't a bad plan, except that Boone has no airport. Dad was known to be leery of strangers and would probably just cut me cold if I walked up to him and introduced myself as his son. But apart from being an attractive young woman, Martina had the charm, wit, and exotic appearance that might well appeal to him. Once she befriended him, she could tell him about me and test his reaction. However, I convinced her to wait until after Sharon's visit. I was sure that Sharon would want to be involved in any plan that might allow her to meet her famous, long-lost grandfather.

    The week leading up to Sharon and Helena's visit was a golden time in my relationship with Martina. I'd never seen her in better spirits. Her anger was gone and she filled her days imagining her first encounter with her idol, my father. As the son of Thomas Pynchon, I enjoyed the benefits of her good humor and happy disposition. At this juncture in our lives, her bi-sexuality did not seem to be an issue. On top of that, my classes were off to a good start, and Martina and I were having a ball with *Piethrower.com*, which continued to grow in popularity on the Web. The day before Sharon arrived we had over 700 hits. I'd been reunited with my daughter, things were seemingly great again with Martina, and I'd finally located my dad. The prospects for the coming fall appeared fantastic.

    When I greeted Sharon at the airport, she looked radiant. She hadn't been in Miami since December, and all the way back to Martina's apartment she commented on how the low skyline and open skies made a welcome change from the sooty Chicago high-rises that block out the sun. Although still hot and thick with humidity, Miami's air felt fresh and clear in comparison to the northern smog. Helena concurred. She and Martina shared the backseat, while Sharon and I made father-daughter talk up front.

    I had to be in school for most of the days when the girls were visiting, but my nights were free. Martina was taking just one seminar. It met once a week on Monday mornings; so she was able to spend considerable time with them in my absence. They took an air boat ride in the Everglades, something Sharon had never done, and hiked through Fairchild Tropical Gardens-- the most splendid place in town, in my opinion. One day they snorkeled above a coral reef off of Key Largo. Another day they went deep sea fishing on a charter boat that left from Miami Beach. That night Martina and Helena grilled their catch and seasoned it in special Czech and Greek spices and marinates that made the occasion especially festive. Afterward, we drove to South Beach and had drinks at an outdoor table on Ocean Drive. The balmy sea breezes caressed me as I basked in the companionship of my favorite women. Sharon savored her rum daiquiris and swayed to the Latin salsa emanating from a live band performing down the street. Helena observed the large number of openly gay male and female couples, and Martina described an article she'd read detailing how the vibrant gay community in South Beach had played a major role in the economic revitalization of the area.

"You need look no farther than Versace and the fashion industry," Sharon piped in.

"Just look what they did to him," Helena reminded.

"Actually, we're sitting only a few blocks down from where he was murdered." I pointed down the street. "Years ago, before South Beach was South Beach, a history professor I knew lived in that building--before Versace transformed it into a palace. I visited him once. It had a lovely interior European courtyard. That's what must have attracted Versace."

"That murder was a tragedy!" Helena remained indignant.

After we finished our drinks, we decided to walk along the beach. Strolling barefoot, carrying their shoes in one hand, Sharon and Helena splashed each other, while Martina and I walked ahead, breathing in the salt air, listening to the waves lap the shore, and watching a huge, shiny, full moon slide in and out among the clouds as it rose over the Atlantic ocean.

Unfortunately, our days of good cheer were marred by the escalating hostilities within the community. The following morning, I was wakened by a phone call from Brian Mulligan. His son's girlfriend, Natasha, had been maimed in a car bombing. She was waiting across the street for her ride to school when her neighbor's Ford Explorer exploded. The neighbor, a teacher who had sponsored a gay teens' support group at a Reform Jewish temple off campus, was killed.

I went to school in a state of shock, horrified at what had happened to the lively little girl I'd dined with a few nights earlier. I was further rattled when I arrived on campus and saw that security had been stepped up. I learned that a group of militant black students had staged a sit-down strike early that morning in front of one of the classroom buildings, blocking access to its entrances. On top of that, for some crazy reason, a few were carrying toy rifles and firing them off periodically to punctuate their demand for separate dorms. The university president canceled classes in that building and told the demonstrators that he would allow them to stay until noon, if they agreed to put aside their toy guns, which were making the campus police very nervous, and to disperse as soon as the campus clock struck twelve. If they refused to disperse, county police would arrest them. Wisely, the students surrendered their rifles, but they refused to disband. Twenty minutes later, phalanxes of policemen armed in riot gear stood across from the twelve protestors who sat unflinching on the ground before each entrance.

Around my department, the faculty split about 80-20 against the students. Two of the Marxists and an old '60s radical supported them, but most of the rest of us thought the action was inappropriate and ill-prepared and that they had not first pursued other, more legitimate ways to achieve their goals. One of our African-Americanists was completely exasperated. She put her hands on her hips and declared, "We put our lives on the line in the '60s so black people wouldn't have to be segregated. And now these *bozos demand* separate dorms. What is this world coming to?"

Our department secretaries told us about reports of bomb threats and plans for counter demonstrations. The last thing anyone wanted was a violent confrontation between the students and the cops, but the president had backed himself into a corner and couldn't easily make further concessions. Plus, he was contending with demands by vocal groups of white and Hispanic students who were outraged that the protestors had impeded their education and by faculty who were just as outraged not only by the disruption to their courses, but also by the assault on academic freedom it implied. On top of that, our law-and-order governor was making clear that he would not tolerate the disruption of a state university for very long. Fortunately, when the clock struck twelve and the police began to ready themselves to advance, the protestors stood and walked away.

I taught an 11:00 class in a different building. When the crisis concluded, I was in the midst of a lecture on how Pericles's famous funeral oration at the start of the Peloponnesian War served both as a genuine tribute to the dead and an act of propaganda that advanced the values of the democrats, who were his power base, against those of his rivals, the landowning oligarches then out of power in ancient Athens. By the time my work day ended, life on campus had returned more or less to normal, although demonstrations and counter-demonstrations were planned for that evening. The planners of each announced they would be peaceful and law-abiding, but I didn't stick around to find out.

When I arrived back home, Martina and the girls were still out; so I worked on the Pie-thrower website until they returned. They'd brought back a six pack of cold Coronas from the beach, and I told them about my day over beers. Naturally, they were all impressed. Martina and Helena, especially, had strong opinions which, to my surprise, supported the demand for separate dorms, even though they felt shutting down classes was premature.

"That's insane," I cried, my voice rising in frustration.

"No, it's your passive acceptance of a racist society that's insane," Martina shouted back.

"And voluntary segregation is going to make the society less racist?"

I argued with them for about fifteen minutes, until I couldn't take it any longer. We were getting nowhere, and I was quickly becoming exasperated. Finally, Sharon called me aside and suggested this might be a good time for a private, father-daughter chat. I hadn't had much opportunity to talk to her alone, and since my efforts to reach Martina and Helena were going nowhere, I agreed. So we excused ourselves and joined Pandora in my office.

After we sat and made ourselves comfortable, I asked Sharon about her studies and if she had plans for graduate school.

"Not yet."

"I think your writing is getting really strong," I told her. "I like how you are developing your own voice. It's both forceful and feminine. That's a rare combination."

"Thanks. I sent a story to the *Chicago Review*, but I still haven't heard anything." She'd never tried to publish anything before, and she seemed a little nervous by the prospect, but excited too.

"Well, I hope they take it. But don't let it get to you if

they don't. Unfortunately, coping with rejection is altogether too much a part of the writing business. Even if the story is great, it just might not be want they are looking for."

"I know," Sharon answered. Then, to my surprise, she sat up and asked, "Why'd you and Mom split up?"

The only version she ever really heard was Diane's. She was a teenager when Diane and I divorced, and after they moved away, she never seemed interested in hearing my side of it. So I was thrilled by her invitation. I think the pie-throwing heightened her respect for me, far beyond what she felt when she read my article. And at this stage of my life, nothing seemed more important than my daughter's respect.

"Where to begin?" I began. "As you know, I never knew my father, and Mom was mostly stressed out from trying to hold it all together as an artist and a single mother. So I didn't exactly grow up in a laugh-a-minute setting. That's why your mother delighted me. When we met, she was this wonderful light spirit, full of play. Not me. I was the nerd in high school who took himself too seriously. I remained pretty much a loner until I met Diane in college."

"How'd you guys meet?"

"Diane never told you?"

"Yeah, but I want to know what it was like from you."

"We happened to sit beside each other at the coffee shop on campus. She said something disparaging about the copy of *Mein Kampf* I was carrying for a term paper. That turned out to be my first research on the politics of eugenics, if you can believe it. We clicked in an instant. Imagine, that bastard Hitler brought me out of my shell and united me with my first true love. We conceived you that very first night while making love to the luscious strains of *Tristan and Isolde*. So Wagner, another rabid anti-Semite, gets an assist."

"I'll never listen to Wagner the same way," Sharon smiled.

"I never have. What thrilled my soul about your mother was how she could turn everything into a big game, a serious joke. It's not that she didn't value the ideas she sported with, but her perspective let her laugh about them too. And her wonderful creative spirit transformed every thought, person, situation, and idea she encountered into fodder for some outrageous but perfectly appropriate frolic. That's what's best about her fiction too, but she hasn't written like that in years."

Sharon pondered what I'd said and then nodded. "I see what you mean. I've always liked her early stuff best."

"We married about a month after Diane learned she was pregnant. Her folks had their doubts about our marrying so shortly after meeting--we'd only known each other for about two months before I proposed. But we were deeply in love, and when they couldn't change our minds, they very generously enabled us both to stay in college and then go on to graduate school."

"Yeah, Grandma and Grandpa are alright."

"Diane had had her MFA in creative writing for a couple years by the time I got my doctorate, but in the Bay area graduate degrees in English are a dime a dozen. So, when the state university in Miami offered me a position in its history program, I wrangled an instructorship for Diane in the English department, and we moved east. You were ten years old then, ready for fifth grade."

"I *know* how old I was. I had to leave all my best friends."

"I'm sorry for that, but we didn't have a livelihood in California."

Sharon paused and then shrugged, "I guess it's time for me to get over that."

"Thanks. We did what we had to do. At first your mom liked it here. Years of working in Berkeley as a part-time adjunct instructor, with no job security, no benefits, no place to meet students after class, and no status within the institution had begun to demoralize her. Her job in Miami was a step up. But four or five writing-intensive classes a semester--classes that required her to comment endlessly on every paper submitted by every student-- left her with little time or mental energy for her own writing. It was clear that she was becoming increasingly frustrated. She simmered like this for several years, less and less playful, less and less content, less and less fun to be with. Then, after she finally published her second volume of poems to considerable acclaim, the department turned down her application for promotion from instructor to assistant professor."

"She's still pissed about that," Sharon informed me. "You should hear what she calls your pals in the English

Department."

"I can just imagine. I never got the full story behind it, but after the rejection Diane turned angry and bitter for real. Then she was no fun to be with at all. 'Have I not seen the loveliest woman born/ Out of the mouth of Plenty's horn...Barter that horn and every good/ By quiet nature understood/ For an old bellows full of angry wind?'"

"What's that quote from?" Sharon shifted in her chair.

"Yeats," I answered. "'A Prayer for My Daughter.'"

"I get the point," Sharon nodded.

"I hope our friends out there do too," I pointed to the livingroom. Sharon said nothing, so I continued. "When Diane's first novel won even greater accolades, the University of Iowa offered her a tenure-track position in their prestigious creative writing program. She accused me of careerism, but that wasn't an issue. I'd have moved to keep us all together, even to a lesser university. Not that Iowa's lesser, but there were no openings for me in their history department--or in any history department in the entire state. History isn't exactly a seller's market. Diane insisted on taking the job, and that was that. I really never had any input in the decision at all."

We both remained silent for a moment. Then I asked, "Is that how Diane tells it?"

"No, not really."

"What does she say?"

"She says that you could have stood up for her more than you did. That you could have tried to get some of your pals in the English Department to support her, but that you were too concerned about your own position to even try. And that you cared more about your career than your family."

I simply shook my head. "That's simply not how universities work. Departments are like little fiefdoms, and no one wants faculty members from other departments telling them what to do. I would have done more harm than good if I'd tried to intercede for her. Not that it would have made any difference, the way things turned out. But I thought she had a good shot at her promotion and didn't want to mess things up.

"As far as valuing my career more than my family, that's simply not true. But Diane didn't make it easy for me to reconcile both. We could have summered together. I could have taken a sabbatical and spent it in Iowa. There were other options. But Diane didn't want to hear about them. She was furious with the English Department, and she took it out on me."

"Well, you asked, and that's what she says."

"OK. Let's just change the subject. Are you seeing anyone special these days? At your party, I thought there might be something between you and your saxophonist friend."

Suddenly, Sharon's expression hardened. "I told you I've sworn off men."

"Isn't that a little extreme?"

"No. No it's not. Every boy I've ever gotten close to has treated me like shit."

"Come now." I kept pressing her for a more meaningful explanation, until finally she broke down.

"Look, I wasn't ever going to tell you this. But you're giving me very little choice." Sharon took a deep breath, as though to ready herself to say something difficult. Her body tensed and jaw clenched. Finally, she spoke. "The final straw came when my last boyfriend invited me back to an apartment he was taking care of for his friend Paul, who was away on vacation. But what he didn't tell me was that Paul had placed hidden cameras in each room, connected them to his computer, and hooked it all up to the Internet. People throughout the world can just drop in and see what's going on at any hour. They can survey each camera and choose the one they want to watch. Phillip says that Paul's making his life an art form. That on the Net he exists separately from himself. The bastard. That night, there were 739 hits on the site."

"That's pretty good."

"You say that now." Sharon's tone was so bitter that I pulled back in my seat.

"Did this guy rape you?" I demanded.

"Not technically, no. But he violated me something awful. Seven-hundred-thirty-nine people from New York to New Deli visited Paul's website--while I was performing oral sex on Phillip. He asked me to dance suggestively for him before we got started. He said it would really turn him on. Seven-hundred-thirty-nine people saw me do a striptease for someone I thought really liked me and cared about me. Can you imagine how humiliated I was when Helena told me that one of her friends had seen it all? He was going to download it but had a problem with his computer. Since then, I've had no use for men. None!"

My mouth dropped, but before I could respond, Martina thrust open the door.

"Get in here!" she commanded. "They've arrested the bastard who bombed Natasha. It's on TV."

We ran into the livingroom and caught the end of an interview with a police investigator who described the suspect as twenty-four year-old white man with a history of arrests for assault. According to the detective, the punk had admitted responsibility for the bombing and was proud of it.

"Poor Natasha," I felt overwhelmed with despair. "I used to think we were fighting the good fight and getting somewhere. But after today, I don't know. I've been battling against pigs like this all my adult life, but where has it gotten us?"

"That poor teacher!" Helena's outburst silenced me. Sharon walked over to the couch to comfort her. "They said on the radio today that she'd gotten an award for her work with troubled kids. Why are those the ones who get killed?" Helena demanded, turning her head toward me for some reason, as though I were somehow at fault. "Meanwhile, jerk-offs like this one live to laugh about it!"

"This just in," blurted the television news anchor. "The group that has taken responsibility for last week's bombing of an anti-gay radio station, the Hysterical Lesbians for Freedom, has issued a statement warning that attacks on homosexuals will be no longer tolerated and that reprisals are imminent."

"Holy shit!" I moaned "That's all we need. Soon there will be open warfare on the streets, like Beirut during the '80s. Either that or martial law."

"Bullshit!" Martina exploded. She walked across the room to interpose herself between me and my daughter. "Force is the only thing these people understand. If someone had killed Hitler in 1929 or '30, the world would have been a lot better off. The conservatives and religious right are getting more powerful everyday. They already control Congress, and they impeached Clinton for doing something that probably 85 percent of all your presidents have done. If not 100 percent."

"Lie, or screw around?" The sarcasm in Helena's voice was thick.

"Both," Martina declared. "You're pretty damn close in this country to something very scary, unless people like us stand up and do something. It's going to be *The Handmaid's Tale*, but for real this time!"

I'd read Margaret Atwood's book about fifteen years earlier. Motivated by the influence of the Moral Majority and religious right during the Reagan days, it's about a Christian patriarchy that represses women after a civil war in North America. But I thought we were considerably farther from that nightmare now than we were in 1985, when the novel came out. Despite its influence in Congress, the religious right no longer held sway in the White House, and the protections of and opportunities for women, and gays too for that matter, were more expansive and more firmly entrenched than ever. Women had flown combat missions in the Persian Gulf War; more women now attended college than men, and the first state, Vermont, had recently legitimized marriage-type contracts between gay couples. Even the Disney Corporation now offered health benefits to the partners of gay employees. What could be more all-American than Mickey Mouse? All of this social progress had occurred without violent attacks against the religious right.

"Court litigation, education, improved social conditions, good jobs, and full integration of schools and communities will help more than violence," I insisted.

But Martina snapped back, "Just like they have in Miami! Where's the political will for those reforms you tout? The citizens of this county won't even pass a penny sales tax to unclog the expressways and ease their own daily degradation in rush hour traffic. Do you think these people are going to allocate resources to improve social conditions for someone *else,* or to foster better understanding? You spend too much time in your ivory tower."

"She's right," Helena jumped in. "We need to fight back."

I looked at Helena and then back at Martina. "Look, I know non-violent reform can be slow, and its certainly doesn't give the same visceral satisfaction as smashing some pig's face with a brick. But it's a lot more likely to yield the results you want. I study history. Believe me, revolutions have a way of spinning out of control and crushing the people who started them. Look at the French revolution. It was begun by moderates fighting against the excesses of the royalty, and it fell into the hands of Robespierre and the other homicidal lunatics who killed the original leaders--and their vision--in the Reign of Terror. Of course, the Revolution's lasting legacy was Napoleon and about fifteen years of warfare that devastated Europe and Russia."

"Napoleon was a great lawmaker," Martina retorted. "He replaced the old king's whims with rule by law and advanced army officers and government officials on merit, instead of heredity. We studied that in our history of revolution classes. They don't teach you that sort of thing in America."

"No, we focused more on the millions of soldiers and civilians who suffered so Napoleon could satisfy his dreams of conquest."

But Martina just shrugged, "Most of the victims were peasants. If they hadn't been soldiers, they would probably have starved to death in the fields during the famines or met some other painful end at the hands of the aristocrats and the czar. It always sucks to be at the bottom of the pecking order. That's why we must fight."

"OK, what about Kerensky in Russia–a moderate who overthrew the czar for good reasons and then was kicked out by Lenin and the Bolsheviks? You grew up under communism. Do you think history was better off for Kerensky's February rebellion? Or how about the revolution in Iran. The shah was bad news, no doubt about it. But do you think the fundamentalists who pushed out the moderates that ejected him have been better for the people of that country than the shah, or worse? Certainly, if you value the rights of women, Christians, Jews, or homosexuals, things are worse. And then, of course, there's Castro. Sure, he expanded health care and educated the underclass, but don't you think that would have happened in the intervening forty years anyway, like it has throughout the rest of the region? Meanwhile, he runs an iron-fisted dictatorship, a personality cult like Stalin's."

"There's no comparison to Stalin," Martina huffed. "Cuba doesn't have show trials and purges that kill millions. The Cuban army doesn't occupy half a continent. My family knew the worst aspects of Stalin. Castro is no Stalin."

"Nonetheless, he's no Thomas Jefferson either."

"No, Castro doesn't own slaves!"

Martina was nearly shouting again, and I, too, raised my

voice in response. "And he didn't introduce democracy and political freedom to his fledgling country, like Jefferson did."

"Sure, for white men."

"Look," I took a breath to calm myself. "I'll grant you Jefferson's personal limitations, and even his vision for the Constitution was badly flawed. Legalized slavery was America's original sin, no doubt about it. We continue to be cursed for it. But at least judge these people according to their times. It's not like many other countries in the world were promoting full rights for women or abolishing slavery. In any case, do you seriously want to suggest that Castro has done more for the cause of personal liberty than our founding fathers? The slaves weren't any freer before Jefferson than they were after. He didn't make things worse for them, even if he didn't necessarily make things any better. The same for women. But a whole lot of people did acquire more freedom as a result of what Jefferson and the others did. And he presented a vision of self-determination to the world that inspired even those who were disenfranchised by the Constitution, and in the long run that lead to the expansion of civil liberties for everyone. Can you say the same for Castro?"

Helena chimed in, "All you know is what you've seen in the American media. Why don't you go down there and ask the women who had to work as whores before Castro closed down the international sex trade. It's what Cuba was famous for before the revolution, when the dictators ran the country for the capitalists. I bet those women feel a lot more empowered now, working at productive jobs, than when they had to sell their bodies just to stay alive."

"Yeah," I answered. "The ones with real jobs. But what about the new sex trade that's popped up in the past decade? Castro's using it to lure European vacationers and investors to salvage his failed economy. So, what's really changed for woman down there after all? It's the same as it was under Batista, except maybe now they get free health care."

"If the U.S. dropped the embargo," Martina interceded, "Castro wouldn't have to exploit his people like that. Besides, the real point we are arguing is not whether Castro is better than Jefferson, but whether revolution is a viable way of effecting change."

"Positive change," I insisted.

"Whatever. Might I point out that despite their differences, Castro and Jefferson were both revolutionaries. Your eloquent defense of your founding fathers makes my point. Revolution *can* work."

I turned to Sharon for support, but she just looked at Helena on the couch beside her and then to me.

"I'm with them," she announced. Then she softened her voice. "Dad, I was trying to tell you this earlier, but we were interrupted. Maybe this isn't the best time to say it, but I don't know when a good time would be." Sharon placed her arm on Helena's shoulder. "I meant it when I said I've sworn off men. I'm gay. Helena's not just my roommate, she's my lover too."

I fell silent. Stunned. It's not that I have anything in principle against a lesbian relationship, but family dynamics aren't exactly rational, and this sort of news is a lot for any father to assimilate.

"I hope you're not disappointed," Sharon said finally.

"No, I'm not disappointed," I answered slowly. "All I've ever wanted is for you to find love and happiness on whatever terms that are best for you. That's still what I want."

"Thanks, Dad." Sharon walked over and hugged me. "This means a lot to me."

.

Chapter 7

Sharon's declaration terminated my argument with Martina. At dinner, Sharon filled us in about how she and Helena had made the transition from friends to lovers, and she gushed about how wonderful it is to be in love. (It turns out that Martina and I had imposed no hardship when we made them double-up during our visit.) Helena was more reticent. I noticed her and Martina trading smiles as Sharon described how it felt to find a soul mate at last, and I wondered if Martina had told Helena that I was her soul mate. Certainly, we shared our passion for Pynchon with no one else; nor did anyone else delight in the absurd in quite the same way. Our creative play together was unlike anything I had known with anyone before. Not even with Diane. My spirits lifted at the thought that Martina had told someone else about how close she felt to me. Her passionate radicalism, which I'd previously only glimpsed, still troubled me, to be sure. But deep down, I still believed her heart was in the right place. Besides, despite her tough talk, Martina had been so concerned about deportation that she wouldn't even ride with me during my pie-throwing caper. Certainly she wouldn't do something even more reckless now that she'd located Dad.

Sharon stopped talking and reached over to grab Helena's hand and smile. While the idea of her apparent bi-sexuality still required some getting used to, I had to concede that Helena was good for Sharon. I'd never seen my daughter so caught up in the throes of romance, so brimming with joy.

After dinner we returned to the living room to see what movies were on the satellite. There was room for only three on the couch, so I pulled up a chair beside my daughter. Martina sat on the side opposite Sharon, and Helena slid in snugly between them. That made me feel a little odd, but I was determined to accept my daughter's life choices. But maybe my body language showed my discomfort, because from time to time I saw Helena giving me strange looks.

Annie Hall and *G.I. Jane* were just about to begin, and I managed to prevail on them to watch *Annie Hall*. Martina and I had seen it before, but neither Sharon nor Helena knew it, and I told them it was important for their cultural education. Despite Woody Allen's current status as a politically incorrect pariah, Martina enjoyed his absurd outlook, and she persuaded them to go along.

They overcame their political objections and were laughing out loud within the first five minutes. When Alvy brought out Marshal McLuhan to silence the obnoxious professor in line at the movie, Sharon said she was sure she'd taken a class with that guy.

The phone rang just as Woody was sneezing into a pile of expensive, hard-to-obtain cocaine at a chic New York gathering. Martina answered, listened a moment, and then took the handset into the bedroom and shut the door behind her. When she returned, Alvy and Annie were broken up, and a frustrated Alvy was taking out his hostility on an L.A. parking lot, much as he used to as a child driving the bumper cars his father operated on Coney Island. Martina walked over to the coffee table in front of us and picked up the remote control. She turned her back to us and switched of the TV.

"Hey," I objected. "The movie's not over yet."

Martina ignored me. "That was Linda," she announced, directing her words to Sharon and Helena, but not to me. "She was my lover some time ago. Now she's with the HLF, the Hysterical Lesbians. They've learned that in two days Marion Hines is going to address a right-wing rally in front of Bayfront Park and then lead a motorcade down Biscayne Boulevard and across the causeway to South Beach, where they will symbolically, and perhaps literally, drive the sinners from Deco Drive. That's us, folks," she looked directly at Sharon and Helena.

I felt my stomach tighten at Martina's words. "What does this woman, Linda, want with you?" Hines was a self-righteous homophobe and anti-abortion activist who commanded a large, vocal, and volatile following, especially among radical elements of the Christian Right. She was rumored to be connected to several abortion clinic bombings, although she'd always denied it and an FBI investigation had been unable to prove the allegations. Two abortion doctors and a twenty-one year-old pregnant woman had been killed, along with her unborn fetus. Hines was also said to have some ill-defined connections with the Aryan Nations and other white supremacist groups. This was going to be bad news, and I didn't want any part of it.

Martina stared at me as though she was sizing me up. Then she asked, "Are you sure you want to hear this? Maybe it would be better if you left the room."

"Of course I want to hear this."

"OK. You asked for it. Look, we all know that Marion Hines has blood on her hands. The only thing we don't know is how much and whether she actually pushed the plungers on those bombs or had someone else do it for her."

"You don't know that for a fact," I objected, but Martina insisted that if I interrupted again, I'd have to leave. I was aghast, but Sharon smoothed things over by asking me nicely just to let Martina finish. Then I could raise my objections.

Martina nodded to Sharon. "Thank you. As I was saying, this woman has blood on her hands." She glared at me, and I glared back but remained silent. "And now she's coming to our city, to our home, to drive us out because she doesn't like who we choose to screw."

"Whom," I corrected defiantly.

"Regardless of the grammar," Martina's eyes narrowed, and she spoke slowly and deliberately, "the HLF is going to off the bitch as soon as she crosses onto Miami Beach. The shooter's going to flee in a getaway car that she'll drive to a prearranged place. Then she'll exchange vehicles. They're going to switch three cars, and they need someone to drive the third one to the drop-off point ahead of time. That's it. Park the car, put the key in the ashtray, and walk away before anyone's even fired a shot. It's risk free. I told her I'd do it. Of course, I'll need someone to pick me up afterward and take me home."

"This is insane," I shouted, but Helena spoke up, "I'll pick you up. Then Sharon added, "I'll go with her."

"Are you people crazy?" I was out of my chair, waving my hands around like a madman. "You'd be making yourselves accessories to murder." I turned to Sharon. "You're finally in love. Do you want to go to jail now for twenty years?" Then I faced Martina, "Do you want to be deported back to Europe?"

"I want to do something important in my life for once," Sharon answered. "I want to take a stand. This woman and her followers must be stopped, and a website just isn't going to do it."

"I'm with her," Martina declared, and Helena concurred.

I'd never felt so frustrated in my life, not even when Diane announced she was moving away and taking Sharon with her. "What you are proposing is not only self-destructive, it's immoral. You're talking as though cold-blooded murder is a righteous act. That makes you no different from abortion-clinic bombers or Timothy McVeigh."

I went on like this for ten or fifteen minutes, reasoning, cajoling, sometimes even shouting. But my efforts were futile. As my arguments received less and less attention, I grew livid. Fearful I might lose all control, I left the apartment and took a long, long walk.

I've never felt as conflicted as I did then. On the one hand, my responsibilities as a citizen, as a moral human being, called out for me do whatever I could to thwart the assassination. But in the starkest terms, that meant informing on the two women I loved most, and I was loathe to do that. After all, I didn't want to send my daughter and my girlfriend to jail for conspiring to commit murder. And even if I struck a deal to protect them, at the very least, they'd feel betrayed and would hate me forever. Me, who'd always been indignant at the careers ruined by McCarthy-era informing. Friends against friends. Family members against family members. Yet, if I did nothing and allowed this woman to be killed, would I ever be able to live with myself?

How could I rise above my quandary and accomplish two seemingly antithetical objectives at the same time: stop the assassination and retain Sharon and Martina's love and respect. This was a paradox worthy of Zeno, but I was no Bertrand Russell.

However, once I started thinking about my situation as a paradox, my mind began to open up. Without being aware of it, I discarded my defeatist attitude and entertained the possibility that I might actually figure out a solution. After all, in reality, paradoxes are transcended all the time. Most fundamentally, matter and energy have been shown to be apparently mutually exclusive expressions of the same phenomenon; love and hate co-exist in our feelings for the same person. Maybe I could transcend the no-win choices before me?

When I thought about my situation like that, it reminded me of Thomas Pynchon's novels. For him, either-or choices inevitably spell doom. But his more successful characters sometimes escaped those restrictions through bizarre acts of creative insanity. That's what I needed now.

And then I thought. "Damn it, that really is what I need now. Some kind of *hocus pocus* that will take the problem to a new dimension. Like we did when Batman and Mighty Mouse tossed those pies at Perry Norwich."

I returned to the apartment about an hour later. The women were in the kitchen, drinking wine and speaking excitedly. I walked up to them and before anyone could say anything, I announced, "I have a counter offer. Are you willing to hear it?"

Initially, there was silence. But then Sharon spoke up.
"Sure."

"If I can convince you that we can subvert the rally and make Hines a laughingstock, will you disaffiliate from those terrorists?"

"How can you do that?" Martina demanded.

"I'll explain it, but only if you agree to try it instead of assassination, if it makes sense. If we try it, and it doesn't work, there will be nothing to stop your friends from going on with their plans. Only you won't be involved."

The three of them exchanged glances and Martina finally conceded, "If it makes sense."

"Absurd times call for absurd actions," I replied.

My plan was simple. I still had my Pie-thrower costume from Chicago. With their help, I'd do a repeat performance, but we'd put some paint in the pie, and maybe something really smelly too, so Hines wouldn't be able just to wipe it off and go on.

"The putrid delay might, by itself, cancel the Miami Beach 'drive-out.' But just to be sure, one of you can videotape the pie-throwing from up close and then post clips of the stuff dripping down her face on *Pie-thrower.com*. We can tell the TV stations and other media to monitor our site for a scoop on the rally. Martina can upload the video from her laptop as soon as we get home. Meanwhile, one of my grad students works for Kinkos. I won't give him any details in advance, but I can have him waiting to accept a big job online. We can e-mail him a particularly ridiculous-looking shot of Hines and print up hundreds of copies to distribute around the beach. We'll put the website address on the flier too. If the motorcade ever arrives, she'll be laughed back to Ft. Lauderdale."

"Or shot down before she reaches Alton Road," Martina rejoined.

"If it comes to that, but I don't think it will."

"I know a guy from high school who's a street artist on South Beach," Sharon offered. "He could probably get the picture distributed in about an hour."

"OK. Now we' re cooking." Then I turned to Martina and Helena and asked, "What do you say?"

Two days later, on Saturday afternoon, a car decorated with bright balloons drove down Biscayne Boulevard toward Bayfront Park. Colorful billboards on the front door of each side read *Ileana's Parties for Boys and Girls*. The balloons conveniently covered the licence plate–a trick Martina had learned in the Czech feminist underground.

Sharon drove; Helena sat beside her with a miniature video camera in her palm, and Martina sat in back beside me. It's about a fifteen minute ride from Martina's apartment to Bayfront Park, and while the others tended to their various chores, I sat alone with my thoughts, dressed in my flamboyant pie-thrower outfit, wondering how my life ever came to this. "But even if I'm beaten, arrested, and fired from my job," I told myself, "it will still better than watching the women I love partake in murder."

At last we pulled up by the crowd thronging the Torch of Freedom, a few yards from the street. Standing on a makeshift platform behind it stood Marion Hines exhorting her supporters, who numbered perhaps 35 or 50. And perhaps a quarter of those were the local homeless and winos just seeking entertainment. Certainly, this gathering was a far cry from the legions of Nazi storm troopers Martina and her activist friends had imagined in their fantasy of an anti-gay pogrom on Miami Beach. Certainly this small knot of homophobes did not pose sufficient clear and present danger to justify murder.

Oddly enough, Hines had assembled a Rainbow Coalition of her own, united by their common hatred, intolerance, and fear. Most of the crowd were men, although a number of older and middle-aged women had come as well, but very few younger ones. The males, on the other hand, ranged from teenagers and college kids to Baby Boomers and beyond. About half appeared to come from the working class, but, as we noted later when we reviewed the videotape, quite a few looked affluent, or at least financially comfortable. A handful of young men carrying signs that read, "Young Republicans for a Moral America," wore coats and ties and otherwise appeared especially neat and presentable. According to Martina, who cited Freud as her authority, their inordinate concern for neatness suggested a repressed anal fixation. Martina further reasoned that their homophobia resulted from a fear of gay men, because gay men embrace the anal eroticism that these excruciatingly straight ones are afraid to acknowledge in themselves.

"Maybe," was all I chose to answer.

About two-thirds of the crowd were Hispanic; Anglos comprised most of the rest. Four or five skinheads stood at the fringes listening attentively; a smattering of black men were also present, cheering on Hines when she denounced homosexuality as an abomination against God.

"Today they walk openly, hand-in-hand down Ocean Drive, kissing, and cuddling, and cooing–and worse! Churning the stomachs of upright, God-fearing Americans who must cover their children's eyes as they walk past. South Beach is no longer fit for a family day at the beach!"

"Amen," answered voices from her audience. Then one of the Young Republicans demanded, "What next?"

"I'll tell you what next," Hines answered in a shrill voice. "They will be in the high schools first, and then in the elementary schools. Recruiting!"

"No, no, no!" the crowd chanted.

"Yes. It's already happening now! The teachers are openly queer, and the students have so-called Gay-Straight Alliances--which are really no more than queer clubs--right there in our public schools. Imagine what goes on in those!"

"It can't be!" shouted a voice from the back.

"It's true!" Hines hollered back. "They're officially sanctioned by the high schools in *your* county. Soon they'll be fondling six-year-olds for their community service!"

"That's outrageous!" insisted another voice.

"You bet!" added a man up front. Then one of the skinheads screamed, "Kill the fagots!"

Sensing that the time for action had arrived, I grabbed a handful of balloons in one hand and my pie in the other. The graham cracker crust was filled with globs of bright red, yellow, green, and orange-colored paint that we'd covered with rancid whipped cream and generously sprinkled with flakes of rotten tuna fish that had baked in the sun for a day. I'd chosen an oil-based, marine paint that I knew would be especially difficult to wash off.

"Special delivery for Marion Hines," I shouted as I worked my way toward her. "Special delivery for Marion Hines."

Surprised by the interruption by a pie-bearing, comic-book intruder, the crowd offered no resistence. Ostensibly I had come as a friend bearing gifts, and the throng of supporters parted easily for me as I made my way forward.

In an instant I was face to face with Mrs. Hines. At first she appeared irritated at the interruption, then perhaps amused by my costume. Then, like Perry Norwich before her, her eyes filled with sudden terror as I produced the putrid pie and pummeled her with it. Helena already knew to keep the camera focused tight on her face, and in an instant a stream of electronic ones and zeroes was making its way onto the videotape, where they later reassembled to show the vomit-colored cream and hideous paints dripping from the demagogue's eyes and her nose and mouth, then onto the double-breasted navy-blue pant suit she had chosen especially for the gay-bashing occasion.

Naturally, I did not linger to enjoy the show. Instead I pushed and shoved through the stunned crowd and made way back to the street as fast as I could. I had the advantage of surprise. Nonetheless, one quick-thinking man pulled at my cape and nearly caught me before a piece of the fabric broke off in his hand and I broke free from his grasp. An elderly Cuban woman swatted me with her purse, and a skinhead tried to tackle me as I hopped into the car. He grabbed hold of my leg, but Sharon sped off and that knocked him off balance. He had to release me to break his fall, and it's a good thing he did; otherwise we would have dragged him down Biscayne Boulevard. As soon as we roared away, Martina, beside me in the back, cut down the party billboards we'd used to disguise our rental car. A block later, she severed the string holding the balloons over the licence plate, and we entered the freeway without incident or identifying features and quickly disappeared into traffic.

We drove home in great spirits. Helena recounted everything for the others, while Martina helped me remove my costume and make-up in the back seat. Helena played back the video on the camera's monitor, and we were convinced that it was the most hilarious political film clip since George Bush barfed all over the Japanese premier at a state dinner. The camera work was masterful. Helena caught Hines's expression in all of its ridiculous horror. For a good three seconds she stood frozen with her mouth agape, colors oozing down her chin. Her eyes revealed the depth of her terror, and for a moment she seemed almost human.

The video ended abruptly as Helena raced back to the car. We couldn't wait to see it on television. Plus, we were all anxious to learn if my absurdist attack had canceled Hines's "drive out." At the very least, we knew she'd have to postpone it until she could clean up. So we decided to wait for her to announce her plans before ordering up the posters of her paint-splattered face. After all, the fewer outside people we involved, the better. And if the news broadcasts announced the website address, people everywhere would be able to laugh at the bigot, and we wouldn't need the posters after all.

In any case, my Pynchon-inspired act of guerilla theater had resolved my paradox, and as we pulled into Martina's parking lot, I basked in the admiration of the three women beside me and in the conviction that I had saved them all from becoming parties to a murder.

Chapter 8

As the Scottish folk poet Bobby Burns concluded in 1785, "The best-laid schemes o' mice an' men/ Gang aft a-gley,/ An' lea'e us nought but grief and pain,/ For promised joy." A few minutes after we switched on Channel 7 News, anchor Rick Sanchez reported that Marion Hines had "died following a massive heart attack after she was unexpectedly assaulted by an imitation superhero wielding a foul-smelling, paint-filled pie in a cowardly hit and run attack."

The broadcaster's words took my breath away. I had achieved the one thing I had struggled hardest to avoid. Now I was a murderer and the women I wanted to protect were my accomplices. I slumped back onto the sofa and groaned.

"I've ruined our lives!"

Martina switched off the television, and she and the others circled around to comfort me. She stroked my head and declared emphatically, "No! You haven't ruined our lives, you've defined them for us. We said before that this is war. Now, we're in it for good. There's no turning back."

"We've just signed on for the duration, like in the Army," Helena concurred. Her tone was harsher and more strident than I'd ever heard before. "I was prepared to help assassinate that bitch two days ago. Nothing has changed really, except the manner of her execution."

"And the fact that she looks like an imbecile in that video," Martina snickered. "Seriously, if we can keep that picture out before the public, it will defuse the sympathy. After all, who could get worked up over someone whose eyes are bugging out of her head like that, with all those crazy colors dripping from her face? Her true self came out. She died looking like the complete idiot she was. Who's going to go ballistic over a clown?"

"We'll find out, won't we?" I replied. Their callousness appalled me. I looked to Sharon, but she was too stunned to say anything. She sat in a chair across from me, bent over with her elbows on her knees and her face in hands. Her complexion had turned ghostly pale. Helena walked over to comfort her, but Sharon shooed her away without looking up. Helena persisted, however, and a moment later Sharon threw herself into her arms, sobbing.

"There, there," Helena whispered as she embraced my daughter and gently ran her fingers through her hair. "It's going to be alright. This was a good thing."

"I know it was," Sharon answered. "I know it was. But she's dead."

"Yes," Helena now lightly caressed Sharon's shoulders. "But think of the people on South Beach who are still alive and safe in their homes because of what we did. That's why we did it. That's why we had to do it. It was for a good cause."

"I know," Sharon raised her head and rubbed away her tears. "It's just the thought that I helped my father kill a woman. It's so," she hesitated, searching for the right word. "Enormous. It like takes my life to a whole different level."

"That's what André Gide wrote about," Martina turned from me and walked over to the girls. "It makes you feel more alive, no?"

"Yes," Sharon nodded.

"Gide was a criminal," I cried. "A criminal who wrote well and used some twisted version of existentialism to rationalize his pathology. So did Hitler. 'Triumph of the will' and all that *shit*. This isn't about achieving a heightened sense of reality. It's about fundamental notions of right and wrong. And murder is wrong!"

"And so is gay bashing!" Martina snapped back.

"That's right" Helena echoed, and Sharon slowly nodded to concur.

For the second time in three days, their murderous radicalism ignited a rage within me that threatened to burn out of control. I stormed out of the room before I exploded and sought refuge behind the closed door of my study.

Swiveling nervously in my office chair, I tried to review the situation. In Vietnam our soldiers maintained they had to destroy a village in order to save it. I had tried to save Marion Hines and destroyed her in the process. What a crazy, unexpected twist to my life, and just as things seemed finally to be getting back on track again.

"How Pynchonesque," I thought to myself bitterly. "I hope Martina enjoys the irony."

Martina. What a disappointment. Maybe it was because she'd been raised under communism, but she had the ethics of a Stalin. She subordinated everything to her ideology, and rationalized everything according to it. How was it I hadn't seen this sooner? Was I blinded by lust? By the joy I found in our splendid flights of fantasy? By both? In any case, Martina now looked more like a monster to me than the exotic soul mate I had mistaken her for. A monster who apparently held sway over Helena, who in turn held sway over Sharon.

And what about Sharon? She'd sided with Martina and Helena. Was she a monster too? I thought long and hard about this. Maybe I was just in another state of denial because she's my daughter, but I finally concluded that Sharon was under her lover's spell; otherwise my child would never condone murder. This didn't absolve her–or any of us–of responsibility. But I didn't want to believe that my ex-wife had, in my absence, raised our daughter to have the ethics of a terrorist.

As my temper cooled, Pandora emerged from under the desk and jumped into my lap. Running my hand through her fur soothed me. "Nice Kitty," I whispered to her. "Nice Kitty." Soon the cat was purring loudly and, still in my lap, she rolled on her side against my thigh. I scratched her beneath her chin until she stood on all fours so she could lean into my fingers and surrender completely to my touch. After a while, I tickled her behind her ears, and Pandora again threw herself against my hand. I petted her like this for another few minutes, until she curled up on my legs and went to sleep.

Pandora purred softly as she slept. I sat watching, stroking her gently from time to time and thinking my thoughts. When she awoke and jumped down to chase a chamaeleon that suddenly darted out from the closet, I rose as well. I needed to talk with the women about what we should do.

They'd adjourned to the kitchen table and were drinking wine and talking excitedly when I came back out. I had a profound moment of *deja vu* from two days earlier, when I returned to propose my pie-throwing alternative to assassination. The repetition of that same kitchen scene unsettled me. For the first time ever, I sensed some inevitable destiny shaping my life. Like Oedipus, I had tried to alter fate and failed miserably.

As I walked over to them, Sharon picked up the bottle and offered to pour me a glass, but I waved her off.

"Look," I said in a controlled voice, "we need to decide what we're going to do about this mess."

"Yes, we do," Martina's tone was even, but her eyes challenged me.

"Well, I say we do nothing," Helena insisted. "As long as you made sure no one can trace you back from that Pie-thrower web address, there's absolutely nothing to link us with this woman's death. No one knows but us. If we keep our mouths shut, we're fine."

"Don't worry, I uploaded the site through an underground server in Prague. The connections relay through several other countries before it gets posted on the Web. It won't be easy to trace. Too many feuding governments need to agree." Martina reached over and patted Helena reassuringly on the hand. Then she sat up erect and looked over to me. "Our business with Marion Hines is done. What I plan to do is go to North Carolina next week and meet your dad. Sharon's grandfather. Remember him?"

I glanced at Sharon, but she lowered her head and said nothing. So I addressed Martina. "Look, a woman died at our hands. She was a person, a human being. We can't just go on with our lives as though nothing happened."

"You still don't get it yet, do you?" Martina sneered. "This is war. Marion Hines was a casualty on the battlefield. It's us or them, Sweetheart."

"Who are you? Lady Macbeth? Well, not all the perfumes of Araby will remove the stench of blood from our hands."

"Or the stench of that pie from yours," Helena joked coldly.

But Martina was livid. "I don't know what Workers' Paradise you grew up in, but in my life power struggles are for real and the winners take all. That's life, baby. I can't afford to live by your ridiculous bourgeois morality. You get all bent out of shape because you scared the crap out of some fascist, pig woman, and she shat in her pants and died. But until we forced you, you've never lifted a finger to end the routine persecution and torture of homosexuals that take place every day in this country. What about the assholes who walk into gay bars and just open fire?"

"Or tie them up and drag them behind moving automobiles," Helena pitched in.

"Keep your perfumes," Martina continued. "I'll take my chances with soap and water, thank you. And for the record, I resent being compared to Lady Macbeth."

Martina's eyes blazed as they bore into mine, but I held my ground. "We're not behind the Iron Curtain, we're in America. We're an imperfect society, but at least we have a history of progressive change, however slow and costly, and at least the system works reasonably well for most people. That might not be nearly good enough, and we shouldn't be smug. But we're a far cry better off than places that have given up on rule by law, or never tried it. Do I need to remind you of *their* record on women and homosexuals? That's where you're leading us."

"And where would you take us?" Helena challenged me.

"I think that in times like this it's important to think about the people you most admire and imagine how they'd act."

"What would Jesus do?" Martina growled.

Ignoring her sarcastic reference to the popular bumper sticker favored by the Christian Right, I continued. "I spent a lot of time back there thinking about Socrates. At this moment, I think the best thing we can do for ourselves *and* for the cause is to turn ourselves in. We then plead 'not guilty' and insist on a trial, in which we make our case to the world, take full responsibility for our actions, and accept the judgment that a jury of our peers renders."

Helena looked at Martina in utter amazement. Then she turned to Sharon.

"What planet do your people come from?" Finally, she looked at me. "This isn't a high school civics class. It's our lives, damn it! You may be over the hill with nothing more to look forward to, but I'm not going to spend the prime of my life in prison."

"So, you'll kill for your cause but not sacrifice yourself for it?"

"Don't lecture me!" Helena's face was turning red.

Sharon, sitting beside her, began to sob. I took a step forward, but Helena intruded. She wrapped her arm around my daughter's shoulder and pushed aside a strand of hair from her face.

"Honey, I don't want to fight with your father," her tone was suddenly soft and comforting. "But he wants us to spend the next twenty years locked up with a bunch of mean, fat, smelly, over-sexed dykes just to satisfy some principle he read about in a book. And I'm telling you right now, I'm not going to do it. I'm not going to do it!" Then she hugged Sharon harder. "I'm not going to let you do it, either."

"I won't let you either," Martina spoke even more forcefully.

Sharon looked up at Helena, then across to Martina, and finally at me. "I love you, Daddy," she said. "But I don't want to go to jail."

No one said anything for the next minute or so. Once again, I wrestled with the most excruciating conflict in my life. I've always taken my civic responsibilities seriously, and I knew the right thing to do was to own up to our actions and surrender. But Helena's picture of a prison brimming with predatory rapists made me cringe. I feared that fate for myself. Worse, how could I consign Sharon and the others to such a gruesome existence. And if I did, I knew Sharon would never speak to me again.

Finally, I spoke up. "Look, we're not getting anywhere here. We've got to stick together or this is going to blow up in our face. So, I'll consider myself outvoted." I looked at Martina. "We'll do it your way and do nothing for now."

"For now?" she challenged. "What if you change your mind tomorrow?"

"If I do, I promise I won't implicate anyone else. Just myself."

"And if they torture you?" Martina was relentless.

"This is America."

"I know that," she answered dryly. "Do you?"

"I assume responsibility for my own actions, no one else's," I reiterated.

"That's not good enough," Martina shook her head. "They'll find out that we live together and find a way to bring me into it, no matter what you say. They'll deport me or send me to jail"

"I don't think so."

"Well, I don't want to risk my future on what you think. I'm leaving tomorrow for Blowing Rock. I guess I'll have to trust you to keep that to yourself. Just remember though, you'll never meet your father if you turn on me."

Martina's mistrust stunned me. "First," I spoke deliberately, with exaggerated calm, "I said that I'm not going to do anything. Second, I said that if I should change my mind, I won't implicate anyone else. I'm responsible only for myself in this."

"Be that as it may, I'm going to Blowing Rock," Martina repeated.

"I'm going with you," Helena seconded.

"Me too," Sharon followed. "I want to meet my grandfather." Then she turned to me. "If that works out, I'll let you know when you can come up and meet him too."

"What about your school?"

"We have another week before classes begin. And if I have to miss the first few sessions it's no big deal. Nothing much happens till the third week anyway."

So I agreed to stay in Miami, keep silent, and continue teaching as though nothing had happened. Meanwhile, they'd drive to North Carolina the next day and try to look up my dad.

Chapter 9

The next several weeks were among the most excruciating of my life. Alone with Pandora in Martina's apartment, I continued teaching my classes and remained silent about our role in Marion Hines's death. My shoulders drooped with the weight of unacknowledged guilt, and I walked around with my head hung low. My friends asked if I was alright, and I told them I missed Martina while she was away doing research. But each night I suffered as I turned on the nightly news and witnessed the fallout from my deed.

Atrocity followed atrocity across the county. Apparently not wanting to wait for retaliation, the HLF struck the first blow, torching the home of a city official who had spoken out against homosexuals and urged swift justice in finding the killers of Marion Hines. The arsonists waited until the family had left for church. After they knocked down the back door, they even freed the dogs and cat before they doused the floors and walls with kerosene and struck a match. The caged bird in the home office at the back of the house wasn't so lucky. In retrospect, he was like the proverbial canary in the mine shaft--the first to feel the fatal consequences of impending disaster.

Whether they sincerely thought they were retaliating or were just getting into the spirit of things, in the next few days neo-Nazis and skinheads firebombed two temples and a gay bar. A fascist underground group calling itself the Iron Swastika claimed responsibility. The temples were deserted, but the gay bar was packed. Three men were killed outright, two more died afterward. In the pandemonium following the explosion, the fascists managed to pull aside an additional five or six victims and brand swastikas onto their arms, foreheads, and asses. The next night a motorcycle gang crashed into a lesbian hangout, trashed the place, and raped three of the women. The police were remarkably slow to respond to the distress call.

I sat on inactive on the sidelines and watched my city spin deeper and deeper into a whirlpool of self destruction. Tourism, our stock and trade industry, was dwindling by the hour, and other counties stole away companies that had been planning to relocate in sunny Miami. Each new act of violence was another gunshot in our collective feet, but we were consumed by conflagrations fueled by long-repressed resentments that spontaneously combusted as they boiled to the surface. Well-intended civic leaders were impotent, while the demagogues fanned the flames for their own petty purposes. During those awful days I thought often of another line of poetry from Yeats: "The best lack all convictions, while the worst are full of passionate intensity."

For what little it might be worth, I decided to use *Piethrower.com* to show how dangerous and absurd the situation had become. Ever since the Hines incident, the site had become very popular, logging thousands of hits daily. Immediately after Martina left, I pulled the video clips of Hines from the site; it would have been tasteless and vindictive to leave them there. But by then, the pictures had already made their way around the world several times over and were featured prominently on the copy-cat sites that were suddenly springing up across the globe. They even made the front pages of the national scandal sheets like *Star* and the *National Enquirer*. Inquiring minds wanted to know. I replaced the pie-throwing video with a statement expressing shock and sorrow over Hines's death. I asserted that my intention had been to use absurdist, guerilla-theater tactics as an alternative to violence, not as a promulgator of it. Announcing my official retirement from pie-throwing in deference to Ms. Hines, I went on to decry the situation in Miami and followed with a series of cartoons ridiculing people from every extreme who were willing to destroy the city in order to pursue their selfish goals.

Sharon called me every night after she, Helena, and Martina left. They arrived in Boone after driving for two days. Staying in a motel while they scouted out the situation, they found the coffee shop early the first morning and stayed there until Pynchon came in for his usual breakfast. They recognized him from the description her friend on the listserve had given her, and

Sharon told me Martina gasped when he came in the door. That made him suspicious, and he immediately sat down on the opposite side of the room with his back to them. It was clear they were going to have to slowly gain his confidence before approaching him, so, armed with my Visa card, they rented a cabin outside of town for a couple of weeks.

According to Sharon, Martina showed incredible self-restraint during the first four days. By the fifth, Pynchon no longer scowled when he looked at them, and on the sixth Martina went over and introduced herself. He was defensive at first, but, as we had anticipated, her charm, good looks, and exotic presence provoked his interest. The next day he consented to meet Sharon and Helena. Sharon said he took an instant liking to her and really seemed to enjoy her sense of humor. So a couple days after that, she took a chance. First reassuring Pynchon that she wanted nothing from him, Sharon told him she was his granddaughter. That night she told me on the phone how he reacted.

"I was afraid he'd think I was trying to scam him and get angry. But he wasn't like that at all. He just smiled the warmest, gentlest smile and shook his head slowly from side to side.

"'I wish you were my granddaughter,' he said. 'I'd love nothing more than to claim you. But I assure you, you are not.'

"He laughed when I told him all about Grandma and her studio in Greenwich Village. 'I remember that episode very well. It's not the sort of thing any man would be quick to forget. But I'm not your grandfather.'

"So that's the bad news," Sharon reported. "The good news is that he's willing to meet you anyway and answer whatever questions he can."

I taught my last seminar of the week the next morning, and caught an early afternoon plane to Asheville, where I rented a car and drove through Boone to Blowing Rock. The Pynchon compound, as he jokingly called it, consisted of about ten acres of remote, forested land right at the foot of the mountain. On the property stood a full-sized wooden house and two winterized log cabins for guests. I had to drive down two different, poorly marked dirt roads to find it. Fortunately, Pynchon's directions were clear and impeccable, and the view was stunning. The leaves were just beginning to turn, and the golden late afternoon light revealed a rustic landscape awash in green, pink, yellow, and red.

That evening I found myself inside a pine-paneled living room, sitting in an easy chair across a fragrant, blazing fire from Thomas Pynchon, the man I'd believed for almost forty years to be my dad. The scene was cosy, familial, and surreal. Shadows from the flame continually flickered across his face, so even though he sat directly before me, he seemed almost as ephemeral as ever. Sharon lounged on the rug by my side. Helena lay beside her, her head resting on my daughter's lap. Martina was scrunched beside Dad, if Dad he was, on the love seat opposite me. I can't really say that I was jealous. I had lost all respect for Martina after Marion Hines died. But seeing my lover nestled against my father was nonetheless unsettling.

I remained convinced Pynchon really was my father, and I rehearsed my arguments on the drive over from Asheville. But when I finally raised the subject, he dispelled in seconds the belief of a lifetime.

"These are my dog tags from the Navy. I always wear them as a reminder." Pynchon removed the tarnished, metallic rectangles dangling beneath his shirt and held them out to me. "Take a look at the blood type and tell me if there's any way we could match?"

A quick glance at the printing stamped on the tag convinced me that I was not his son. He had extremely rare blood, while mine was all too common. His driver's license, a photo ID that identified him as an organ donor in case of fatal accident, likewise indicated his unusual blood type. Sharon assured me that he'd shown her the tags when she first informed him she was his granddaughter; so it wasn't as though he had manufactured them to deceive me. Plus, I'd seen dog tags before, and these looked real. My face went ashen, and I apologized profusely.

As he'd been with Sharon, Pynchon was exceedingly gracious. "I liked your mother," he said as he pulled out his collar and dropped the tags back inside his shirt. "She was wild. She had a lot of spunk. And we did get it on for a while. So I guess I could have been your dad. But I've always kept close track of my offspring. I would have known."

"Do you have any idea who my father might have been, then?"

"I can't speak with certainty."

Martina abruptly interrupted, "That's what they should put on your gravestone. It's the central axiom for everything you've written"

Pynchon smiled at her and squeezed her hand. "Perhaps that's so." Then he returned his attention to me. "Nonetheless, I have an instinct that says your father was a fellow we used to call Burnt Umber, a real character. He went through a bunch of names back then. I can still remember some of them: Duck 'n' Cover, Foggy Bottom....The last time I heard of him, which was a long time ago already, he was calling himself Lift 'n' Separate. When I met him he was using something akin to a real name, Bertrand Russell." Pynchon looked up to the ceiling to check the name against his memory and then corrected himself. "No. No, it wasn't Bertrand. It was Freddy Russell. That's right, Frederick Russell, Hair Stylist to the Stars."

"You're putting me on," I replied.

"No. Not at all. Burnt was this brilliant, talented but incredibly eccentric character who was always trying on new personalities. I don't think he was clinically schizophrenic, or even more neurotic than most of us. He did it deliberately. He said that's what life should be about--having as many different kinds of experiences as possible. And what better way than to be different people? I remember we had a long conversation about that one time."

"This really scares me," I cringed. Knowing how loose my mother's connection to reality was, the thought that my father might have been even farther out than she was unsettling. But Pynchon reassured me that beneath the wackiness Burnt Umber had been one of the sanest people he knew.

"How'd you meet him?" Sharon wanted to know.

"I first saw Burnt from across a busy street. It must have been in 1959, because that's when I was living in Greenwich Village and working on *V*. It was a sunny spring day, and I was writing at a table of an outdoor café in Washington Square. Suddenly, I heard a shaggy man with long hair and a scruffy beard arguing with a cop who was moving him along. The bum held a sign and was soliciting for spare change. He gave the cop a big piece of his mind and then abruptly turned away and plunged into the street, stepping in front of cars as though daring them not to stop. I thought he must have been drunk or demented, but he made it safely across, and I went back to my writing.

"Some time passed, and I looked up and saw the same bum about a block away. He was walking toward me and holding his sign out to people, who mostly ignored him, though a couple turned their heads in apparent puzzlement after he passed. When he came close enough for me to read the sign, I saw why they were confused. On a weathered piece of cardboard he had hand-printed in big, black letters, 'VICTIM OF PARADOX. GIVE GENEROUSLY.'

"I returned to my work. But he caught me looking, and before I could say anything, he'd pulled up a chair at my table and started talking.

"'Sure, they'll help out heroin addicts,' he grumbled. 'They'll give dollar bills to drunkards who refuse to take control of their lives, to all sorts of people who are...' and here his voice dropped and he twisted the words contemptuously, 'down on their luck.' Freddy--he called himself Freddy then--spat. 'They're down on their luck because they're too lazy to figure out what they need to do, or if they've figured it out, they're too lazy to make the effort to do it.'

"I looked at Freddy again. He was not as old as I had initially thought. He was closer to my age, perhaps in his late twenties or early thirties. His clothes were dirty and torn; his shoes lacked polish, and he could use a bath with some industrial strength cleaner, if you catch my drift. I surely caught his. Most of all, Freddy was completely unshorn. His scraggly hair fell below his armpits, and his long, bushy beard had no discernable shape. He looked like a *bona fide* derelict to me. But he didn't talk like one.

"'If you don't mind my saying,' I answered, 'you seem down on your luck, yourself.'

"'Well, duh! Aren't you the bright boy.' Freddy mocked.

"'At least I pay my own way. What makes you so different from those other losers?'

"'They are victims of their own laziness and lack of imagination.' Freddy paused a moment to let the statement sink in. Then he proclaimed theatrically, 'I am a victim of paradox!'

"'Yes, I can see that from your sign. So what's this paradox bullshit? You're well spoken. You sound educated. Why don't you clean yourself up and get a job? For God's sake, at least get a shave and a haircut and make yourself presentable.'

"'Ah, a shave, a haircut. A shave *and* a haircut. How poignant. How ironic.' Freddy's face fell as he manufactured a look of despair.

"'Look,' I said. 'I'll pay for the haircut. But I insist on going with you. I don't want you wasting my good money on cheap wine or rotgut whiskey.'

"'If only it were just a matter of money,' Freddy sighed wistfully. 'Or whiskey.'

"'O.K., I'll bite. What is it?'

"'I am a hapless victim of paradox.'

"'So what's that supposed to mean?'

"Freddy sat up straight and looked me in the eye. 'Are you ready to hear the saddest story you've ever known?'

"'Go on ahead,' I commanded. 'I can take it.'

"So Freddy rose and began to recite his tale of woe."

Martina suddenly reached around Pynchon's shoulders and hugged him in an expansive embrace. "This is already a fabulous story," she said. "And we don't even know where it's going from here."

"Incredible," Sharon muttered. Like me, she was in a state of awe and incredulity.

"That's some family you come from," Helena joked, looking up at my daughter from Sharon's lap.

Pynchon cleared his throat and reclaimed the floor. "Do you want to hear the man's tale?"

"Absolutely," we agreed.

"Alright." Then he altered his voice, making it louder and theatrical. "'Once upon a time, not so long ago,' said the bum, 'I was a success. I was Frederick Russell: Hair Stylist to the Stars. Rich and in love, I styled starlets and Broadway divas. I even coffered the wigs for manikins in upscale stores. I had developed my own line of fashion products, and business was good.

"'But of all things in the world, I loved two the most. First was my dearest love, my sweet Penelope, a beautiful, gifted, radiant young woman of many talents, capable of conferring numerous pleasures. After Penelope, I loved to shave beards. I know this sounds ridiculous,' Freddy insisted, 'but there's something about a man's beard that projects character and inner strength and beauty. Whenever I shaped a beard, I sculpted a soul.'"

"Was this guy crazy, or what?" Helena demanded, but the rest of us silenced her and encouraged Pynchon to continue.

He nodded and went on, "I told him, 'You must have sprung a leak somewhere, fellah, because your inner beauty is oozing out all over.'"

"'Ah, yes. You mock me,' Freddy slowly shook his head. 'That is part of the oh-so-ironic curse of paradox.'

"'What's with the paradox?' I demanded, by now exasperated and anxious to get back to my writing.

"'The paradox is the crux of everything.' He glared at me defiantly. 'I'm just coming to it, if you can hold on a few moments longer.'

"I sat silently and stared at him until Freddy continued. 'I have an evil brother, Bertrand. He's a clever liberal, a conniving intellectual, and an envious son-of-a-bitch. He could not abide my professional success, nor my bliss with Penelope. So...' Freddy paused ever so slightly for effect, 'he devised a cruel plan to play one against the other in order to deprive me of both.'

"Freddy looked down to gauge my reaction, which I guess was satisfactory, because then he continued. 'I'd long wanted to dedicate my talents to sculpting beards, and Bertrand knew this. He also knew that Penelope expected the finer things in life and insisted upon a very high standard of living. Consequently, I devoted myself to the better-paying heads of prissy *prima donnas*, although I really wanted to apply my art exclusively to men's jaws and chins. If only I could be assured of shaving enough beards to generate sufficient income, I could satisfy both my passions. But that seemed out of reach.

"'Then one day Bertrand slyly approached me with a proposition. "If I can guarantee that you will shave every man in a half-mile radius of your home who does not shave himself," he asked, "would you be willing to restrict your clientele only to men who do not shave themselves?"

"'Now, I knew Bertrand had some shady dealings with the Mob, and though it sounded improbable, he probably had the wherewithal to enforce the terms of such a contract. Organized crime ran everything in my neighborhood, and the gangsters could definitely send a lot of business my way. I figured they were putting the screws to some barber who was holding back on his protection fee, and Bertrand had recognized an opportunity for both of us--he'd get a quarter of the profits. Whatever the real story was, his proposition sounded like a good deal for me, so I agreed.

"'That night, Bertrand dropped by just as I was preparing to celebrate my good fortune with Penelope. When I greeted him at the front door to my apartment, my face was lathered, my shirt was off, and a towel lay draped over my shoulder.

""""Just in time. I got here just in time," Bertrand declared, snatching my razor from my hand as he pushed his way inside.

""""Hey, give that back to me," I demanded. "I've got a date with Penelope in half an hour."

""""Unless you want your kneecaps broken, you'll court her unshaven."

""""What are you talking about? You know Penelope detests beards."

""""I'm talking about your contract. You are to shave only men who do not shave themselves."

""""So?"

""""So, do you shave yourself?"

""""Yeah, I shave myself."

""""Then you are outside the category of men whom you are permitted to shave. You may only shave men who do *not* shave themselves."

"'Now I'd long suspected that Bertrand lusted after Penelope and wanted her for his own. Clearly, this sophistry was part of some fiendish plan to pull us apart. But since I could not readily refute him, I simply shrugged my shoulders and said offhandedly, "This is crazy. I'll have Louis shave me then."

"'But Bertrand held up his hand. "No way. You're not allowed. If someone else shaves you, then you fall into the category of men who do not shave themselves, and you and only you are permitted to shave such men."

""""So, you're telling me that I am not allowed to shave myself and no else is allowed to shave me?"

""""That's right." Then he snickered, "'Penelope will love your new look."

"'I clenched my fist to knock the insipid grin from Bertrand's face, but at that moment two goons carrying baseball bats stepped into the room. They introduced themselves as members of a free enterprise society. Their job, they said, was to enforce business contracts. "The inviolable sanctity of the contract lies at the heart of any free market economy," one of them proclaimed in a thick, New Jersey gutter accent. He sounded like a thug from *On The Waterfront.*'

""""We live in the neighborhood," announced the big one whose arms were thicker than the bat he carried, "and we'll be stopping in from time to time for a shave."

""""Yeah, and we'll want to see how your beard is coming along too," his partner guffawed.'

'"The first one added, "We'll live up to our end of the bargain. We expect you to honor yours."

'"Then they left the room. Bertrand followed, pocketing my razor as he left. I hope it cut him.'

""""You won't be needing this," he smirked as he shut the door behind him.'

'"That was nearly a year ago,' Freddy sighed, exhausted from his narration. 'I'm the victim of a cruel paradox engineered by my evil brother. Unable to shave my beard, I've lost everything: my livelihood and my love. I look like a bum. Penelope despises me--she is now Mrs. Bertrand Russell. And my business has collapsed. By terms of the contract, I surrendered my models, actresses, and other non-bearded clients. But as my looks deteriorated, all the men in my neighborhood took to shaving themselves. Soon, perhaps because of Mob collusion, I had no customers. When my own business failed, I tried working for other boutiques who only months earlier would have paid a small fortune to employ me. But their businesses could not abide an ill-groomed barber any more than mine. As it turns out, no one can afford to hire the unkempt. I live on the street now, with no hope of redemption. A deal, after all, is a deal.'"

Pynchon looked around from one of us to another as we hung on every word of his fantastic tale. Then he continued, "Freddy looked at me, expecting some kind of response. I ordered him a glass of beer, then told him, 'I never knew paradox could be so debilitating.'"

"'Oh, paradox strikes much more often than you might imagine,' Freddy assured me after the waitress delivered a Schlitz and he took his first sip. 'Have you ever seen an inexperienced job seeker. No experience, no job. No job, no experience. It's not a pretty sight.'

"'Why don't you at least cut your hair? The deal doesn't cover that, does it?' I had an appointment, so I packed up my manuscript and stood to leave. Freddy was looking at me expectantly, so I took out my wallet and handed him a couple bucks.

"Freddy pocketed the money. Then he answered me. His voice was suddenly in a more natural register. 'Too much contrast with the beard. It would ruin the entire look.'

"'Right.' I winked at him as I walked away and wished him luck with his dilemma."

"'Luck!' His voice regained its theatrical timber as he called angrily after me. 'What is luck to a victim of paradox? Paradox is impervious to luck!'

"I saw him around often after that, and eventually we became friends. After a day of writing, I enjoyed sharing drinks and listening to his wild stories. I followed him through two or three more of his identities. I'm pretty sure he was Burnt Umber when he knew your mother."

"Do you know how they met?" Sharon asked.

"They met through me, I suppose. I remember they were already together the evening when Burnt told us how the government was after him because he'd escaped from some secret experiment they were doing on him. They wanted to breed a superior race to lead the fight against world communism, or something."

"You're kidding!" Martina was flabbergasted.

"Oh, I remember it well." Pynchon grinned at Martina beside him. "We were all at a party in somebody's loft, smoking weed, listening to Bird and Train on the hi fi, awash in the smell of linseed oil that had been freshly applied on the canvases scattered about the room. We were talking shit. Everyone was trying to be more outrageous than the speaker before. Anyway, one guy suddenly got really serious and said the Army had experimented on him with LSD. Then Burnt said the government had used radiation and behavioral psychology on *him*.

"'They kept tabs on everything I did for a year,' Burnt maintained. 'They even charted my sexual escapades and mapped them against power drainage within a two-block radius.' According to Burnt, his love making was so intense it would suck all the electricity from the power lines and blow out the transformers when he came.

"Of course, we all took Burnt's boast for the bullshit it was, except for Gertrude, your grandmother." Tom looked at Sharon.

"Whose *they*?" she asked. "The government scientists?"

"Your grandmother wondered the same thing, but Burnt roared back, 'No, my women!'"

Tom grinned at the memory. "Burnt said he'd managed to sneak out of the compound two years earlier and had been hiding out ever since. That's why he used so many different names–although on other occasions he offered different explanations for his multiple identities. He was getting nervous again, though, because he thought he'd spotted some agents roaming around the Village a few days earlier.

"Everyone else in the room thought Burnt and the other guy were just being stoned. But something about the look in their eyes made me sort of believe them. Burnt had claimed the government was trying to identify which set of attributes was really better suited for survival of the species: high IQs and physical strength or creativity. And which could be more easily passed on to new generations."

"'For some reason,' Burnt opined, 'they seemed to think brilliance and brawn are incompatible with creativity and optimism,' although he said that hadn't been true in his experience.

"Burnt said his group of four arts majors from Oberlin College was being tested against another experimental group of subjects from Harvard whose intellect and physiques were being enhanced. The idea was to create Houyhnhnms, a superior species, to supersede *homo sapiens*. But first they needed to settle once and for all what traits are truly most useful for the success of the species."

Pynchon's reference to Houyhnhnms startled me, but before I could interrupt, he had already moved on, and I didn't want to violate his narration. "Burnt told us he had been a music major known for his high spirits and upbeat attitude. Actually, he played a mean honky tonk piano whenever he could hold a gig. I used to hear him sometimes playing in dives in Greenwich Village. I think they recruited him and the others by telling them the project was a work-study program. As I recall, he said they were paid and even received credit towards their degrees. They were taken to a very remote town in the Midwest where their movements were restricted to a limited community. They had no access to any vehicles, and they were miles from nowhere. So, although they weren't exactly imprisoned, they certainly weren't free.

"After about half a year of behavioral therapy, the geneticists started administering radiation treatments. And that's when Burnt got the hell out of there. He said we were getting enough gamma rays from the radioactive clouds that passed overhead each time the government tested an H-bomb. This was before Kennedy's nuclear test ban treaty, remember, and both the Americans and the Soviets were regularly exploding nukes above ground. That was plenty enough radiation for Burnt. Who knows what he was like before the experiments, and how much of his wild behavior resulted from them—assuming there was some truth to his story and the government conducted any experiments on him at all.

"Anyway, I thought he might be telling the truth. I'd heard similar stories from credible sources. Plus, some of my military buddies suspected that the Navy had conducted some bizarre, scientific drug testing on us in the mid-'50s. The doctors told us they were giving us experimental vitamins to fortify our immune systems, but the side effects seemed pretty strange for vitamins. I remember walking around with a heightened sense of awareness. Everything seemed in especially sharp focus. Anyway, the experiments were halted without explanation after about two weeks, and that's the last I thought about it until a few months before the party, when one of the guys from my unit called me long distance-- back when calling long distance was a big deal--and asked if I'd noticed any unusual people lurking around. Actually, the first person I thought of was Burnt, your dad," Pynchon looked at me. "But I didn't mention him to my friend. I just told him I'd keep an eye out."

Pynchon paused momentarily to relive those memories from over forty years before. He took a deep breath and continued.

"When I heard Burnt's story, I decided the time had come to get the hell out of New York. That's why I remember that evening so well. I figured no one would search for me deep within the military-industrial complex, so a few weeks later I moved to Oregon and took a job with Boeing working on the Minuteman missile project. To tell you the truth, I've never been sure if Burnt really did escape from a secret experiment. Sometimes I wondered if he really was a government agent sent to watch me and, for reasons of his own, he told that story to warn me. Or maybe he was just the crazy character he seemed to be, or a guy who'd figured out that some girls really dig fugitives and weirdos. Your mother sure did. But somewhere in my gut, I always thought he was telling the truth."

Pynchon then looked me in the eye. "So, Ben," he asked. "How's it feel to be a first generation Houyhnhnm?"

Chapter 10

That night Tom, as I now called Mr. Pynchon, let me sleep in the spare bedroom in the main house, as he hadn't been expecting company until the day before, and the guest cabins were not ready for use. Sharon and Helena camped out in the living room by the fireplace, while he and Martina retired to his room. My sleep, when it finally came, was punctuated by wild and disturbing dreams about beatniks, nuclear testing, Marion Hines, my mother, Martina, and centaurs running through grassy meadows spouting lines of poetry. The next morning I announced my intention to return to Miami. Not surprisingly, Martina elected to stay with Tom, who promised to protect her and keep her safely hidden. Sharon and Helena decided to go back to Chicago and begin the new semester until other options shaped up more clearly.

Over the next few weeks I heard from Martina only twice. She needed me to send her some computer disks and other belongings in her apartment. But Sharon e-mailed me almost every day. Ironically, we had never been closer. I was still deeply distraught over Hines's death, but I had promised not to act independently on it, and like the poet says, "A promise made is a debt unpaid." Publicly, at least, the police were claiming to have no clues about the identity of the masked pie-thrower who'd provoked her heart attack, so I tried to deal with my guilt as well as I could and get on with my life. The semester was in full swing, and my teaching routine gave my existence a modicum of normalcy.

Sharon and I exchanged a few messages debating whether we should track down Burnt Umber. I didn't think we had much of a chance but agreed to let her try. To my surprise, she located him on the Internet the next day. After numerous dead-ends she'd tried a simple key word search on "Lift 'n' Separate," and there he was, listed between a porn site and Maidenform bras. He had his own website that featured all kinds of weird things: abstract art, surreal short stories, wild jazz, and links to various conspiracy theories. The site included nothing on the Houyhnhnms, however.

Without asking me first, Sharon e-mailed him directly and told him she thought she was his granddaughter and wanted to meet him. She even offered to go to his home, wherever that might be. I didn't think that was so smart. After all, he might just be a demented kook and not a relative at all. For that matter, he might actually be my dad and still be crazed. There were no guarantees there. But my daughter was nothing if not headstrong. Anyway, Burnt didn't want to reveal where he lived, but after Sharon elaborated on our conversation with Pynchon, he agreed to come to Chicago to meet us on October 31.

Halloween fell on Tuesday. I arranged for someone to cover my Wednesday class, and when I finished teaching Monday morning, I caught a plane and made my way back to Hyde Park. When I arrived that afternoon, Sharon was unexpectedly subdued. She'd been so excited just the day before, but when I appeared at her apartment, she started to cry. Eventually, she managed to tell me between sobs that earlier in the day Helena had confessed that she was in love with Martina. Sharon was devastated. It seems that Helena and Martina had secretly become lovers back during our visit in August, and then later in Miami and again in Blowing Rock, before Martina finally met Tom. In fact, their first tryst had been at Sharon's birthday party, while I was out throwing my custard pie at Perry Norwich.

"No wonder Martina was so anxious for me join in that escapade." I made no effort to conceal my disgust. "She made me feel like a hypocrite when I didn't want to go along. Now it's obvious that she was just looking to get rid of me."

"I know. Helena told me." Sharon fought back her tears. "That's why they were in the bedroom together when you got back. They turned on the TV so they'd have an excuse for going there. It was just a fluke that they happened to see you in that clip for the headline news."

"I'm so sorry, Honey," I wrapped my arms around my daughter, and she sobbed freely on my shoulder. As I held her silently, I was once more struck by how strange my life had become. As if the pie-throwing, the death of Marion Hines, and my bizarre heritage were not enough, now my live-in lover had cheated on me with my daughter's girlfriend.

The shock of learning that I'd become a killer had disoriented me and left me feeling detached and disconnected for the previous two months. I suppose that was some kind of instinctive coping mechanism that also inured me to the pain of Martina's betrayal and the emergence of her cold-blooded side that I had only glimpsed previously. But this newest development, this effort to hurt me by breaking my daughter's heart, ripped through the shield that had been protecting me from my outrage. I clenched my teeth to hold back my fury as I tried to comfort Sharon.

Finally she stopped crying and wiped the tears from her eyes. "Helena left this afternoon for Blowing Rock. You might have passed her at the airport. She's convinced that Martina's fling with Tom won't last, and she wants to be there to pick up the pieces."

"The bitch," I muttered as I pushed aside the last tear trickling down her cheek. "They're both bitches. Feel sorry for them, if you have it in you. Being Martina must be its own punishment, and Helena has just thrown away a gem and set herself up for major heartbreak. I don't know. Maybe it's a result of growing up under a totalitarian regime, but it's pretty clear to me now that Martina doesn't know what the word 'loyalty' means. Even if she and Tom do break up, she won't stay long with Helena either. She doesn't have it in her."

Sharon thought a moment and nodded in agreement. Then she laughed weakly. "And here I thought once I gave up on men, I'd be through with pricks."

We went out for an early dinner at a nearby pizza place, and Sharon seemed to cheer up some as we anticipated meeting Burnt Umber, a.k.a. Lift 'n' Separate.

"That's some crazy family you come from," she joked. "How'd you manage to stay so sane?"

"I had to for the sake of my daughter."

"Thanks for doing that and for saying that." Sharon kissed me quickly on the cheek. Then she began to fill me in on the details of Burnt's visit. "He seemed suspicious and aloof in his initial e-mails when I first contacted him. The details from Tom's account of the party in Greenwich Village and his tryst with Grandma seem to have convinced him. But he's still doubtful."

"Me too," I answered, wondering about the wisdom of aligning ourselves with the crackpot Tom had described.

But Sharon did not share my reservations. "Burnt insists that our initial meeting be outdoors in some public place and that we all show up in costume. I'm to dress as a pioneer woman, and you must come as an astronaut. We're supposed to wait for him alone on Halloween by the Henry Moore statue in front of the Regenstein library. He'll be in costume too, but he won't say what. He says that he'll recognize us. We're to be there at 9:00 tomorrow night."

Although Sharon found the weather temperate the next evening, I felt cold and ridiculous walking through Hyde Park. Virtually everything about the University of Chicago signals a common quest for higher knowledge and greater understanding, the things I most greatly prize. And here I was parading along in a fake astronaut suit I'd bought downtown that morning. Walking past the medieval-looking classroom buildings and faculty offices that abut one another for entire city blocks, I felt as much out of place in the modern world as the campus itself.

The difference is that the university is insular by design. The architects, over a hundred years ago, tried to recreate a medieval college protected from the corruption of the city that teemed beyond its gates. Instead of opening out to the messy, harsh, external world, the rows of buildings face inward, onto an inner sanctum of quadrangles. At the same time, the edifices offer their back sides to the street. As I walked along, I looked up to see stone gargoyles in parapets grinning down hideously at me on the sidewalk below. More than one made me think of Martina and how she must have been gloating.

We stood before the library and waited, Sharon in a 1960s granny dress she'd found in a second-hand store and me in my fish-bowl helmet that looked like a cheap parody of the large, bronze, nuclear mushroom cloud that Henry Moore had sculpted to commemorate Enrico Fermi's atomic chain reaction. My outfit did little to ward off the chill, and I shivered as the wind from Lake Michigan sliced through my clothes.

"You've lived in Miami too long." Sharon laughed at my

discomfort. "It's only about 40 degrees out. You should come up in December and see what cold really feels like."

"Thanks. I think I'll pass." Rubbing my arms to warm myself, I hunched over to shield against a sudden gust. Another band of costumed party-goers walked by laughing. One of them howled with the wind. I watched them closely, but all of the revelers were far too young to be my father.

"It's not the intensity of the cold that bothers me," Sharon blew on her hands. "It's the duration. Winter up here lasts forever. Each year a few Chicagoans get cabin fever and go crazy. You'd be amazed at what they do after being stuck inside for months on end. There was one guy a few years back who couldn't take it anymore, so he hijacked a snowplow and...."

Before she could complete her tale, a man wearing blue jeans, a maroon sweater, and a brightly colored, papier-maché horse's head sauntered up.

"Hi, I'm Mister Ed."

I hesitated a moment and then grinned beneath my helmet. "Of course."

"Of course," Sharon echoed. "You're Burnt Umber, aren't you?"

"My friends call me Lift 'n' Separate," he offered his hand and she shook it. "You must be Sharon." Then he turned to me and said with less warmth in his voice, "I guess you're Ben. Your daughter here tells me I'm your dad."

"After all these years." I stared at the half-horse, half-man before me. "I've been looking for you for a long time."

"Obviously not in the right places. How about we get rid of these masks and find some place warm to talk."

"We can go to my apartment," Sharon offered while I removed my helmet and Burnt took off his yellow, blue, and red horse's head and revealed himself. His hair was long and gray, and his complexion, like mine, was fair. The beard he sported was bushy and gray. Deep lines radiated from his eyes, which shined bright blue under the crime lights, also like mine. His face wrinkled when he smiled from time to time at Sharon. Still, there was a youthfulness to his look despite his age, which I guessed to be around sixty or sixty-five.

On the way back Sharon walked between me and my ostensible father. We filled the sidewalk, three generations of

Umbers lined up like ducks in a row. A far cry from the sobbing, broken-hearted little girl I greeted the day before, Sharon now overflowed with excitement. I was more cautious, but my daughter peppered her grandfather with a thousand questions before we arrived at her place. Had he really met Gertrude, her grandmother, at a Greenwich Village pot party? What did he remember about her? How long had they dated? Where had he gone after leaving New York, and did he ever think about Gertrude? Did he want to call her or see her again? What did he think about Thomas Pynchon, and did he like Tom's books? Should she call him Grandpa Burnt, or Lift 'n' Separate?

Burnt just brushed off her queries and said she'd have to wait until he could warm himself up before a radiator and, this being Chicago, perhaps dispel the cold with a mug of Irish coffee. "I'm an old man," he reminded her. "And my bones chill much easier than when I was young."

So, when we finally got back to the apartment, checked our head gear at the door, and settled in the livingroom, the first thing Sharon did was set three cups and a bottle of Jameson's on the coffee table. Then she went into the kitchen to put on a pot of Maxwell House.

While she was away, Burnt poured a shot into his mug and downed it straight. "Aaah," he sighed. "There's nothing like whiskey for a family reunion." He tipped the bottle in my direction, but I said I'd wait until Sharon came back with the coffee. Burnt shrugged and poured himself another shot. "Blood may be thicker than water," he said after downing his drink. "But whiskey trumps them both, don't you think?"

Sharon soon returned and fixed a round of Irish coffee for each of us.

Burnt took a sip. "Nice place you have here? You live alone?"

I looked anxiously at Sharon, who winced at the question but answered simply, "My roommate is out of town."

The answer contented her guest, who leaned back against the sofa, propped his feet up on the coffee table, and asked, "So tell me, now that you've found me, what can I do for you?"

Sharon reiterated her questions from before, while I was content mostly to sip my coffee and take in this whirlwind who claimed to be my father. Not at all reticent, he spent the next three hours regaling us with tales from the last forty years. Convinced that government agents had tracked him down in Greenwich Village, he had secretly joined the merchant marines a few months after meeting Mom and shipped out as a deck hand on a cargo ship bound for South America. He didn't know she was pregnant when he left, although I doubt it would have made any difference.

"She was quite a pistol, your grandmother," he told Sharon. But he wouldn't elaborate except to turn to me and add with a wink and a grin, "There was good sport at your making."

He'd spent a few years at sea and then jumped ship in Singapore in the mid '60s and eventually ended up in Thailand. He was vague about what he did there, but I suspect he was somehow mixed up in the Southeast Asian drug trade that flourished during the Vietnam War. He returned to America in the early '80s and took a job briefly as an auto worker until the recession closed his plant. After that, he joined a commune in Oregon where he practiced organic farming and free love with a group of second-generation hippies. But he left a few months later when two of the girls discovered they were pregnant following a wild celebration of the full moon in which they had tried to reenact the ancient Greek bacchanalia. Apparently during the Reagan years he'd impregnated a string of young women from one end of the country to the other, while supporting himself with odd jobs.

"I was a regular Johnny Appleseed back then," he boasted. "But it wasn't apples I was planting." Then he waved his hand dismissively. "Oh, don't thank me. I was just doing my bit to create a bright future for my country."

Sharon and I exchanged horrified glances. We were appalled by his cavalier attitude, but Burnt just went ahead with his narration, as though he had nothing to be ashamed about. In the '90s his life became slightly more settled. He traveled with a circus for almost three years, although he wouldn't say what he did. After that, he and the snake lady opened a store in central Florida where they sold New Age products and read tarot cards.

"Did you ever run across a fortune-teller named Natalia?" I asked, not really expecting him to say yes. "She lives in Texas."

Burnt—I never could make myself call him Lift 'n' Separate, despite his insistence that all his friends did—Burnt eyed me suspiciously.

"A gypsy on San Padre Island?" he asked cautiously. I'd

finally said something that caught his interest. Until then, Burnt talked only about himself. He never even asked me what I did for a living.

"Yes, that's the one!" The coincidence left me flabbergasted.

"We were partners for a while a few years back. I think I was using Tom Pynchon's name then," he answered. "We had a good thing, but it didn't last. There was an unpleasant misunderstanding, and we went our separate ways. That was right after I left Florida. How do you know Natalia?"

When I told him my story, and how she tried to kill me after I told her Thomas Pynchon was my father, Burnt roared with laughter.

"That's the same Natalia, all right. She was a spirited gal, like your Mom, a real pistol. We didn't exactly part on friendly terms."

"Daddy, you never told me that story," Sharon complained.

"Well, your mother didn't approve of my efforts to track down my father."

"Why not?" Sharon demanded.

I shrugged. "I don't pretend to understand what your mother approves of or disapproves. Ask her."

Sharon and I tried to find out why Natalia wanted to kill him, and to learn of his more recent experiences, but Burnt clearly did not care to reveal much that was intimate about his past or his current situation. Finally, I asked him to tell us about the Houyhnhnms.

"The Houyhnhnms were a Cold War experiment in eugenics." he began, his tone suddenly serious. "Someone in the government figured we'd be in an indefinite, nuclear stalemate with the Russians. He managed to convince some official with power that we might prevail thirty or forty years down the line if we could create a race of supermen--the next step in human evolution."

Sharon shuddered. "That sounds like what the Nazis did during World War II. Didn't we convict them of war crimes for that sort of thing? And this was only what, a decade or so after the war ended?"

"It's not a war crime if you do it to your own people," I

answered. "As far as I know, no one was ever prosecuted for ordering American soldiers into the atomic test sites in the New Mexico desert right after the war. But there would have been plenty of tribunals, and heads would have rolled if we had made POWs march up to ground zero minutes after a nuclear blast."

"That's right," Burnt nodded. "Plus 1957, the year the experiment began, was also the year the Russians sent up Sputnik."

"Sputnik?" Sharon looked puzzled.

"It was the first satellite ever to go into outer space," I told her, appalled anew at how little contemporary history her generation of young Americans knew. Even my own child, the daughter of a history professor, was ignorant of the most basic facts about the Cold War which, after all, had dominated the politics of the second half of the twentieth century. "Sputnik scared us Americans silly. After that, you could justify just about anything, so long as you made some minimal case that you were doing it to fight communism."

"That's right," Burnt concurred. "The Houyhnhnms were going to beat the communists and create an American utopia. Most of the subjects were chosen for their scientific aptitude. But a handful of us were selected for our artistic traits. I was a musician back then. I played honky tonk on the piano and sang a little back up. I don't think they ever believed we'd contribute much to the new species, but we were included so they could say they tested those qualities but didn't find any positive results. Well, I'm still alive and fertile, which is more than the left-brained geeks in the other test group can say."

"What finally happened to the program?" Sharon couldn't take her eyes off the strange man before her.

"Ironically, the experiment was shut down when some right-wing Congressman caught wind of it and thought it might be a commie plot. Remember, this was the '50s, and even though old Tailgunner Joe McCarthy was out of power by then, the Red Scare was still going strong. Anything strange or different was likely to be attacked for being communist. Eisenhower ended the experiment to avoid a scandal, but I'd already escaped before then, along with a handful of others from the humanities group. Unlike our counterparts with superior IQs, we instinctively distrusted the government scientists."

Burnt pointed his finger at Sharon. "That's a survival skill I hope I passed down to you through our common DNA. My time in the hands of behavioral social scientists had been bad enough; I wasn't about to let them fry my brains with radiation on top of that. It was evident that they either didn't know what the hell they were doing, or they didn't care. Me and my buddies figured out early on that we were just experimental lab rats as far as they were concerned. But the geeks in the other group were all gung-ho for science and couldn't believe those clowns with all their advanced degrees and fancy equipment didn't give a damn about their personal welfare. Of course, it later turned out that the x-ray process sterilized all the subjects who had been stupid enough to stay around for all the treatments. So much for spawning a new generation of supermen. They only zapped me once before I found a way to get the hell out of there. That didn't seem to have had much effect. Naturally, there was a big cover-up. By now the scientists are either dead or senile. But I trust no one. I've been on the run one way or another ever since."

"Are you in contact with the others who escaped with you?" I asked.

"We didn't all leave at the same time, but yeah, we've stayed in touch. At first we didn't want to have anything more to do with the program, or with each other. But one guy, Sam, started wondering if maybe the traits we were selected for--creativity, intuition, and optimism--really might give us an advantage in the Darwinian jungle. 'They definitely make for a better quality of life,' he argued.

"'How come we artists aren't exactly flourishing then?' I asked. But Sam said that over the years truly creative people had been rejected so often for being weird or different that they'd become alienated and overcome by despair. 'They've lost their optimism and sense of purpose,' he said. 'Without those, nobody's going to make a big splash in the gene pool.'

"It made sense to me, and I've been doing my bit to upgrade the gene pool ever since." Burnt looked at me and winked. "Look how well you've turned out."

"I'm not sure how well I've clung to my optimism, but thanks for the compliment," I answered. This was the first positive thing he'd said to me since we met.

"Well, you better cling on for dear life, son. I'm not kidding you now. This is some real fatherly advice I'm giving you here."

"It's a little late, don't you think?" I suddenly felt bitter.

"Better late than never. A positive attitude is the best life raft you can have in the sea of pain and violence we all get tossed into sooner or later."

"So who was responsible for the Houyhnhnm website?" I asked. "I stumbled across it once, not too long ago. But then it disappeared."

"Sam ran the website. Over the years, he tried to keep track of us and fill us in on what was going on with the others. He figured it might be a good idea to know if anyone suddenly developed any peculiar symptoms. Sometimes two or three years would go by without anyone hearing from him, but then somehow he'd track us down. When the Internet came along, we agreed to go online and keep in touch through e-mail. Then he got the idea of a website. He used the government code name *Houyhnhnm*. In *Gulliver's Travels* the Houyhnhnms are a breed of super-rational horses that Gulliver regarded as superior, more highly evolved beings. But Sam had to close it down a while back."

"How come?"

"Apparently a group of skinheads and neo-Nazis ran across the site. They've somehow got it into their thick skulls that Houyhnhnms are part of some great Jewish conspiracy to take control of the world by creating a race of super-Jews."

"Holy shit," I groaned.

"Yeah, it's true," Burnt nodded. Then he poured some more whiskey into his cup and drank it. "At first we didn't think they posed a serious threat to us, but a couple months ago we started getting e-mails at the website suggesting they might know more than we were comfortable with. So Sam shut it down. He didn't want those assholes trailing us."

I tried to get Burnt to tell us more about his life, especially his relationship with my mother, but for some reason he always refused. Finally, he announced that it was getting late, and we retired to bed. I took Helena's room, and Burnt made himself comfortable on the couch.

Chapter 11

The next morning after breakfast we went into Sharon's room and pulled up chairs around the computer on her work table. Except for a quick peek when Martina and I had visited her over the summer, I hadn't been in my daughter's bedroom since she and Diane moved away five years earlier. The walls in the room from her teenage years had brimmed with posters of movie and video stars, collages of friends sharing good times, decoratively written lines from sentimental songs and poems, and, of course, pictures of actual and would-be boyfriends. Her floor then was so deeply carpeted with plastic CD cases, school books, notes from friends, and other personal debris that I often had to wade across the room just to kiss her good night.

The chamber that now served both as Sharon's study and sleeping quarters at the University of Chicago was similarly blanketed with the flotsam of her life, but these revealed a very different person, an adult with a unique identity that had already begun to sharpen and take full shape. CD cases still littered her floor, but now the compact discs were more likely sophisticated computer data bases than entertainment. The musical CDs Sharon did own were mostly classical and jazz (remember Carlos the saxophonist from her party), but she also had a fair sample of Chicago rhythm and blues. There was no longer room on the walls for posters of idols and heartthrobs; book cases now occupied that space. Sharon was just beginning her junior year and had declared her English major only the spring before. But already she'd surrounded herself with paperback novels from every era; volumes of contemporary poetry, mostly by women and minorities; manuscripts of her own writing and that of her friends, and library hardbacks of literary criticism and theory--much of it

Marxist and feminist from what I could see at a quick glance. I also noticed some textbooks about political theory and sociology. Her bed wasn't made, and her night stand was a mess. But Sharon's open closet revealed a well-cared for wardrobe that included some brightly colored blouses and a couple of feminine-looking dresses. These offset the faded blue jeans and sweat shirt that dangled from her reading chair, a bra carelessly thrown on top. As I looked around her room, I wondered what kind of butterfly would eventually emerge from such a cocoon.

Gone too were the youthful photographs of boys she pined for. Instead, above the reading chair hung a tastefully framed reproduction of one of Auguste Renoir's female nudes, and over her bed was a lush Monet landscape. These conferred a softness that was otherwise missing from the environment. Next to the computer monitor on her work table stood a simple, silver-framed picture of Sharon and Helena holding hands by the frozen bank of Lake Michigan. Sharon discreetly turned it over when she entered the room and booted up the computer for me. Burnt didn't seem to notice.

We were there because I wanted to show him *Pie-thrower.com*, and Sharon's computer was in her bedroom. After all the talk about his wild past, I thought my website might appeal to his nonconformist sensibilities. If I had been thinking more clearly, I never would have made such a foolish move. But I was short on sleep and still a little stunned at finally meeting my father, whom I suppose I wanted to impress. Burnt recognized the home page as soon as I called it up. His past dealings with the neo-Nazis had brought him there, as Martina and I frequently spoofed them on the website.

Burnt silently checked out the new features on the site, while I proudly looked on. But after a few minutes he turned to me and grinned.

"So, *you* killed Marion Hines. My own bastard is a murderer. It's the seeds of Cain and Abel, I tell you. Try as we might, we humans just cannot escape their curse."

I felt the blood rush from my face. Burnt had obviously seen our posting of my throwing the pie at Marion Hines, or had read about it on other websites. My secret was out. I recognized instantly that my fate was now in the hands of a brilliant, bizarre stranger who played by his own set of rules. Ostensibly, Burnt was my father and we were on the same side. But so far he'd demonstrated little warmth to me, only to Sharon. And I'd known him for less than twenty-four hours. At times he'd been fascinating, even inspiring. But on other occasions his eyes flamed like a madman's, and I was scared. Was he grinning because he approved of my killing Hines. And if so, was *that* a good thing? After all, I never intended any harm to her at all; her death haunts me still. What would it say about Burnt if he reveled in it? On the other hand, maybe he was grinning because he'd learned my secret and felt he suddenly had gained power over me. Perhaps he had. Would the Pie-thrower fall prey to the Victim of Paradox? All these thoughts raced through my mind as Burnt's grin lit up his face.

When he noticed Sharon blanching behind me, Burnt laughed out loud. "So you're in on it too. What'd you do, drive the getaway car?"

Sharon seemed momentarily discombobulated, but then she regained her composure. She sat up straight, raised her chin, thrust back her shoulders, and declared proudly, "As a matter of fact, I did."

When we'd finished showing Burnt the website, he announced that he had compelling business on the east coast that afternoon and an old flame to look up that night. An hour later he was stepping into a cab on his way to O'Hare. The farewell was cordial, if not exactly warm. I noticed he hugged Sharon a couple times extra before hopping into the taxi. Maybe there was some grandfatherly affection there, or maybe he was just copping a feel from a cute, young woman. Perhaps both. To me, he only repeated, "the seeds of Cain and Abel," and shook his head. His motives were as difficult to decipher when he left as when he arrived.

I stayed on until the afternoon and then caught a flight back to Miami. I had a window seat on the plane, and, as I gazed down onto the clouds below, I contemplated my life anew, again. Several years earlier my unanticipated divorce had abruptly reconfigured the circumstances of my existence, and I'd felt as though I'd entered into a new world. New rules, new expectations, new identity as a suddenly single man. Then my whirlwind summer romance with Martina changed everything again. Now, the events of the previous few months and days promised to reassemble my life one more time. Although I'd at least found Tom Pynchon, the completion of that quest failed to bring closure to my mission to establish some kind of bond with my father. Quite the opposite. It demolished the belief of a lifetime that my father was a masterful artist whose genes I had always taken secret pride in carrying. Instead, my dad now appeared to be some kind of brilliantly demented eccentric, a rolling stone who exhibited precious little interest in his long-lost son–if, indeed, I was in fact his child–but had a keen interest in exploring the margins of society and the edges of civilization. On top of that, I might be a first-generation Houyhnhnm, the next evolutionary step for humanity, the product of the unbridled lust of a drop-out from a 1950s genetic engineering experiment gone wrong. Plus, my girlfriend--now my ex-girlfriend--had proven to be a heartless revolutionary who stole away the lesbian lover of my daughter, and then abandoned her for the man I thought had been my father. And, most unsettling of all, I had committed manslaughter, if not outright murder, during the preposterous act of pie-throwing. Where would I go from here?

Where did I want to go? I had no idea. So when I arrived in Miami I did the only thing I knew to do. I drove back to Martina's apartment, fed Pandora--a neighbor had been looking in on her while I was away--and thrust myself back into my work.

Meanwhile, the presidential election came and went, although the final outcome remained in abeyance. The only communications I received from Martina were mass mailings she sent to everyone in her address book denouncing the claims of a Bush victory. She was demanding a full and fair Florida recount and investigations of the disenfranchisement of African-American voters who'd been stopped from voting there and of the notorious butterfly ballot.

Naturally, I shared her outrage over what seemed more and more to be a stolen election, but I was also overcome by a sense of impotence, an inability to do anything about it, or about anything else in my life. Apart from the period of my divorce, I had never felt so out-of-control. The country was being hijacked by the Right, and no one seemed all that upset about it, except radical extremists like Martina. Once again I thought of that line from Yeats: "The best lack all convictions, while the worst are full of passionate intensity."

Was the Second Coming indeed at hand? The election shouldn't even have been close. The nation had prospered as never before during Clinton's two terms, we'd won the air war against Serbia and were otherwise more or less at peace; we'd balanced the budget and wiped out the national debt, and we enjoyed strong economic growth with low inflation. Even with the Republican shenanigans, it shouldn't have been a contest. But because of Monica Lewinsky, Gore distanced himself from all of Clinton's achievements, and so the election boiled down to whether the voters trusted Bush the frat boy more than Gore the geek to steer the nation during turbulent times. It was sobering to realize that, in any event, roughly half of them trusted the inarticulate frat boy–in part *because* he was inarticulate. Moreover, it was evident that virtually every tie-breaking mechanism was controlled by Bush supporters, from the Florida legislature to the U.S. House of Representatives to the Supreme Court. Events were swirling around me with potentially horrifying consequences, and I felt as though all I could do was watch and hope and duck when the time came.

The time came sooner than I expected. The day before Thanksgiving Dick Cheney suffered a mild heart attack, a Republican-led mob closed down the voting recount in Miami-Dade County, and, late that evening, Martina and Helena showed up suddenly at my door, suitcases in hand.

"We're back," Martina announced as she marched in. Helena's greeting was distant but polite. Certainly less brash.

"What about Tom?" I finally managed to ask as they dumped their belongings on the floor.

"What a disappointment he turned out to be." Martina slammed the door closed behind her.

Her declaration astonished me. She'd seemed so enamored of him when I last saw them in Blowing Rock. "Maybe no one could live up to the expectations you'd built around him," I finally offered. I was stunned by their unexpected appearance, and I looked from Martina to Helena back to Martina as we stood in the foyer. I didn't know what to think or say. Helena seemed pale and perhaps stressed, but Martina was filled with self-righteous animation.

"It's not that," Martina indignantly dismissed my suggestion. "He's as brilliant and creative as I ever imaged. But he's totally apolitical. He supported Nader, for God's sake. He says there's no difference between the Democrats and Republicans, that it's all big business, which is more true than we like to admit. But you can't tell me there isn't a huge difference between Bush's agenda and Gore's. Tom insists change has to come from the bottom up, not the top down. But he won't do anything to make it happen. He won't lend his name and prestige to help rally the troops and fight back against this right-wing coup that's taking place in front of our eyes. He won't even send an anonymous letter or join a demonstration march. He just retreats farther back into his little cabin and writes his books. Like you."

"That's not fair and you know it!" Here she was, digging at me again.

"Oh, yeah! Well what have you done to keep the Republicans from stealing the election? Were you downtown this morning mixing it up with those thugs who shut down the democratic process right here in your home town? Did you march out to the courthouse demanding an investigation of this mob rule, which, we now know, was orchestrated by a Republican boss from New York? Did you write letters to your Congressmen and newspapers and governor demanding the resumption of the Miami-Dade hand count? Demanding that every vote be counted. Isn't that what democracy's supposed to be all about? Have you lifted one finger during any of this to protect the Constitution you say you value so dearly? Or did you just go back to teaching school?"

Martina's hard blue eyes seared into me. Angry as she had been at Marion Hines, I'd still never seen her so possessed by venomous rage.

"You flew all the way back here to attack me?"

"No. I flew all the way back here to fight the fascists; so they don't steal this country right from under your nose, while you and your liberal friends just sit there whining and complaining and pretending to be appalled."

"What do you want us to do? Go down there and punch out some right-wingers? How will that help Gore?"

"It'll send a message that you aren't about to be intimidated and that you aren't going to just lie down and let them pluck the presidency right out from under you."

"No, it won't send a message!" I was furious at her affront. "It'll only land me in jail, cost me my job, and render me even more marginal than I am. This thing is going to play out in the courts, and there's nothing any of us can do to stop that. And at this stage of the game, I don't want to stop it. The courts are our best hope. Not the streets. We have to play out the process and accept wherever it takes us."

"Coward." Martina's disgust was palpable.

"You forget I killed a woman in defense of a political cause, *your* political cause, just a few months ago."

I was horrified to hear myself speak those words, but Martina dismissed them with a flick of her wrist. "It's not like you *meant* to kill the bitch, or anything."

Even Helena appeared shocked by Martina's callousness. She stepped back and almost tripped over one of her suitcases, which she then bent down to pick up. "I'm going to start putting things away," she announced, as she grabbed her bags. Her voice was agitated. "Where should I take these?" When she looked up to Martina, I could see that Helena's face had fear written all over it.

"Help yourselves to the bedroom," I answered. "I'll sleep in the office with Pandora. I'll start looking for a place of my own tomorrow."

I found a very satisfactory one-bedroom apartment close to campus the following day, but the current tenant, a visiting biology professor, wouldn't be vacating until the end of the term in mid-December. As I wasn't up to moving twice during the crunch time of the semester, Martina, Helena, and I were compelled to share the same space for the next few weeks. I stayed away as much as possible, working into the night at the library or in my office at the university. But some evenings we spent together. On those nights, the three of us would gather around the television to learn the latest developments in the vote count. We hissed at Governor Jeb, George's brother, when he urged the Republican-dominated Florida legislature to perform an "act of courage" by calling a special session to select an alternate set of representatives to the electoral college. And we cheered as we watched the convoy of rented vans haul over a million ballots from West Palm Beach and Miami-Dade to Tallahassee, where, if the process permitted it, the votes might be fairly counted. But mostly Martina and I avoided one another.

Martina and Helena spent most of their days participating in recount protest demonstrations and contemplating how to respond if the Republicans should, indeed, snatch the election. One day Martina came home with a black eye from a pro-Bush Cuban exile she'd locked horns with on a picket line. "You should have seen the other guy," was all she said. That was the day the court ruled that the infamous butterfly ballots in Palm Beach were valid, despite their somewhat confusing format that had apparently caused the notoriously liberal county to vote overwhelmingly for Patrick Buchanan, instead of Al Gore.

"The system's stacked against us," Martina ranted. "Anyone knows those Democrats up there didn't deliberately vote for Buchanan. He's farther to the right than Bush, for God's sake!" I sighed and shook my head, both at the ruling and at Martina. She seemed prepared to lay into me again for surrendering--I did feel helpless to influence the recount process--when the phone rang. It was Linda, Martina's contact with the Hysterical Lesbians for Freedom. Martina had been speaking a lot with Linda since returning from Blowing Rock. She took the call in another room.

Her mood improved considerably a few days later when, to the surprise of all of the TV pundits, the Florida Supreme Court ordered hand counts throughout the state, wherever undervotes had occurred. It also restored 168 votes in Miami-Dade and 215 in Palm Beach counties, narrowing Bush's lead to a mere 154 votes. Maybe there was hope after all. Hope, I pointed out to Martina, that came not from street protests and violence but from the Constitutional process. But some 96 hours later, on the same day the Florida House voted along party lines for an alternate set of electors who would vote for Bush, the U.S. Supreme Court overturned the Florida Supreme Court and ended the recount. Bush had won.

I moved out a few days later. Martina and I were barely speaking by then. Helena seemed increasingly intimidated by her outbursts of rage and indignation, and she withdrew into herself as the days went on. After Gore conceded, Martina was on the phone more and more frequently with Linda and the HLF. She always made the calls in private, so I wasn't privy to their machinations. But the night before I left, Helena stepped into my room. We hadn't spoken much since their return, so her appearance surprised me. But in the previous week or so I'd noticed she'd become, if not exactly more friendly, at least more open to me, perhaps because, like her, I too was a target of Martina's tyranny. Helena looked nervous or anxious, as though she was waiting for something bad to happen.

"Ben, I just wanted to say goodbye." She held out her hand and I shook it. "And I want you to know that I appreciate everything you've been trying to do. Martina's been pretty hard on you, and that's not fair. Throwing that pie at Marion Hines was not only heroic, it was an act of love. I'm sorry everything went haywire."

I looked up from the suitcase into which I was packing my Pie-thrower cape and mask. "Thanks," I told her. "I appreciate your saying that. Martina doesn't seem to see it that way."

"I know," Helena shook her head. Then she added, "Tell Sharon that I'm sorry I hurt her. I never wanted to. She was always very special to me."

My feelings for Helena had soured considerably after she abandoned my daughter, and until now she had neither said nor done anything to make me feel better about her. But the look in her eyes and the tone of her voice seemed sincere.

"I'll tell her." We stood silently for a moment. Finally, I decided to take advantage of Helena's unexpected overture to find out what was going on with Martina and the HLF. "Are they plotting something dark and mysterious?" I asked.

Helena smiled. "I wouldn't exactly describe it that way. Although it will certainly have a dark side to it."

"I don't get it."

"Well, I'm really not supposed to tell you, but what can it hurt? You're the Pie-thrower, after all. They're planning a mass protest at Bush's inauguration."

"What are they going to do? Organize a huge sit-in along Pennsylvania Avenue?" I closed the suitcase lid and zipped it shut.

"No, not a sit-in. A Shit-In."

"A what?"

"A Shit-In. They're going to place protestors in the crowds, who, when Bush's car drives past, are going to pull down their pants and take a crap. While they're evacuating their bowels, they'll hold up signs saying, "This election stinks!" and "Bush is full of shit." Things like that. Martina's organizing it. I think the HLF has a few other plans as well, but this is Martina's assignment."

"My God!" I tried to imagine the scene. "Leave it to Martina to organize a Shit-In. The dark side, for sure. Are you going to participate?"

The mirth left Helena's face. "What choice do I have?"

Chapter 12

Gore conceded the election on December 13, the same day I turned in my grades for the semester. I was off until the beginning of January, and there was nothing really to keep me in Miami; so once I settled in to my new place, I bought a bargain rate airplane ticket and flew to Hyde Park to spend the holidays with Sharon.

I'd experienced cold before, but nothing as bitter and bone-chilling as Chicago in the winter. The trees were barren, the sidewalks icy, the sun barely rose in the sky, and it set behind snow-filled clouds by 4 P.M. *Bleak* pretty much summed it up. All in all, it was difficult to accept that I was again staying in the same apartment in the same city where I'd so happily begun my pie-throwing career less than half a year earlier.

But Sharon and I did our best not to succumb to despair. While Bush basked in his stolen election and Martina plotted with her HLF pals back home, my daughter and I strolled through Chicago's Art Institute and admired its stellar Impressionist collection, renowned throughout the world for its stunning Monets and sensuous Renoirs. We listened to crisp, clean performances of Beethoven and Mahler by the Chicago Symphony and to swinging jazz and honky tonk blues in Old Town; we feasted on bratwurst and moussaka.

When Chanukah arrived, Sharon produced a menorah, and we lit the candles together each evening at sundown. The ritual had never much spoken to me before, but this year the holiday's message of deliverance from dark defeat and stifling oppression offered a ray of light on those frigid Chicago nights as we watched news accounts of the presidential transition. I have fond recollections of staring at the menorah, seeking visions in the flickering flames and trying to connect to our Jewish past as we retold how the Maccabees, Jewish freedom fighters of the second century B.C.E., overthrew their conquerors. We spoke of how the eternal light in the temple, a tribute to God's immortality, was never to be allowed to expire, and how it miraculously remained aflame for eight days after it should have exhausted its supply of fuel.

Sharon had gotten off to a slow start that semester, but she had poured herself into her studies after Helena left and finished the term with good grades. This was in spite of occasional bouts of depression, due to her failed relationship and, perhaps, unacknowledged mixed feelings associated with the death of Marion Hines. She was reluctant to speak much about her love life. I noticed that the picture of her and Helena beside Lake Michigan remained on her dresser in her bedroom, but Sharon never mentioned Helena by name.

She was more open to discussing Marion Hines. Although I remained haunted by my own role in the demagogue's demise, and was still torn by conflicting allegiances to my daughter, on the one hand, and rule by law, on the other, Sharon insisted that Hines's heart attack had stemmed from her preexisting medical condition and unhealthy lifestyle and that we bore only incidental responsibility for it. And she became furiously indignant when she inventoried all the documented instances of Hines's homophobia, something she clearly took very personally.

The day before Christmas I was reading in the living room when Sharon came out of her bedroom to tell me she had just received an email from Burnt Umber. She'd remained in touch with him after Halloween, although he never communicated with me. Their exchanges had been friendly and witty, and he sometimes sent her reports and news accounts of bizarre happenings throughout the world. "Nothing suggestive or pornographic," she insisted. "Just weird stuff, mostly. And sometimes off-beat articles about little people who changed history. That's what he calls them, *little people*. People like the Serb nationalist who killed Archduke Ferdinand and started World War I."

"How about the guy who knocked the arm of Giuseppe Zangara?" I asked. "When he tried to shoot Franklin Roosevelt in Miami in 1933, just a few weeks before FDR's first inauguration. If that anonymous man in the crowd hadn't stepped up, there might never have been any New Deal, Social Security checks, and maybe no atom bomb. Who knows which side would have won World War II, or if we'd have even been in it. Or how the Cold War would have begun."

Sharon simply went on. "I told Burnt that when he calls them *little people* they sound like leprechauns, but he says he admires them, or at least some of them, because they're the wild cards in history. According to him, the little people who assert themselves at unexpected moments keep history unpredictable, and unpredictability, in the long run, guarantees freedom."

"There's a thought worthy of Thomas Pynchon."

"Burnt has all kinds of theories about why we need to shake things up from time to time, just on general principle." She sat down on the couch across from my easy chair. "He says we shouldn't try to contain the future, or even try to direct it too much. We should leap into life and go wherever it takes us. Don't just study it." Sharon added the final point with a shrug as she looked at me.

"Contain the future? Is that what he calls planning and forethought? Civilization and sanity?" Why was it that, almost 2500 years after Socrates pointed out how the unexamined life is not worth living, almost everyone I met lately was attacking the life of the mind and the basic premise of my being--that our lives are most rewarding when our actions are well informed by knowledge and wisdom. Martina had ridiculed me for thinking this way. She called me an antique, an Enlightenment sensibility living in a postmodern era. "Life is messy," she once berated me. "From the Big Bang forward the one constant in the universe has been explosive, cataclysmic change. That's what's what it's all about. And that's what's wrong with you *petit bourgeoise*s. You're afraid of change. You're afraid of life. You're afraid of the universe." It seemed that Burnt Umber was on her side.

"You can ask him about it, yourself." Sharon straightened the pillow beside her. "He said he's flying in to O'Hare this evening and will come by tomorrow. I told him we'd go down tonight and meet him at the airport, but he insists that the hospitality at the Admirals Club on Christmas Eve is unsurpassed, and he doesn't want to miss out on it. He'll "pop in" for lunch. And he insists on taking public transportation.

"Hellooo, Buckos!" Burnt greeted us with an exuberance and good cheer that I frankly had not expected, although Sharon didn't seem surprised. He showed up at her front door around 10:45 on Christmas morning; his breath already reeking of alcohol.

"Hello, Grandpaw," Sharon ran up to him and gave him a hug. I followed behind more tentatively.

"For God's sake, don't call me *Grandpaw*. Especially on Christmas. Makes me feel like we're the Waltons and I just walked into the little house on the prairie. Or maybe we're the Real McCoys and I'm Grandpappy Amos." Burnt then uttered a high-pitched imitation of Walter Brennan's semi-suppressed giggle.

"What should I call you then?" Sharon asked as she helped him out of his overcoat.

"You know. Lift 'n' Separate is what I go by these days."

"That's just too sexist and too strange. I'll call you Grandfather Burnt from now on." She spoke *grandfather* in an affected, pseudo-aristocratic, excessively nasal voice, emphasizing *grand*, which she pronounced *grond*, and prolonging each syllable.

Burnt grinned as Sharon took the coat from him and started toward the hall closet to hang it up. Then he suddenly reached out to grab her shoulder. "Wait a second, Missy." He reached inside the interior breast pocket and removed a thin, silver flask. "My Jameson's." He held it up for us admire. "I used it this morning to liven-up the glasses of eggnog they served me at the Admirals Club. I was hoping maybe you'd be able to fill it up for me?" Burnt's look suggested this was more an order than a request. "Between my Jameson's and the danishes, croissants, cookies, and coffee they put out for us to help ourselves, I had a particularly satisfying Christmas breakfast; thank you for asking. Particularly satisfying." He smiled a self-satisfied smile and then stepped past us into the living room. The scent of his whiskey permeated the air as he went by.

"What? No Christmas tree?" Burnt feigned shock. "What kind of heathens are the product of my loins?"

"We're Jewish, *Grond*father," Sharon reminded him.

"I guess I knew that. Your mother being Jewish and all. Just never gave it any thought." For the first time since his arrival Burnt looked at me. "But that still doesn't mean you can't have a

Christmas tree. How can we be the Waltons without a yuletide log in the hearth and a Christmas tree?"

"I guess we'll just have to settle for being the Branches," I said.

"Or the Twigs," Burnt grumbled as he plopped down into the easy chair where I'd been reading.

"Can I get you anything, *Grond*father?" Sharon asked.

"A Christmas tree."

"Sorry, it's a little late for that," she smiled. "You should have given me more warning. But we can light the candles when the sun sets."

"You gotta menorah?"

"Yes, and we've been lighting it every night."

"Well that's good," Burnt shook his head approvingly. "A father should pass down respect for religion to his children, whatever religion it may be, although my personal preference is for the shamanistic cults of the Native Americans."

I couldn't discern to what extent Burnt's words were just drunken bullshit and to what extent they expressed his sincere beliefs. Certainly he'd made no effect to pass down anything to me. I wondered if his parents had ever done so for him. It was suddenly strange to imagine Burnt as a little boy. Who *were* his parents, my grandparents? Where did he grow up? Under what conditions? Was he well adjusted? Did he play well with others and get good grades in school? What did he want to be when he grew up? What would the 16-year-old Burnt Umber (or Tommy or Bob or Lance or Biff or whatever his name was back then), what would he have thought of the man that he became?

Sharon brought out a tray with coffee and a bottle of Jameson's, which Burnt quickly pounced on and poured into his black coffee. "Don't mind if I resupply my stash?" he asked Sharon as he carefully transferred more whiskey from the bottle to the flask.

"Of course not," Sharon laughed. "I bought it for you."

"Next best thing to a Yuletide log," he said, saluting us with his coffee mug. He offered to pour some Jameson's into my cup, but I declined.

I tried to ask him to tell us about his youth. However, although he never directly refused to talk about his childhood, Burnt avoided discussing any of his life before the Houyhnhnm experiment. Instead, he launched into an array of wild, and very hard-to-believe stories. He spoke for almost two hours about his escapades with Marcella, the circus snake lady, a devilish twenty-three year-old back in the 1990s who loved to play practical jokes on people by placing her boa constrictors in unlikely places. Sometimes her jokes were very practical, indeed. More than once the girls, as she called her snakes, had unexpectedly turned up slithering among the sheets and inside the pillowcases on the Pretzel Woman's bed, spoiling the hussy's efforts to make furtive love to the Strong Man, who was married to Marcella's best friend.

"Is that where you met Natalia?" I asked him. "In the circus?"

"Close. A carnival, not a circus. I met Natalia before I ever knew Marcella. I was playing honky tonk in some dive in some town in Virginia, and I had time to kill before my midnight set. So I checked out the traveling side show that had set up just a few blocks down the street. You know, a Ferris wheel, a roller coaster, some games of chance, freaks, a fortune teller, and lots of cotton candy. Natalia was the fortune teller. When she took my hand to read my fortune, a spark jumped between us so bright it lit up her gypsy booth. Just ask her. She'll agree, unless she's lying out of spite. Anyway, we partnered up after that.

"Not a bad life if you like cotton candy." Burnt took another sip of his Irish coffee. "That was back in the days when I was calling myself Thomas Pynchon. That's right, I was Thomas Pynchon, King of the Carnies." Burnt chuckled at the memory. He went on to regale us with tales of his life as a carney, stories that amazed and amused us. But try as we might, we still couldn't draw Burnt out on what he had done to so greatly provoke the gypsy's fiery wrath.

At noon the grocery down the street opened, and I ventured out to pick up some more food for lunch. I had intended to pick up cold cuts for sandwiches but Burnt insisted on muffins, Sara Lee blueberry muffins. As I made my way to the store, a stiff wind skimmed off Lake Michigan and smacked me in the face. The trees had lost their leaves, and the sky was gray and forbidding, like the buildings beneath it. When I finally entered the store, my cheeks were bright red and numb with cold. I blew on my hands to warm them, and then I went about my business.

They didn't carry Sara Lee, so I selected half a dozen muffins--three blueberry and three assorted--and made my way to the check-out counter and then back outside into the cold.

When I returned, Sharon and Burnt had moved into the kitchen. I gave Sharon the muffins to warm in Helena's toaster-oven. Then I sat down beside Burnt at the little wooden kitchen table, where he was sipping coffee spiked from the bottle of Jameson's. I poured myself a mug without the alcohol and leaned back into my chair. Although Burnt remained guarded, the whiskey was opening him up, and eventually he became more willing to talk about himself.

"If it's not prying, do you mind if I ask where you live?" I inquired of my father.

"Here and there."

"Hey," Sharon called over from the toaster, "that's not much of an answer. Can you be a little more specific?"

"I don't like to stay in one place for very long."

"But where have you been staying lately?"

"Airports."

"What?" I shot forward and sprayed the coffee I was sipping into the air.

"Airports," Burnt scowled as he brushed aside the brown droplets that landed on his sleeve. "I said I live in airports. You deaf as well as unmannered?"

I started to apologize, but Sharon wasn't about to be intimidated, even by her cantankerous grandfather. "I'm not deaf either, but you're the only person I know who lives in airports."

"You just don't travel in the right circles."

"I guess not."

"Well, don't blame yourself. You may get there yet."

"Do you mean to tell me that there's a whole underground of people who live in airports?" I interjected.

"Something like that. Most of us don't live there year-round. But from time to time they provide a nice break from the routine."

"Sleeping under fluorescent lights in those uncomfortable plastic chairs is a *nice* alternative?" Sharon arched her eyebrow. "I don't think so."

"Only losers sleep in those cattle pens for coach." The disdain in Burnt's tone was pronounced. "Losers and the mentally ill. I go first class."

"How is that?" I asked while cleaning the table with a napkin.

"I belong to American Airlines's Admirals Club. Any fool with $200 can join. I made that back the first night I stayed over in New York. A hotel with as many frills would have cost me that, easy."

"So let me get this straight," I leaned forward on the table. "When you need a change of pace, you fly into a strange city and take up residence in American's Admirals Club?"

"Depends on the city." Burnt grabbed a muffin from the plate Sharon presented before him. "Sometimes I enjoy the hospitality of other airlines. I don't take up residence. I use their facilities like a hotel. After my flight arrives, I go the Admirals Club, leave my bag in the cloakroom, find transportation into town, look up friends if I have any there, go out to dinner, perhaps check out some art or jazz or take in a show.

"Maybe I'll get lucky and meet some babe who wants me to spend a night or three at her place. If I don't, I splurge for a taxi back to the airport. Then I flash my card at the receptionist and avail myself of the finest service American has to offer. Maybe I'll help myself to a complementary cup of coffee or, if it's very late and I don't want to disturb my sleep, some herbal tea. If I feel like something more fortifying, I'll add a little whiskey from my private stock," he patted the silver flask beside him.

"After I enjoy my nightcap, I usually drop by one of the computer stations and go online for a while. I can check my e-mail, handle my investments, conduct some e-business...do whatever needs to be done. With a Visa platinum card, many things are possible. And I get frequent flier miles when I use it, which means future stays at other Admirals Clubs.

"When I complete my computing, I'll either make my way to the reading area and settle into a cushy chair with a newspaper or magazine, or head for the lounge and ease into one of those fancy leather recliners that mold to my body. I can watch TV or just zone out or meditate. Did I tell you that I meditate? It's so very important every day to experience that calm place within you. Keeps you from going mad, like your mother." Burnt looked at me.

"You think meditation would have helped Grandma?"

Sharon pushed the butter to him.

"Well, I didn't know her very well or for very long," Burnt tore his muffin in half and cut a hefty slice of butter. "And it was a long time ago." He watched the butter melt into the warmth of the muffin. "But she always seemed dissatisfied to me. And bitter. As though life had let her down. She was always angry about this, protesting about that. Always ready to become righteously indignant. Actually, that's what made her such a good painter."

Burnt bit into the muffin and smacked his lips. He chewed while he talked. "To this day, some of her pieces stand out to me. That's how powerful they were." Burnt pushed aside a crumb from his mouth. "She had one that literally exploded off the canvas. Blues and yellows and reds and greens flying every which way in utter chaos and horror. It was her reaction to the Chinese invasion of Tibet, I think. She also executed some amazing responses to civil rights and, of course, nuclear bombs."

Suddenly Burnt's eyes brightened and a smile spread across his face. "I hadn't thought about this in years," he told Sharon, "but your grandmother detested Charles de Gaulle. Hated him with a passion. I always got such a kick out of that. She did a whole series of paintings making fun of him that year. In one she had pasted a magazine cover photo of his face onto a canvas and then splattered it with heavy cream and beaten eggs and mounds of butter, along with thick oil paints and gooey linseed oil. Great muffins by the way," Burnt added before continuing. "And she threw in, literally, other ingredients from those French sauces that everyone used to swoon over before they discovered cholesterol. For the *pièce de résistance* she took a jar of snails she'd collected from somebody's garden and poured them all over the food-splattered photo. Of course, they'd leave their slimy paths across de Gaulle's eyes and mouth and ears. Gertrude displayed that work in a show she and a few other artists had at a beatnik coffee house that summer. I think she called it *Escargot*.

"I believe I knocked her up the night of that opening." Burnt then looked at me. "There was something about de Gaulle's big nose covered in all the goop that made me feel virile. It's hard to explain, but I had this feeling that my boys were going to hit the jackpot that evening. I've got to tell you, it gave me considerable satisfaction to think that my son would be the product of anti-

Gaullist antipathy."

I felt Burnt Umber was putting me on, but it was hard to tell. Certainly my mother was given to fierce hatreds, and many were political. I was unaware of the de Gaulle series, but clearly *Escargot* had not been made to last. Besides, she'd always been careless about documenting her work. So her passionate stand against de Gaulle, if she'd indeed taken one, didn't surprise me.

"But you were saying that Mom should meditate," I reached over for one of the remaining two blueberry muffins, but Burnt slapped my wrist and I pulled back.

"Maybe you'd prefer strawberry instead?" he suggested as he helped himself to the one I'd been about to select. He placed it on his plate beside the muffin he'd already started. I began to object, but he waved aside my complaints. "Quit whining," he commanded. Then he returned to his recollections of my mother, and I contented myself with strawberry.

"Of course meditation would have helped her. She had a tunnel vision that kept her focused on what disturbed her and blocked out the things that might make her happy. That probably energized her and made her a good artist, but it kept her dissatisfied. There's always going to be some social injustice in the world, and if you insist on being perpetually pissed off until it's all cleared up, then you're never going to be happy. It's not a big leap from there to despair, and then to madness. Attitude is everything. She needed to see the bad stuff smaller and the good stuff bigger. It could have kept her sane. Or closer to it anyway."

"Wow," Sharon nodded in agreement. "I never thought about Grandma like that. But I think you're right. She's always seemed so angry. I hadn't connected that with despair."

I was impressed not only at the details Burnt could recall after forty years but by his insights as well. I asked him about it, and he said that daily meditation seemed to help with that too. Somehow, it allowed him to summon forth from his unconscious an entire array of associated images, sensations, and associations.

"It's all very Proustian, very Freudian" he declared nonchalantly as he chewed his food. "Anybody willing to sustain the effort can become proficient in a matter of weeks."

"How can you meditate at the Admirals Club?" Sharon wondered. "There must be so many distractions."

"Not at all. First, you can always find some private cubical and meditate there. But I prefer to wait until the club closes and everyone leaves. I get such a sense of self-indulgence when I lean back into my Sharper Image recliner and realize that I have all to myself the finest hospitality of its kind that corporate America has to offer. Makes me feel peaceful and secure."

"You stay there after closing?" I asked.

"Well, it wouldn't be much of a hotel if I had to leave in the middle of the night now, would it?"

"And how do you manage to remain after hours?"

"You don't have to be a master thief to hide in a hospitality lounge while the help closes up. I mean, it's not like they're searching for stowaways. They usually take a quick look, turn off the lights and lock the door behind them. After all, it's late and they just want to go home. I set the alarm on my watch for ten minutes before closing time, and then I find a place to hide for half an hour or so. The bathrooms are too obvious, but there's always a little cranny somewhere. I've stayed at the Admirals Club at Kennedy for a week at a time on three different occasions."

"You weren't caught?"

"Nope."

"Have you ever been caught?" Sharon wanted to know.

"Just a couple times."

"What happened then?"

"You'd be surprised at how cooperative a janitor can be if you offer him fifty dollars, cash. Twenty-five now and twenty-five in the morning after he opens up. Especially if you give 'em a sob story about how your flight was canceled and you have to be back early in the morning for the next available." Burnt bit into the last of the blueberry muffins and licked his lips.

"That's mighty fine cooking," he told Sharon.

She just shrugged and pointed to me. "Thank Dad. He went out and bought them. I just heated them up."

"You didn't get Sara Lee," Burnt grumbled at me. Then he turned his attention back to Sharon. "No, the clean-up crew wasn't the problem. But one time I ran into another "vacationer" in the middle of the night. We scared the shit out of each other. After we finally calmed down and accepted one another as fellow travelers, he told me about an underground cell of rootless voyagers he belongs to."

"An underground of wayward travelers?" I was incredulous.

"Yes. Right now, there are forty or fifty people who spend their entire lives migrating from hospitality lounge to hospitality lounge throughout the world. They run their businesses from their computers using the Internet hook ups, and from cell phones. They pay their bills with credit cards, get cash from ATM machines in the terminals, keep current with the hit television shows and top sporting events, read newspapers from throughout the world, and dine out every night in food courts. They've chosen to exile themselves from the tyranny of physical space, which they consider a prison for the soul. They refuse to be restricted by the traditional three-dimensions that define physical space. Instead, they embrace the fourth dimension, time."

"How can they do that?" Sharon was excited by the idea. I admit I found it intriguing as well.

"They cross time zones as often as possible, or better still, straddle them; they conduct simultaneous transactions on their electronic gadgets. Most of all, they immerse themselves in the visible, auditory, yet intangible world of the Web. They retrieve data from the past, leave messages to be accessed in the future, all while carrying on a present-tense conversation with someone on the opposite side of the world, where day is night. They live in a time-warped world of airports, e-mail, instant access to worldwide information, and multi-windowed computer displays where real and virtual time continually weave in and out and finally become indistinguishable."

"I've never heard of such people," Sharon exclaimed.

"They sound like they climbed out of one of Tom Pynchon's novels and into the twentieth century," I pitched in.

"They call themselves refugees in cyberspace and gypsies of the global economy. But my friend said they have a secret name too, so they can identify themselves to one another, should the need ever arise."

"Did he tell you what it was?" Sharon was now on the edge of her seat.

"Yes, and because I'm your grandpa and you fed me such a tasty muffin, I'll tell you too...in case it ever comes in handy sometime when you're in some tight spot. The secret name is W.A.S.T.E. It stands for Well Armed Surfers of the Technology Economy. But spell it out as an acronym. If you pronounce it like a word, *waste*, they'll know you for an impostor."

"And these people, these refugees from the postmodern world who have carved their niche from within the W.A.S.T.E. of our high-tech, consumer culture, they wander like you, hopscotching among airport hospitality lounges throughout the globe?" I was doubtful.

"Some of them do. That's right. You don't know everything. There's lots of things in this world a whole lot stranger than that."

I nodded and gave Burnt his due. "You have me there." I took another sip of coffee and pondered the point.

Frequently helping himself to more whiskey, Burnt regaled us with more stories for another hour or so. Then he suddenly declared that he needed a nap and promptly stretched himself out on the couch. Sharon and I went back into our rooms to read and reflect on what he'd said. Burnt's insights into my mother seemed very apt, but I still had trouble accepting that this Victim of Paradox who called himself Lift 'n' Separate was really my dad.

Finally, I too took a nap. By the time I woke up, around 5:30, the sun had already set and it was dark outside. Burnt was still asleep, snoring loudly and sometimes mumbling incoherent words. But Sharon was in the kitchen, checking out the contents of the refrigerator. We finally agreed to order in from a nearby Italian restaurant that was run by a Syrian family. It was the only restaurant open on Christmas. Burnt awoke just before dinner arrived, and we all sat down to a feast of spaghetti and meat balls.

After dinner Sharon took out a DVD of Mel Gibson's *Hamlet*. Glenn Close co-stars as Gertrude, but she'll always be *Fatal Attraction* to me. She's very good at portraying the kind of woman who can really creep me out. Anyway, spicy food mixed with subterfuge, retribution, and redemption seemed an ideal way to conclude our postmodern family Christmas.

"Hold up," Burnt said as Sharon popped in the disk. "I've got dessert." He removed from his shirt pocket a small plastic bag containing four joints of marijuana and lit one up. He took a hit and offered it to me. I declined.

"Oh, go on, you sissy Puritan," he insisted. "It's not even such good stuff."

"Go on, Daddy. I'll have some too. We can all get high and goof on the movie. God, I haven't done that in ages."

"The last time I smoked, I became the Pie-thrower, and look where that led." I thought again of Marion Hines and a wave of regret passed through me.

"You did that for me, and I'll always appreciate it," Sharon came over and hugged me. Then she took the joint from Burnt Umber, inhaled on it deeply and passed it over to me. "Go on," she held it before me like Eve tempting Adam with the apple. I could see her mother's eyes looking into my own, and suddenly I was back twenty-one years earlier, in Berkeley. "You'll feel better. That's all that really counts in the long run, isn't it?"

I shrugged my shoulders. "What the hell. It's Christmas."

The stuff kicked in subtly, so I was never really aware of becoming stoned. But soon I was high. I became caught up in the film's opening sequence, which, unlike Shakespeare's original play, begins with the burial of Old Hamlet, Mel Gibson's father. No new dialogue is added, but the scene does a lot to establish the context of the action, and I thought it worked. I found myself becoming deeply attuned to the action on screen, imagining what it would feel like to be a sensitive, young, bipolar prince whose father, a warrior king, had been murdered by his mother's lover, who was also his uncle and the new king.

"Try some of these." A plate cannolis suddenly appeared before me, and my thoughts about incest were gone, replaced by the smell of cinnamon and the slippery sensation of thick, whipped cream on my figures and then on my lips. I popped one into my mouth, and as I savored the flavor, Hamlet's suicidal desires fell back deep into the recesses of my mind.

Then Sharon's face was once again in front of mine. She was asking what similarities I perceived between Hamlet and Old Hamlet and the first George Bush, whom she called Old Bush, and the current one. Surprised to discover that I had any thoughts upon the subject at all, I found myself answering that the similarities to *Henry V* seemed far greater. "'W' is less like Hamlet than Prince Hal, the uncouth profligate who, upon assuming power, vows to 'keep the promise never made.' I only hope that 'W' will likewise astound us all and rise to the occasion."

"Forget that nonsense," Burnt's voice boomed from the

easy chair beside me. "What would you do if you learned I'd been murdered by higher ups in the government?"

"What?" Burnt's pointed question threw me off balance. "What the hell are you talking about?"

"Like Hamlet. That's what we're watching, isn't it? Would you risk your very soul to avenge me?"

"And save the country at the same time, maybe," Sharon piped in. "I mean if Burnt's secrets are really that important...."

"Forget the country," Burnt insisted. "Would you do it for me?" He looked hard into my eyes.

"What have you done to deserve it?" It was my turn to try to spread a little guilt.

"I brought you into being. What greater thing can a person do for another? You owe me your life, you little ingrate."

"Why am I an ingrate? Why are you always attacking me? What have I ever done to you?" Part of me watched in awe as this other, very articulate part of me thrust and parried with my dad—a ritual played out between fathers and sons since men first learned to speak, but one in which, until now, I'd never been able to partake.

"You made me aware of your existence. Isn't that enough?" Burnt snarled.

"How does my existence threaten you? Why should it upset you? You once called yourself a regular Johnny Appleseed. I would think you'd be happy to see the fruit of your labor. Maybe even be proud of what you produced."

"You think that, do you? Well you'd be wrong." The ringing of the telephone punctuated Burnt's emphatic assertion, and Sharon ran to answer it.

Burnt and I called a truce as she picked up the receiver, listened a moment, and then said cautiously, "Merry Christmas to you too, Helena." Sharon paused a moment and then added, "I'm sorry we missed the first night of Chanukah....Me too." Then she took the phone with her into her bedroom and continued her conversation with her former lover behind the closed door.

Burnt and I retained our silence and returned our attention to the movie. Hamlet was watching Claudius, now exposed as the old king's murderer, praying for forgiveness for his deadly sins. As Claudius prayed, Hamlet realized that this was his chance to avenge his father's death and purge his country of the canker that was poisoning it.

"What if you are absolutely convinced that Bush stole the election and that Al Gore should be the president?" Burnt demanded as Hamlet considered whether he should kill his uncle as he prayed. Killing Claudius would rid Denmark of the usurper of the crown and of Old Hamlet's bed; but it would also allow Claudius, now newly purged of his sins, to enter Heaven. Would it be better to defer the revenge and wait instead until Claudius has sinned again, so Hamlet can send him straight to Hell? We watched silently while Hamlet chose that second course and thereby triggered his doom. Suddenly, I wondered if his newly discovered obsession with damning Claudius to Hell was really Hamlet's reason for sparing the king's life. Or was it actually a convenient way to rationalize his fear of doing something momentous? Was Hamlet just afraid to act?

"So," Burnt persisted as Hamlet left Claudius and proceeded to his mother's bedroom, "in your oh-so lofty eyes, Mr. Professor, what should a good citizen who is convinced the election was a fraud do? Just sit there and suck it up for the good of the nation, like Nixon did in '60, when John Kennedy and Richard Daley stole it from him? Tell the Republicans, 'O.K. Now you're even'?"

"Martina says the same thing," I answered. "But what alternative is there? Should we manufacture some connection to the military and foment a coup? Should we try to organize a general strike across the country and bring the economy to its knees until they give us a fair count? Surely you don't think we should assassinate him and make a martyr of the man, while trampling over the Constitution at the same time?"

I truly believed the answers I gave Burnt. But at the same time, in my reefer-induced haze, a different part of me followed another line of thought. "What if they really had stolen the election right from under our noses? What *is* the truly patriotic thing to do? Would the most patriotic action also be the most truly principled course of action? And if not, which should take precedence: principles or patriotism? What if neither principle nor patriotism is the best course of action? And what constitutes the best course of action, anyway? Is it the path that creates the greatest well being for the country? Or for the world? Maybe we should just put all our faith in the Constitution, and follow wherever it takes us. Or not."

Sharon suddenly reentered the living room. She looked happy.

"As I'm sure you have figured out, that was Helena. Things aren't going so well with Martina, and I guess she was getting a little nostalgic on Christmas Day. Even if she's Jewish, she's an American, and let's face it, Christmas is such an American holiday. Anyway, Helena was lonely."

"And?" I ventured.

"She says she misses me and wants to come up for New Year's Eve?"

"And?" I repeated.

"And I said, 'OK'." Then she added, "Look, I really don't want to talk about it. Let's go back to the movie."

Burnt and I renewed our truce, and we all returned our attention to Prince Hamlet's quest for revenge. We agonized over his death, when it came, and then watched as Fortinbras commanded his soldiers to treat Hamlet's body in a manner befitting a soldier and then to clean up the other corpses strewn about the stage. Soon after, Burnt Umber rose from his chair and gathered his things. He had a late-evening flight and wanted to partake in the Admirals Club's hospitality one more time before he parted.

But on his way out he addressed me again. "Well, Sonny," he said. "Stop asking yourself what Jesus would do if Caesar stole the election. We know the answer to that one; he'd turn the other cheek and be crucified. But what should a man of action do, Othello or Edmund or Iago? Brutus was a real liberal. Maybe the first one in history. He tried to do the principled thing and fucked everything up royally. He destroyed the republic he was trying to save because he wanted to be fair to Marc Antony and let him speak at Caesar's funeral. And he didn't want to kill any innocent men. Think about it, Sonny." He pointed his finger at me. Finally, he walked over to Sharon and gave her a long hug. "You too!" he admonished. Then he turned his back on his, proceeded down the hallway to the stairs, and descended back into his murky Burnt Umber world.

"I will, *Grond*father," Sharon called after him as he disappeared from our sight.

Chapter 13

Helena arrived the next day, and, not wanting to be in the way, I booked a flight back to Miami for the day after that. When Sharon went to meet her at the airport, I headed off to the Regenstein Library and spent a pleasant afternoon exploring the University of Chicago's various holdings, exhibits, and special collections, which were far more extensive than what I'd become accustomed to. I didn't leave until 5:00, when the library closed. The sun had already set, and even though Sharon lived only five or six blocks away, making my way to her apartment in the cold and dark became a true test of will. The temperature was in the low twenties and I was walking straight into a stiff wind blowing off frigid Lake Michigan, less than a mile away. I pulled my jacket close, hunkered over, and for the first couple blocks muttered through chattering teeth, "Goddamn cold! Goddamn cold!" Finally, recalling Edmund's words to his suffering father in *King Lear*, I told myself, "Men must endure." As I struggled onward, a sudden flurry of snowflakes assaulted me and covered my eyelashes, rendering me able to see only blurry batches of dark and light. "Men must endure."

"Jesus, it's cold!" I hollered as I unlocked the door to Sharon's apartment and let myself in. My cheeks were red and numb, my ears ached, and I was chilled to the bone.

"It's only 23 degrees outside," Sharon walked in from the kitchen to greet me. They just said it on the radio. Light to moderate snow. It's not bad. Anyway, come say hi to Helena. She's in her room resting."

Sharon knocked on the door and after gaining permission, she led me to the doorway.

"Welcome back," I said to Helena, who was reclining on

the bed. I didn't know what to say, or even how I felt about Helena's return. My view of her had certainly waffled over the past few months. I was bitterly disappointed that she had gone along with Martina's militarism and had been part of the unified female front that compelled me to attack Marion Hines with that putrid pie. Helena seemed weak to me, too weak to stand up against Martina's powerful will and her absolute belief in the virtue and value of her causes. Moreover, I retained a father's outrage against anyone who would hurt my little girl. On the other hand, Helena had tried to befriend me before I moved out, and she had exerted the strength and good sense to leave Martina and appreciate what she'd lost in Sharon.

"Thanks," Helena looked up from her pillow. "I was just resting. I've been tense lately. It's good to be back home where I can relax." Sharon went over to the bed, sat beside her, and held her hand. They looked at each other and smiled. Both seemed genuinely happy. I supposed that was a good thing. I just hoped it would last.

After I washed up we ordered a mushroom-black olive pizza and Italian salads; Sharon opened a bottle of red wine, and eventually the bone-chilling cold that had penetrated my body began to dissipate. Helena put on some soft jazz, and the three of us found ourselves talking about the election. Naturally Martina also became a topic of our conversation. Helena told Sharon about Martina's plan to organize a Shit-In at the inauguration.

"Sounds like Martina." Sharon said blandly. "But it's not going to change anything. She'll just make the rest of us seem crude and uncivilized. How much credibility will Gore's supporters have after that?" Sharon's feelings toward her rival remained understandably cold, but she made a good point.

"Yeah, well," Helena sighed. "If that were all, maybe it wouldn't be so bad. But apparently Martina agrees with you. The Shit-In won't make any lasting difference. So she and the HLF are planning to use it as a diversion for something with greater impact."

I sat forward in the easy chair where I was sipping my Chianti. "What do you mean, *greater impact*?"

"It's all very sketchy do me. But I think they want to do something drastic."

"What, exactly, do you think she's planning?"

"I don't know. I only kind of overheard things and picked up scraps from this and that and pieced some stuff together. Maybe I'm wrong. But I'm pretty sure she's up to something big, and it's tied to the inauguration."

We went to bed not long after that, and the next morning I left for Miami. After liftoff I pushed the seat back, plugged into the classical station, and tried to relax, absorb, and decide. Decide if I truly had the courage of my convictions and was willing to act on them. The election had been stolen, and a new, possibly even more catastrophic assault on the Constitution was fomenting, even as I cruised comfortably from the frigid north to the balmy subtropics, thousands of feet in the air. "These are the times that try men's souls," Thomas Payne wrote in support of the American Revolution. Mine had been tried more in the last year than in my whole lifetime.

And now it was about to be tried again, as I prepared to grapple with Burnt Umber's parting words that still rattled through my mind. In pivotal, but dangerous and uncertain times, what must a man of action do? I recognized that I had already subconsciously embraced his basic point: at such times in history the only authentic response *is* to become a man of action. Hamlet must kill Claudius at prayer. Spin it any way you want, remaining passive while your democracy is scuttled before your eyes is not moderation. It is not respect for law. It's not even the impotence of feeling everything is utterly beyond your control. Deep down, my liberal's passivity was rooted in none of those things. I finally admitted to myself that those excuses were rationalizations, like Hamlet's pretense to himself that he must send Claudius to Hell in addition to taking his life. These are masks our psyches erect so we don't have to admit to ourselves we are afraid. Once I saw through the masks and recognized the presence of my fear, I knew that I could not remain passive and still retain self respect.

By the time I arrived in Miami, I resolved to go crawling back to Martina.

I spent the first part of New Year's Eve alone in my new apartment. Except for Brian Mulligan, who had been caring for Pandora in my absence, I had not mentioned my return to anyone, and Brian had already made plans for the evening. I hadn't finished unpacking before I went to Chicago, so I picked up a Value Meal of chicken, white rice, and black beans at Pollo Tropical and brought it back home to share with Pandora, who especially likes the white meat chicken, while watching the local news. After dinner I switched off the television, and put on a CD I'd burned from Martina's copy of *The Cunning Little Vixon*. I then went about the business of putting things away. But first, I called Martina to wish her a happy new year.

"What do you want?" she demanded.

"Nothing. I'd just like to try to keep things civil between us."

"You would."

What are you up too?" I asked.

"Not much." Her voice showed that she remained suspicious. "Watching campy horror movies on the cable. Maybe I'll get together later with some of my girlfriends. I don't know."

"I'm still puttin' stuff away," I offered, even though she hadn't asked. "Pandora is jumping in and out of the boxes. That's entertaining."

"I know you really mean that." Martina made this sound like an accusation.

"I did."

"Yeah, well, I need to get going now."

"Sure thing. Just wanted to wish you happy New Year."

"OK," and the phone went dead.

Actually, that went better than I had expected. We'd even talked for a moment. I figured that I'd call back about five minutes before midnight and work things from there. But Martina surprised me when she showed up at my door around 10:30. She was wearing old jeans and a work shirt, and her long blond hair fluttered against her shoulder. I let her in and cleared a couple settings on the kitchen table. As I dug out some wine glasses, Martina uncorked the bottle of champagne I'd picked up for the holiday. It exploded open with a loud bang just as I sat down. Froth overflowed from the spout.

"Cheers," Martina offered blandly as she raised her glass.

"Cheers," I replied with somewhat more enthusiasm.

We sipped our drinks, and then she asked, "OK, Ben, what's going on? Why did you call me?"

"I called you because I've been doing a lot of thinking."

"About?"

"Things."

"Such as?"

"Such as a stolen election and what to do about it."

"And what did you conclude?"

"That passivity is no answer; it's only cowardice. I need to act."

"That's quite a revelation. Where'd it come from?" She drank her champagne but kept her eyes on me.

"My father. I met my real father. Burnt Umber. I met him before, on Halloween. But in Chicago I met him again. I don't know quite what to make of him. He doesn't seem to like me much, but he likes Sharon."

Martina looked up questioningly at that last statement, and I continued, "To be honest, I'm not altogether comfortable about that either. But Sharon enjoys having a grandfather, and so far he just seems gruff but harmless."

"So what did this gruff father figure of yours do to whip you into line and make you so ashamed of yourself?"

Was that what Burnt Umber had done? Made me ashamed of myself? Was that really why I back talking to Martina?

"He said that in the face of a threat to the very existence of our democracy, a true man, a real patriot, cannot remain passive. He must become the man of action."

"And you believed him because he's your father?" Martina was suddenly accusing me again. "When I told you the same thing months ago, all you ever did was call me Lady Macbeth."

"Maybe I was still in a state of denial back then. Plus, the election hadn't even taken place yet, much less been stolen. That changed things. A lot. I mean that takes everything to an entirely different level. I didn't want to admit that, but Burnt Umber kept throwing it back in my face. You and I weren't even talking then. But after my weekend with Burnt, I found I didn't have any alternative but to face the stark and unsavory facts."

"That's some father you have." Martina's voice softened some.

"You'd like him. He's Pynchonesque."

Martina raised her eyebrow at my allusion to the man she'd left me for. "So, you want us to get back together? I don't think so."

"No. I don't either."

"So, then, we're back at the beginning. Why did you phone me? Not just to wish me happy New Year."

"O.K. I'll tell you. I was going to work my way to it eventually. I don't know if she was supposed to mention it, but Helena told me you were organizing an absurdist protest at the inauguration, a Shit-In. It sounds clever. I'd prefer something with more long term impact, but it's a start. At least it will make a strong statement and give us something to build on. Can I play a role? I still have my Pie-thrower outfit, if that would help. Remember, he's a wanted man; he could get you some TV time, at the very least."

"*The bitch!* No, Helena *wasn't* supposed to mention it. What else did she mention?"

"That was it. You weren't exactly a popular topic of conversation up there."

Martina calmed down and sipped her champagne again. "Maybe not." Then she put aside her glass, leaned over, and looked me in the eyes. "So, you want to be part of the Shit-In?"

I look directly back into her eyes and said in a strong, clear voice, "Yes, I do."

Martina hesitated for a moment as she contemplated her response. Finally she held up her glass in the gesture of a toast. "Well, Ben, welcome back to the fight."

Only three weeks remained between New Year's Day and the presidential inauguration. That involved a lot of planning and coordinating for Martina, as well as running an email campaign, which was essentially a series of chain letters inviting recipients to come to Washington to participate in the inaugural Shit-In and to forward the email to at least five other potential shitters. "Don't dump on me!" was one subject line I recall. "Dumping for democracy" was another. An angrier one read, "If you didn't move your ass to vote, at least move your bowels to protest!"

"I think we're going to have a big turn-out," Martina announced about a week before the inauguration. I was over in her apartment, helping out with odds and ends in my capacity as the man of action, and we were in the kitchen taking a coffee break. "We're getting a lot of responses," she went on, looking exquisitely self satisfied.

It was bizarre to see her so pleased with herself again, and with me, but Martina had always been mercurial. I felt myself responding to what I'd always found attractive about her, when she wasn't overtaken by some demonic obsession. When she was active and engaged--and sane--Martina could be electrifying. Unfortunately for someone like me, she could be electrifying even when she wasn't altogether sane.

"So what's your role in this for me?" I asked. "You still haven't told me yet."

"You're going to strike the first blow for freedom. You're going to give the "Go" signal to all the shitters along Pennsylvania Avenue."

"Wow, I'm going to start it all off?"

"Yes. In your incarnation as Pie-thrower, since you offered. We're still working out the details, but at the right instant, you're going to hit someone with a pie, and that will be the cue for everyone to pull down their pants and let loose."

"The Bolsheviks fired shots from the battleship *Aurora* to commence the storming of the Winter Palace," I recalled. "You're starting your absurdist revolution with a pie-throwing. That's inspiring."

Suddenly serious, Martina dismissed the compliment I'd intended. "How can you compare a pre-industrial peasant uprising to an electronically engineered populist campaign in the era of consumer capitalism?"

"I wasn't really trying to make a serious point. Just trying to make you feel good. In any case, I'm honored that you've given me such a distinguished role.

"There is a lot of danger for you," she answered. "We'll try to come up with some sort of escape path, and we'll work out a routine so you can get rid of your costume and maybe change two or three more times; but there's going to be a lot of security and you could get caught."

We were silent for a moment. We both realized that if I was caught, I would certainly be identified as the man who threw the pie at Marion Hines, and that meant facing trial for murder.

"The man of action must take risks." I stood to leave. "I'll go rescue my outfit from the moth balls."

"Thanks, Ben. I wasn't sure you were ready for this.

Truly, welcome to the fight." She kissed me briefly on the lips for the first time since we'd fought over Marion Hines, and once again I was taken in by the fragrance of her *Obsession*."

"I'll catch you later," I smiled and moved toward the door. "I have to go home and work on my technique."

"You do that," Martina walked me to the door. "Work on your technique."

Actually, what I had been working on for the past two weeks was a way to figure out what Martina and the HLF were really up to. Helena had spoken of something cataclysmist, and I wanted to know what it was. But it wasn't easy to collect information. Martina never talked about it, and she was very careful not to give out her computer passwords. However, a couple days after she informed me of my mission, while she was in the study reading her email, someone named Jane called. I knew Jane was in the HLF.

I answered the phone and brought it to Martina. As she listened her face tensed and then filled with anger. "Shit!" she exclaimed. "Shit!"

She hung up and then handed me back the phone. "Emergency meeting. I've gotta go," was all she said. Then she jumped from her chair, grabbed her purse and keys and was out the door. "Lock up before you leave," were her parting words.

I had been helping out by writing out plans for inauguration day and working out the exact protocols. Martina intended to scatter her agents throughout the crowd. They'd be passing out X-Lax to protestors who arrived without their own, and they were to be the first to start defecating and would thereby instruct the other shitters in the crowd when they too should begin. These agents, in turn, were to wait for a secret signal, which they wouldn't learn until about half an hour ahead of time, when they would receive text messages emailed from a remote location to their cell phones. Then I was to don my mask and cape and set to work.

As soon as Martina left, I went into the home office that Martina used as her command center. She maintained several email accounts, but when she was called away, she was logged-in to the one she used to communicate with the HLF. It took me a while figure out which of Martina's email correspondents were major players and then to piece together what the radical lesbians were really up to, but by the time I did, I knew that Martina's real strategy would, if successful, have a lot more impact than any absurdist demonstration.

I carefully got up, left the room just as I found it, locked up the apartment and went home. I don't know what time Martina returned home, or what the nature and resolution of the emergency was, but when I spoke with her later that evening, she assured me that "one the more hysterical of the lesbians for freedom" had simply overreacted to something someone had said. It was all a big confusion, and everything was still on.

Chapter 14

I had Pandora purring on my chest that night as I lay down to sleep, and a lot on my mind. Pandora extended her legs along my torso and massaged me with her claws, gently, but hard enough to prick my skin. The moral dilemmas from Martina's HLF plot dug into me much more deeply. It would be one thing to create so much civil unrest that the authorities would have to void Bush's victory and call for a new, clean election. That was an extreme, radical position that I could almost accept—although it would run a number of very serious risks. But to these women, that would just be child's play. They were truly out for blood. No quarter given, no quarter asked.

Unable to sleep, I got out of bed and went to my computer. Although I didn't know him well, or even trust him completely, I felt the only person I could turn to was my father. I didn't want to further involve Sharon. So I emailed Burnt Umber and asked him to phone me the next morning from a pay phone.

"Burnt....Dad," I stammered. "It may not have seemed like it at the time, but I took to heart what you were saying about not allowing those fascists to steal the election from us."

"And?" Burnt's voice was non-committal.

"I came back to work with Martina on some kind of meaningful protest--and also, I confess, to keep an eye on her. She's dangerous."

"So is a stolen election," the voice at the other end insisted.

"So is an assassination." There was quiet on the other end as my words sank in. "Have you seen those emails that have been circulating, telling people to come to D.C. for a Shit-In?"

"Yes, I have. I was planning to go and lend my voice to

the cause, so to speak."

"Well, Martina's been organizing that. I'm supposed to start it off with a pie-throwing. Target to be announced. That's all anybody thinks this is going to be, a disgusting protest of a disgusting political theft. And maybe the start of some grassroots movement to keep Bush and Cheney in check. But that's all just a cover. While the security force tries to deal with a superhero pummeling people with pies and hundreds of people crapping on the president, Martina's going to send a suicide bomber to blow up the limo. I'm supposed to be the front man for all this. Talk about your dupes. I need your help. Are you in?"

"Assassinate the president!" Burnt's voice had a certain dreaminess about it as he voiced the words. But then his tone turned serious. "Of course, I'm in."

On Saturday, January 20, 2001, Martina and I stood among the throngs of people packing the Mall in Washington D.C., hoping to get a glimpse of the inauguration. Despite the mid-winter cold, we had dressed warmly and showed up before daylight to claim a spot on the route where George W. Bush's long, shiny, black limousine would pass by on the way to his swearing in. Naturally, we weren't able to get close to the street, but we were near the front row and would have a good view of the presidential motorcade when it passed. As the morning progressed, the Mall filled with more and more citizens anxious to applaud and protest their new president. It was gratifying to see how many protestors, of all ages and races and ethnicities, had also traveled to Washington and endured the cold and dark to express their outrage over the mockery of democracy that was about to receive official sanction. But an equally large number of Americans had similarly sacrificed to show their approval.

I had layered for the occasion: long underwear, tights, pants, shirt, Pie-thrower cape, sweater, and jacket. When the time came, Martina would help me remove the coat, pants, and sweater, and after I donned my superhero mask, Martina would hand me a gooey custard pie. We'd be surrounded by a knot of HLF supporters whose job was to hide my wardrobe change. Then I was to smite the target with my pie--she'd point out the target at the last second--and run back into the crowd, where another group of HLF members would quickly surround me, remove my cape and mask, provide me with pants, a coat, and hat, and then allow me to pass back into the crowd before I was caught. Meanwhile, as I changed back into my identify as Benjamin Branch, hundreds, perhaps thousands, of Americans would be turning their backs to the president-elect, pulling down their pants, and expressing their most deeply felt convictions about the election.

That was the plan as Martina had explained it to me. At about 11 A.M., Martina called someone on her cell phone, who then sent out an email instructing her agents, pre-planted throughout the crowd, to watch for a pie-throwing close to where she and I were standing. Presumably, the rank-and-file participants would know from Martina's extensive email campaign to follow the lead of her agents.

But Martina didn't know that I knew the Shit-In, itself, was just a huge sleight of hand. In addition to my costume and pie, Martina also carried the remote control to trigger an explosive device. She had sewn it into the lining of her overcoat and sneaked it in past security. According to the plan, while the police preoccupied themselves with defecating protestors, one of the radical lesbians was going to run up to the limo. When she got as close as Martina judged she could, Martina would detonate the napalm, creating a fireball that would certainly kill the woman, and maybe the president-elect along with her.

"That's crazy!" Burnt Umber said when I told him. It'll never work. The place is going to be crawling with police. Maybe Martina can slip by with her remote control, but how is the bomber supposed to get her explosives anywhere close to the street?"

"One of the Hysterical Lesbians is a doctor who specializes in breast work. She treats breast cancer, but she also does enlargements, reductions, and reconstructions. One of her clients is terminal. She's lost both of her breasts, and her cancer is inoperable. She has only has a few months to live anyway. So she's the delivery system. They're going to reconstruct her breasts, but instead of using silicon implants, they're going to fill them with jellied gasoline."

"Napalm!" Burnt interjected. "Where'd they get their hands on napalm?"

"It seems that it's not that hard to make, if you have the right kind of lab. Apparently some of those radical lesbians took some of those 'manly' science and technology courses in college and have access to the right kind of lab. They're going slip electrodes into the reconstructed nipples, and when Martina presses the switch, there'll be a huge fireball. Big enough to swallow Bush's limousine. At least, that's the plan."

"Holy shit!" Burnt Umber exploded when he concluded that the plot actually had a chance to work. I couldn't quite make out whether he was expressing fear, awe, or admiration. Maybe it was all three.

At first, everything went pretty much according to plan. Martina and I camped out in a prime spot close to Pennsylvania Avenue. Bush's motorcade would pass right in front of us, although we were barricaded back several yards from the street. Burnt, I noticed, showed up around 4 A.M. He kept his distance, but I could tell he'd seen us. Martina, of course, had never seen him before. He'd engaged a couple of twenty-something women in lively conversation and was offering swigs from his hip flask, which he'd somehow smuggled in past the security. From time to time women from the HLP would pass by and bring Martina and me a cup of hot coffee, and once a couple held our place while we used the portable toilets that had been set up on the Mall.

The sun rose onto a blustery winter landscape, but the shafts of predawn light colored the sky in rich reds and comforting pinks. Martina held my hand and we watched the sun rise together. "This is going to be our finest day," she announced. Then she kissed me quickly on the mouth. Her lips were cold, and I felt a shiver go down my spine.

The wait seemed like an eternity, but late in the morning Martina finally received a call on her cell phone telling her that the motorcade was on its way. She signaled to a group of women close by who worked their way through the crowd and then circled us. As they pulled close, I noticed Burnt Umber pushing and shoving in my direction. Once Martina and I stood inside our human screen, she pulled off my jacket and helped me remove my sweater. I took off my pants myself. The leotards I wore over my long underwear had helped me endure the frigid night. Now, I let my tattered cape cascade down my shoulder; I donned my mask, and once again I was Pie-thrower, bane of the radical right and defender of the downtrodden everywhere.

When my transformation was complete, Martina handed me a yellow, custard pie she'd been given by one of the women. After she passed it to me, I noticed that she had removed the remote control from inside her coat and held in her left hand. At last, she instructed the women in front of us to move to the side and pointed to one of the security agents on the sidewalk. He was speaking into a walkie talkie. "Him!" she said. "Get him." Then she squeezed my hand and kissed me for good luck just as Bush's motorcade came into view down the street.

I squeezed back, but did not let go. Before Martina knew what was happening, I dragged her up to the barricade. The crowd was chanting, "Bush, Bush, Bush;" people were pushing at one another to get a view, and the plain clothes security agent Martina had targeted was running up to us with a look of alarm as Martina struggled to get free.

In front of everyone, I turned toward the agent, and then spun around and hammered Martina with the pie. Thrusting it into her face with my right hand, I slapped the remote control from her hand and down onto the ground with my left. For an instant, I lingered there victorious, a photo op--my outlandish Pie-thrower cape fluttering self-righteously in the breeze and Martina standing motionless and dumbfounded, custard oozing from her eyes and whipped cream dripping down her cheeks.

Then I pushed her away and slipped back into the crowd as she had instructed me. But as I did, I saw Burnt Umber retrieve the remote, as he and I had prearranged.

A heavy set man standing by the barricades suddenly removed his pants and mooned the passing presidential limousine. Then two or three more people did the same thing, farther up the street. And then a few more. Soon the sounds of defecation could be heard throughout the crowd, punctuating the partisan cheers, jeers, and chants. It wasn't the thunderous outcry Martina had envisioned, and the shitters could be counted in tens, not thousands. But although the press largely failed to cover this most visceral of protests--much as it failed to cover the other protests from that day--Martina's Shit-In did occur. And I set it off. We were part of history.

Once the shitting started, the police became less preoccupied with catching me and more with containing the defecation, or simply avoiding it. People were shoving and pushing to see the president-elect, whose car had just made its way to our position, and everyone was shouting and crapping and jumping up and down and farting. Pandemonium reigned, and the security police were running every which way. Suddenly, a woman, probably in her forties and nearly bald, perhaps from chemotherapy, leapt over the barricade and ran toward Bush's car. The security detail, preoccupied by the shitters, responded slowly to her intrusion, and she came within perhaps 20 feet of the limo before she was intercepted and tackled to the ground. I looked over to where Burnt Umber now stood with the remote, not far from where Martina, her face still covered with pie, was on her hands and knees searching frantically for it. Burnt seemed transfixed by the woman struggling on the street with Secret Service agents. As Bush's limo came to an abrupt halt, Burnt slowly and deliberately lifted Martina's remote and pointed it at the woman, now pinned to the ground. I could see him mouth the word, "Bang!" and I stood motionless, impotent, in horror. The temptation to be one of those history-altering *little people*, the wild card that could change the course of human events, had finally been too great for Burnt Umber to resist. I had gambled by taking my father into my confidence, and I had lost. Once again, my best plans to thwart Martina and save innocent lives had horribly backfired.

But then everything went back again to normal. Normal? Laughing to himself, Burnt pulled back his arm, opened the back of the device, removed and pocketed the batteries, and then smashed the remote control with his boot. Martina, still on her hands and knees about ten feet away, looked up at him. He grinned back at her before disappearing back into the raucous throng. Martina stood, furious, and started to go after him, but the crowd was too dense and agitated. All she could do was retrieve the broken fragments of her gadget.

The Secret Service quickly subdued the would-be suicide bomber and cleared the street, so Bush's entourage could continue. The woman would probably be charged with a misdemeanor and set free. Presumably no one would think to check whether her breast implants were filled with jellied gasoline, and she would be released. Martina, it now seemed, would appear to anyone interested simply as the victim of a random pie-throwing at the politically charged event, and even the

Pie-thrower would now be able slip back into retirement. The crisis had passed.

I soon found the group of lesbians and lesbian sympathizers who had been assigned to wait for me. Grabbing the clothes a young woman handed me, I kicked off my sneakers and then quickly pulled a pair of trousers over my leotard, while the women closed ranks around me. Then I put on a pair of hiking boots, a flannel shirt, a ski cap, and an overcoat. I rolled my cape and mask into a ball and then made my way back into the crowd, shoving my Pie-thrower costume deep into the first trash barrel I came upon and then making my way toward the Lincoln Memorial. While George W. Bush safely took his oath of office, Burnt Umber and I rendezvoused among the bronze statues of Korean War infantrymen on patrol. Then we got the hell out of town.

Chapter 15

Burnt had rented a car, which he'd parked in College Park and then taken the Metro to the Mall. So we reversed the course, caught a train to College Park, and retrieved the rental. We drove west around the beltway and then headed south on Interstate 81. We hadn't decided where we were going, just that we needed to leave the scene of what was almost the crime of the 21st century. Finally, we stopped for lunch at a roadside restaurant outside of Roanoke, Virginia. We sat in a little booth in the back, and I ordered a soup and sandwich, along with a hot cup of coffee. Burnt had eggs, bacon, Virginia ham, and grits.

  For the first time since we'd met, he finally seemed to show some warmth for me. "Well, my boy, we did it, didn't we?" he grinned as he settled back into his seat. He removed his flask from his coat beside him and poured some into his coffee. "Maybe just a handful of folks will know," he continued, "and no one's going to be anxious to tell. But we were players. We made history! Maybe we played defense to Martina's offense, but that's still history and we created it!"

  "Created?" I found the word choice provocative.

  "God created humans," he said. "And humans create history."

  "God also made with weather, natural disasters, and vicious animals," I answered. "Look, pneumonia did to 'Old Tippecanoe,' William Henry Harrison, what Martina tried to do to 'W.' It nailed him on inauguration day. Just took another month to finish the job."

  "More wildcards," Burnt answered. "And thank the Lord for them. They're our greatest long-term protection against an evil empire."

Just then I noticed a news story on the television set over the lunch counter. I couldn't hear what was being said, but there was closed captioning at the bottom of the screen, so I could read the words. The story was rehashing the inauguration news, when suddenly I saw myself smashing Martina with the pie. They showed a close up of me and then one of Martina, covered with custard. Then the picture switched to the woman who had tried to blow up Bush's car. Someone with a video camera had caught her climbing the barricade and running towards the limo. She was shouting something, but there was no captioning for that. Then the Secret Service agents pounced on her and wrestled her to the ground. Interviewed after her arrest, the woman maintained she was just a Bush supporter caught up in the excitement. The reporter asked if there was any connection between her and the pie-throwing that occurred just before she breached security, and she answered that she hadn't been aware of any pie-throwing. But the reporter concluded her coverage by pointing out that "A man in a similar, makeshift, superhero outfit was responsible for the death of religious activist Marion Hines, and he is still at large. Police are pursuing the lead."

"You're back in the limelight, my boy!" Burnt was ecstatic. "You're becoming a real player."

My own response was less enthusiastic. I knew there would now be an even more determined manhunt to establish my identity and track me down. But I had accepted that risk when I offered to appear in my Pie-thrower costume and became the man of action.

We decided to stop for the day in Roanoke, so we rented a room at a Super 8 close to the highway. Burnt wanted a nap, but I decided I needed to check my email; so I borrowed the rental car, found my way to the Roanoke public library, and went online. I had two emails in my Inbox. The message from Martina was short but to the point: "We know where you live." The other was from Thomas Pynchon: "Great work!"

I sat back in my chair, surveyed the volumes of books that filled the shelves around me, and pondered my next move. How safe would it be now to return to Miami and resume my teaching? Martina had already demonstrated her capacity for ruthlessness and revenge--I recalled her story about the young woman who had betrayed her underground movement in the Czech Republic. Surely her reaction to me would be more severe. Nor would the Hysterical Lesbians for Freedom, a group that had already shown its bloodlust and a taste for murder, easily forgive the fact that I'd thwarted the assassination. In their minds, no doubt, they were patriots and I was a Benedict Arnold, worthy of execution.

I flipped through some news stories on the Internet and spotted photos of Martina and myself on several. Our identities were still listed as unknown. My face was fully masked and Martina's was smeared beyond recognition with custard. Still, with all of the sophisticated technology, I wondered if the FBI might be able to reconstruct what Martina looked like, and, if so, would they match that against her passport photo or some other data base. My prospects didn't look good. Finally, I reopened Tom Pynchon's email and hit Reply.

"Would I be able to stay with you until things settle down?" I queried. Then I emailed Sharon and told her about how I'd thwarted Martina's plan which, if successful, could have set off a backlash of bloody retribution unlike anything this country has ever seen before. It might have destroyed the republic and set off a civil war. I added that I was with my accomplice, her grandfather, and that I'd try to stay in touch by email, but I was going to have to go underground for a while for my own safety. "At this point," I told her, "I'm more afraid of Martina and her cohorts than I am of the feds."

I busied myself for another couple hours checking out the holdings of the Roanoke library. Finally, when I checked my email around 4:00, I'd received a response from Tom. He said I could hide out with him.

Chapter 16

I didn't think Tom would want for Burnt Umber to know the whereabouts of his hideaway, and I didn't think Burnt was anxious to meet up again with the man whose identity he had stolen long ago. So the next morning, I had Burnt drive me to Asheville. He dropped me off near the city center, and I made my way on my own to the Greyhound station. A couple hours later, I was on a bus to Blowing Rock. I didn't know Tom's phone number, just his email address. So I had no way to let him know when I arrived. I hiked the last three miles over the packed, frozen snow on the road that led out from town and then up the dirt path that led from the road to Tom's compound. It was already late afternoon, almost dusk, when I left Blowing Rock. About twenty minutes after I set out, it started snowing.

"Man must endure," I told myself as I once again hunkered down against the cold, a Miamian contending with mountainous elements in the dead of winter. But then I realized how differently I felt from when I'd quoted that same phrase a month earlier in Chicago. It wasn't just that the snow flakes now were big, white, and clean and fell gently, bathing me in their softness instead of assaulting me in a Lake Michigan gale. But ever since I struck Martina with the pie, the bleakness of the previous month had lifted. Bush would still be president, the election would still be stolen, and Marion Hines would still be dead. I couldn't help any of that. But I no longer felt overcome by defeat and despair. I had thwarted Martina's insane plan.

  I hiked the last quarter mile in the dark, slipping several times when I stepped on an icy patch. Finally, I arrived at Tom's cabin and knocked at the door. A moment later he opened it and I passed from darkness into light as I entered the living room.

"Welcome, Ben. Come on in. My you're cold. What can I get you? Whiskey?" A roaring fire lit up the living room, the smell of burning pine filled my nostrils, Miles Davis wailed on the stereo, and the warm cabin air caressed my frozen cheeks. For the first time in my life, I felt the compelling attraction of the family hearth.

"Belkis, come out here," Tom called into the kitchen. A moment later, an attractive woman entered the room. She was about forty years old with lively brown eyes and banana curls that cascaded down her long black hair. "Ben, this is Belkis. Belkis, Ben."

The most recent woman to attract Tom's interest, Belkis was a Cuban Santeria priestess he'd recently met. She spoke with energy and zest and peppered her speech with wonderful, rich images. Although I could tell that Belkis and Tom enjoyed one other and felt comfortable together, it wasn't clear to me what the nature of their relationship was. Belkis, who young enough to be Tom's daughter, was staying in the one of the two guest cabins on the property. I was to stay at the other.

Belkis's ability to read people's lives by throwing cowrie shells and communing with their dead ancestors fascinated Tom, and I had to admit that I found it interesting as well, although I retained a lot of doubts. Tom believed Belkis truly had some special talent along these lines. "You'll see," he told me.

"I'll throw them for you later," she offered. "When the time is right."

Tom was intrigued by her practical advice that was based on the myths and parables indicated by the shells, and by how Belkis would seek guidance for herself and others by consulting the forces of nature, which she identified as *orishas*.

"Santeria is actually a misnomer," she maintained a few days after my arrival, when Tom, Belkis, and I were hiking up one of the mountain trails. It was cold in the late January air, and the path was covered with snow that crunched beneath our boots, a far cry from the steamy African jungles where her religion had originated. "It should be called *orisha* worship."

"What about all those dead chickens?" Tom asked, alluding to the animal sacrifices that had made her religion notorious, especially in 1993, when the Supreme Court ruled that the ritual sacrifices are protected by the Constitutional.

"First of all," Belkis insisted, "I've never performed one. Only specially trained and ordained priests or priestesses are permitted to do this. Of course, we have our share of sleaze bags who are cynical, ignorant, and reckless. What religion doesn't? Some of these phonies are in the religion just as a power trip or to scam people, and they harm the animals, That's not just horrifying, it's blasphemy. Those bastards should all be locked up, and they should throw away the key too!

"They're just like television evangelists who preach only for the money, or priests, rabbis, and mullahs who exploit their congregations," she went on. The topic clearly had struck a nerve. "It's a shame when these people get all the attention, because outsiders think they speak for their religion. But these frauds who slaughter goats and chickens without doing proper homage to the *orishas*, or to the animals, no more embody the true spirit of my religion than Jimmy Swaggart or Tammy Faye Bakker represent genuine Christian piety."

Tom conceded that she had a point, and Belkis continued. "Look, I'll be honest with you. I'm still not totally comfortable about this part of the religion, but if you truly believe, as I do, that the sacrificial chicken, dove, or goat is literally being sent off to perform a divine mission, then their death is a blessed thing to be thankful for."

"Isn't that the mentality of a suicide bomber?" I asked.

"Like everything else, faith can be used for good or ill. When our religion is used in a constructive way to help people, as opposed to cursing or harming them, then, no, it is not the mentality of a suicide bomber."

"What happens to the carcass after the sacrifice?" Tom asked. Then, as we approached a wooden bridge that spanned a frozen stream, he added, "Watch out here. Use the hand rail. This bridge can get icy and very slick. I know from painful experience."

I crossed first. Tom waited for Belkis and held out his hand to steady her. She accepted it with a satisfied smile. When she reached midstream she uttered "Oshun" to the frozen water and then continued on. I was curious what that meant, but once she reached the other side, she addressed Tom's question.

"The animals are well cared for, and, when sacrificed properly, they are killed quickly and painlessly. Why would we want to abuse or bring pain to the spirit that is delivering our prayers? Afterward the animal is dead and its spirit has departed, we have a ritual feast in which the carcass is eaten. Those who consume the meal ingest a special spirit into their being. Is that worse than if we raised the chicken in its own filth, pumped it up with chemicals, killed it in a slaughter house, and sold it to you in a grocery store so you could make *arroz con pollo* for your friends? Or if we served it to you at a fast food joint?"

"Like in the *Odyssey*," I noted, struggling for air as I spoke. Being from flat Miami, I had to stop periodically to catch my breath on the steep mountain path. Belkis, too, required frequent breaks. "The Greeks would sacrifice oxen to the gods and then gorge themselves on ox meat in their celebrations and ritual meals," I finally elaborated.

Walking slightly ahead of us now, Tom stopped at an overlook to catch the view and let us rest. "Actually," he declared when we caught up, "there's a lot about Santeria, *orisha* worship, that reminds me of Greek mythology. It's all about tapping into the forces of nature. Think about the river god Xanthus in the *Iliad* who saves the Trojans by rising up against Achilles."

"Exactly!" Belkis agreed. "All of nature is filled with spirit. Rivers possess the spirit of Oshun, a female *orisha* who fills our lives with love and sensuality."

"Is that what you said when you went over the bridge back there?" I asked.

"Yes. It is considered respectful to acknowledge Oshun by speaking her name when crossing a river or stream."

"Aphrodite came from the sea," I noted, "but Oshun sounds sort of like her. Is that a fair comparison?"

"Aphrodite came from her father's castrated testicles that were cast into the sea, didn't she?" Belkis replied. "So I guess you can say she came from the sea. That's not Oshun's story. But she shares some things with Aphrodite, yes."

Belkis walked over beside Tom, who was watching a line of low clouds race across the sky and cover the mountain tops. She rested her arm on his shoulder and pointed.

"These mountains are the spirit of the chief *orisha*, Obatala. He's a powerful Zeus-like figure associated with creativity. That's why Tom likes the mountains so much. I bet he's an Obatala. But his spiritual mother is probably Chango."

"What's that mean, for someone to be an Obatala?" I asked. "And who is Chango?" I went to where they were standing and admired the vast expanse below me. I loved being in the mountains.

"It means that Obatala's spirit dominates and shapes the personality." A lightning bolt flashed in the distance, and Belkis pointed to it. "Chango, the warrior divinity, is associated with lightning and thunder. He enjoys confrontation and likes to stir things up. People whose *orisha* is Chango are like that. I think Martina's probably a Chango. You seem more like an Obatala. They tend to be peaceful and accommodating, more interested in justice and consensus. They're like mountains, stable but capable of unleashing great power."

"I'd still have a hard time letting an animal be sacrificed for me," I returned to the earlier topic.

"I understand," Belkis answered. "But remember, we never sacrifice dogs or cats or domestic pets. We kill only barnyard animals, the ones that farmers slaughter every day for food. Compared to the millions of turkeys that are ritually slaughtered and consumed in Christian America each Thanksgiving, our sacrificial animals at least are treated lovingly before they go to their deaths, and their spirits are followed by prayers and blessings."

"I guess," I conceded reluctantly. "But I don't think the goat that's about to die would see it that way."

"The sacrifice is an act of religious communion," Belkis answered, "just like in the Catholic Church. If you are a Catholic and accept the doctrine of transubstantiation--and it's blasphemy not to because it's the core mystery of Catholicism--then you are eating the body of Jesus in order to be filled with, to commune with, a holy spirit. Our rituals do the same thing. Only we don't believe in human sacrifice."

I couldn't really argue with her logic, but I thought of poor Pandora, whom I'd hastily arranged for Brian Mulligan to care for again in my absence. Belkis said that only barnyard animals were sacrificed and that she had many Santeria friends who owned and doted upon their pets. Still, I resisted the notion that it is necessary to kill an animal, or a person, in order to commune with the divine.

As we continued our hike up the path, I decided that I too

liked Belkis. She wasn't pushing her religion onto us, but she clearly felt comfortable in it and was happy to share her experience of it. She was at once spirited and serene, animated and enthusiastic about life, yet seemingly stable. I looked forward to spending more time with her.

I wasn't looking forward to spending more time with Martina, but it seems to have been in the cards anyway. A few days after I arrived Tom made an announcement while the three of us were having dinner in his cabin. "I've got some news that's probably not going to be all that welcome for you," he began, looking at me. "Martina is going to join our little gang of fugitives here at the Pynchon compound."

Belkis and I turned to each other, each with a similar look of shock and consternation. Meanwhile, Tom was getting off on the idea. "If we ever get found out, we'll be as notorious as Butch Cassidy and his Hole-In-the-Wall gang. They'll call us Tom Pynchon and his Blowing Rock Babes," he chuckled with self-satisfaction. Then he looked at me. "I guess we'll have to include the Pie-thrower in the name too, somehow. Anyway you cut it, it should make for interesting times."

"Why is she coming here?" I demanded.

"It turns out that she's in the same boat as you. Her HLF pals aren't real happy about the way things turned out at the inauguration, and they're blaming her for bringing you, a man, into the plan. She's already had some party discipline inflicted on her, but she knows that some of her rivals want a stronger punishment, and she doesn't have many remaining allies. In short, she's running for her life. Like you, she came to me for asylum, and like I did for you, I'm giving it to her."

"And where will Martina be staying?" Belkis wondered.

"I haven't figured that out. I guess we'll have to make some alterations in the present arrangements."

"I guess so," she grumbled. Then she pushed her plate aside and stood. "I'm not so hungry anymore. I'll be in my cabin, resting."

Tom and I exchanged glances. After she left Tom whistled, "Oh boy, this sure is going to make for interesting times." He seemed to relish the anticipated bouts between Martina and Belkis.

"I think I understand now why Belkis sees some Chango in you too," I told him. Then, returning to my dinner, I wondered what things would be like for me, now that Martina was back in the picture.

Chapter 17

Martina drove all night and showed up just before lunch the next day. Tom, who insisted that we all be present when she arrived, greeted her warmly at the door. Then he introduced her to Belkis, who tried to be civil but could not mask her icy demeanor. After Martina sneered in reply and hissed "Meow," Belkis stormed past her out the door and back to her cabin. Then I emerged from the livingroom.

Martina's face turned red with rage. "What's *he* doing here?" She spat at my face but missed. I backed away before she could spit again or attempt something more violent.

"Take it easy," Tom grabbed her arm to restrain her. "Ben's hiding out here. Same as you."

"Let me go!" Martina tried to pull her arm free to get at me, but Tom held on tight. "I'm not staying here if he is!" Cursing at me all the while, she fought to free herself, but he was bigger and stronger. Finally, after a few minutes, she stopped struggling.

"You can always leave," Tom told her when Martina was calm enough to listen. He nonetheless maintained his hold on her arm, and I continued to keep my distance. "You know me. I'm a big believer in free will."

"Why didn't you tell me he was here?" she demanded.

"Because then you wouldn't have come, and I've missed you."

Tom's answer caught Martina off balance. I could see the confusion on her face. Then he added gently, "You've had a long drive. Come on." With his free hand he picked up her overnight bag and, keeping his body between us, led her back toward his bedroom. Martina spat at me again as they passed, but she allowed Tom to guide her into the back. Later, after I returned to my cabin, he brought the rest of her things from the car into the bedroom, where he and Martina spent the remainder of the day. Apparently, the alterations in the living arrangements had been determined.

After our initial encounter, Martina kept her distance from me and I from her. Belkis and she were superficially polite but hardly friendly. So Belkis and I spent more time together by ourselves, or alone in our cabins, while Tom and Martina reunited. Tom retained his good cheer and remained friendly with all of us, but I could tell it was sometimes difficult for him. The night after Martina arrived, when I was in my cabin emailing Sharon, I could hear her in their bedroom screaming, "I want that sonofabitch out of here!"

But Tom didn't say anything about it the next day, and I stayed on. I felt safe under Tom's protection and wasn't about to let Martina force me out. She obviously couldn't manipulate Tom as easily as she could me. So, after a few more outbursts, she quit trying. Most of the time we avoided each other and went our own ways, except for meal times, when Tom insisted that his gang of fugitives dine together. Even then, Martina and I didn't speak to one another, and our dinner conversations consisted mostly of Tom's monologues in which he remarked on current events or discussed ideas he was considering for his new novel.

Perhaps I have some Obatala in me after all, because I always come alive in the mountains. I delight walking among the thick pine forests that cover them, and I passed many of my days hiking the mountain trails. The snow-covered ground was hard, the trees were bare, and the cold air bracing. But I dressed warmly and walked five or six miles pretty much every day. This immersion in nature had a calming effect that I needed more than I'd realized. Normally, at this time of year I'd be stressed by the flurry of paper grading, class preparation, and committee work. But my interlude at the Pynchon compound offered an opportunity for introspection and regrouping. What did I really want, I asked myself, and how would I get it?

One afternoon I encountered Belkis alone on one of my hikes. Bundled up in scarfs and a powder blue ski jacket, she had stopped at an overview that looked down and across at a waterfall.

The river close to the bank had frozen, but the water in mid-stream poured over the cliff and fell into a pool of swirling ice floes below. I walked up beside her. Belkis acknowledged me and gestured silently for me to join her. We stood quietly together, taking in the scene.

"Even in the dead of winter the spirit of Oshun fights to survive," she declared after a few moments. "That explains why I am a daughter of Oshun."

Belkis's cheeks, rosy red from the cold, set off her long black hair that flowed from beneath a blue and white ski cap and splashed down between her shoulder blades. Although cold, the day was sunny and bright, and her eyes sparkled in the sunlight. Pictured against the snow-covered mountains and bright blue winter sky, Belkis was animated by an exciting, sensuous spirit. Although I didn't exactly *see* it, I became aware of a golden yellow aura around her.

I stood tongue-tied for several seconds. Then to fill the awkward silence I asked her how she came to be here with us in the Pynchon compound.

Belkis looked me directly in the eyes. "The short answer is that I killed a man. I'm a fugitive too."

I was astounded. "You're joking, right?"

"I wish I was."

"There's an explanation?"

"Of course," her tone was emphatic. "There's an explanation for everything." I looked at her questioningly, and she continued. "I was born in Cuba but lived in the United States since I was a little girl. I was naturalized when I turned eighteen. But until recently I lived in Mexico on and off working for the religion. Oshun instructed me to do that. I used to come in and out of Mexico on tourist visas and was paid under the table. Tom likes to joke that I'm a wetback in reverse.

"About three months ago, a government official started coming to the store asking for powders and things. I didn't recognize him, and he went by a phony name, Ricky Ricardo. But one of my friends stopped by one day when he was there, and she recognized him. She told me he was a pretty high-ranking official in the government, and that he had ties with a business cartel that included some prominent Americans. From the things Ricardo was buying, I could tell he was having some heavy-duty rituals performed, but I didn't know by whom. It might not even have been Santeria, it could have been some form of black magic like voodoo. We use some of the same herbs and powders, but Santeria isn't about black magic.

"Ricardo asked me a lot of questions about the religion, and I answered them as well as I could. About a week after his first visit, he asked me if I could do a reading, so I threw the shells for him. It was a very ominous reading. Oshun told him that he was surrounded in darkness and needed to change his ways. Ricardo didn't like to hear that. He became very indignant and stormed out of the store. But on his way out, he pointed his finger and warned me never to mention anything about him to anyone. Of course, my friend had already recognized him, but I just nodded my head yes, and he turned and slammed the door behind him."

"Wow. Scary."

"Let me tell you, I was frightened. But the first thing I did was thank Oshun for protecting me. She instructed me to burn a stalk of sage in the room to cleanse the store of his bad energy. And she warned me of coming danger.

"Three days after that an influential businessman known for his opposition to U.S. corporate interests was murdered, and there were rumors throughout the city that Ricardo might be involved. The following evening he reappeared at the botanica. It was just before closing and the store was empty. He had a crazy look in his eyes, and I prayed silently to Oshun for protection. He pulled me out from behind my counter and tried to strangle me with his bare hands. I struggled, but he was overpowering me. Finally, I had one of those sudden bursts of adrenaline you sometimes hear about. I pushed him away, and he stumbled backward into a display of *orisha* statues. The display crashed to the ground and so did he. He fell right on top of Chango's spear. It took him about three minutes to die, and I didn't know what to do. I'd was too terrified even to scream. I just stood there in horror, my hands across my mouth, and watched him try to pull out the spear. Then he fell back onto the floor and cursed me with the dying breath."

"How awful," I commiserated. "What a terrible thing to go through."

"That was just the beginning. When Ricardo finally died,

I was careful not to touch him or look into his eyes. I didn't want his spirit to enter mine. I did cover his body with an Indian blanket though. Then I left everything as it was and locked up the store and left. I ran to my apartment, collected my passport, some clothes and a few belongings, and headed straight to the airport.

"But when I got there, I noticed that my tourist visa had expired. I was afraid of being detained by the police and questioned. Maybe Ricardo had even given my name to the airport authorities to make sure I couldn't escape. I was afraid to go through passport control. I didn't know what to do, but I had use of a friend's membership in the American Airlines Admirals Club, and I decided to go there to think things out. For one thing, it would probably receive less scrutiny than the regular waiting areas. I stayed for several hours, and when it was time for it to close, I hid in one of the bathroom stalls and then came out later to sleep on one of the couches.

"Don't tell me," I interrupted. "You ran into someone from the W.A.S.T.E. underground of dispossessed travelers."

It was Belkis's turn to be astounded. "Yes! How did you know?"

"It's a long story. It turns out that my father is a fellow traveler, so to speak."

"Incredible!" Belkis's eyes widened. "Well, it took a couple of days of hanging around the Admirals Club, but my new friend was able to call on some of his contacts and help get me out of Mexico and back to the States. I had to reenter illegally, because I was afraid that if they knew about me, the U.S. officials might extradite me back to Mexico to stand charges for Ricardo's death. I thought Ricardo's friends might be looking for a scapegoat, someone to pin both murders on, and that they'd make me out to be some deranged cultist obsessed with murdering prominent Mexicans. I didn't want to be sacrificed for their cause."

"So how did you come here?"

"Once I made it into the United States, I entered into some kind of vast underground railroad that took me from the W.A.S.T.E. travelers to a secret society of shamans who use peyote for hallucinogenic visions, to an organization dedicated to saving lives of political prisoners, to a radical lesbian group. They had a connection to Tom, and that's how I ended up here. I arrived the day after Christmas."

"My God," I said. "Was that the Hysterical Lesbians for Freedom."

"Yes." Once more Belkis was astounded by my knowledge. "How did you know?"

"That's Martina's gang. Martina brought you here, or at least she's responsible for getting you here."

Belkis had nothing to say to that, but she seemed uncomfortable to learn she was so deeply indebted to her unpleasant rival. "How long do you think you'll stay?" I asked to change the subject.

"Under the circumstances, I'm not sure."

"Me neither. This is awkward for me too. I don't know how much you know, but before she was with Tom, Martina was with me. But she'd probably like to see me dead right about now."

"What a soap opera," Belkis answered. Then she turned her attention back to the forest and we continued walking in silence.

After a while, we stopped by a mountain stream to rest. It had frozen over completely, but Belkis pointed out how water still trickled downstream beneath the surface. She sat down on a boulder beside the bank. I tried to make myself comfortable on the one beside it, but the cold penetrated through my jeans to my legs and buttocks.

"Wait a minute," Belkis said. She stood and removed a blanket from her backpack. She spread it over both rocks.

"Thanks," I offered, feeling a little more comfortable.

"Have you ever had a spiritual experience?" Belkis suddenly asked.

I thought a moment and then concluded, "Yes, I believe I have."

"Can you tell me about it?"

"It happened a few summers ago when I was trying to track down my dad--or at least I thought he was my dad--Thomas Pynchon."

"You thought Tom was your father?" Belkis again looked amazed. "And you shared the same woman!"

"Well, the sharing wasn't exactly my idea. Remember, I

was with Martina first. But until about half a year ago, yes I did think Tom was my dad. That was all cleared up before he and Martina hooked up. Of course, I don't know how Tom would have felt if it hadn't been, but Martina wouldn't have minded. I'm pretty sure of that. Anyway, now I know, or I think I know, that he's not my real father. A strange character named Burnt Umber is."

"He's the one in the W.A.S.T.E. underground? I never ran across him. What an odd name."

"Everything about him is odd. Burnt Umber is what he used to go by when he got my mom pregnant. No one knows his real name. Right now, he tells people to call him Lift 'n' Separate, but I can't bring myself to do that."

"Lift 'n' Separate!" Belkis laughed. "I never met him, but I heard stories about him from the W.A.S.T.E. people." Then she looked at me with new eyes. "And he's *your* father?."

"Seems to be."

"This is just too much. Tell me more."

I shifted my weight on the boulder and then began. "I'd been visiting people who claimed to have known Tom, and my last stop was Natalia, a gypsy who lived on Padre Island on the Texas coast. She tried to kill me."

"Is that what made it spiritual?"

"No, not at all. It's sort of a long story. You're not too cold, are you?"

"I've got time if you do. Start at the beginning. But first, maybe it is a little chilly. Let's have some hot coffee." She removed a thermos from her backpack and poured me a cup. I savored its steamy warmth.

Martina was the only other person to whom I'd told my full experience with Natalia, but I felt compelled to tell it now. "After a long day checking out worthless leads along the Gulf Coast, I finally crossed the bridge onto Padre Island as the sun was setting. This was in the summer, and I remember admiring the shafts of red and yellow sunlight that thrust upward from beneath the horizon and then arched majestically over the marshes and pastures stretching out toward the mainland. On the opposite horizon, a blue sky tumbled into the sea."

"How beautiful you make it sound." Belkis smiled at me and sipped her coffee.

"It was. Natalia lived alone in her shack on a desolate stretch of highway on the Gulf side of the island, and it took me a while to find the place. The briny smell of seaweed and salt almost overpowered me as I approached the house.

"When I knocked at her door, her dog Skippy barked ferociously from the other side. I stood there while Natalia calmed him and made him sit. He was a German shepherd-greyhound mix with long sinewy greyhound legs, a broad shepherd chest, oversized ears, and a brindle coat. He was affectionate when you got to know him, but a fierce watch dog. The only things I noticed as I entered were Skippy's snarling lips, his bright-red gums, and his long, sharp German shepherd fangs. Let me tell you, I walked in real slow. Skippy growled angrily, but Natalia had him under control, and he didn't attack.

"Natalia pointed for me to come inside and instructed Skippy to lie down and behave. We both did as we were told. Natalia gestured for me to take one of the overstuffed maroon chairs across from the fireplace. She took the other one. Natalia was probably in her mid-thirties, but it was hard to tell, and I never asked. She had long, jet black hair and dark, intense, deep-set gypsy eyes. Her angular face had sharp features. She was dressed flamboyantly, yet sensuously. She looked just like a gypsy was supposed to look.

"Once the threat from Skippy subsided and I became less preoccupied with basic survival, the heavy smell of incense caught my attention. At the same time, I noticed shadows dancing across the walls, curtains, and window shades. These were cast by numerous candles flickering throughout the house. Over the fireplace hung a large, black, ominous-looking, iron pot. The heads of two rag dolls, a boy and a girl, peered over the lid. Someone had placed handwritten signs around their necks, 'Hansel' and 'Gretel.'

"'Pretty funny, eh?' Natalia laughed when my glance lingered overly long on the dolls. 'I call it Meddlesome Child Stew.'"

"Oh, I like this woman's sense of humor," Belkis chuckled.

I answered seriously, however. "It may be installation art to you, but Hansel and Gretel looked creepy enough at the time, and given that Natalia later tried to tear out my larynx, I think the dolls may have been more than just an ironic, artistic statement.

Anyway, she quickly got down to business. I followed her into the back of the house where she had her 'office.' A heavy curtain covered the window and tapestries hung on the walls. Beneath them were shelves stacked with jars and bottles of various shapes and sizes. One was very conspicuously labeled 'Eye of Newt.'"

"More installation art?" Belkis offered.

"Perhaps," I conceded. "Natalia struck a match and lit a new stick of frankincense. The only other illumination came from a glass candelabra atop one of the shelves and two large candles in pewter holders on either side of a large wooden desk. A crystal ball and a tarot deck lay between them. She commanded me to take one of the two wooden chairs facing the desk as she walked around and seated herself in a worn leather recliner.

"First, she demanded fifty dollars for the reading. After I paid, she grabbed the tarot deck and began shuffling the cards. She did this repeatedly for several minutes without speaking. I sat silently across from her, watching as her breathing became slower and deeper and her eyes lost focus. Natalia appeared to be entering an altered state."

"Yes," Belkis agreed. "That's often how it is when I read the cowrie shells."

"At last, she stopped shuffling and turned over the top card.

"Natalia, who had a bad cold, sneezed twice before speaking. Looking at the upturned card and then up at me, she counseled, 'Beware the Hanged Man.' Then she added, 'Do not fear death by water.'

"'But what does this have to do with me?' I demanded.

"'There is a Hanged Man in your future,' she predicted. 'He may be your father, or he may be someone else.' Natalia went on to explain that in the tarot, the Hanged Man is the Fool who has lost his way by becoming caught up in his own vanity, envy, greed, ambition, or preoccupation with worldly matters. To be the Fool--curious, optimistic, innocently motivated, enthusiastic about life, and oblivious to the praise and censure of others--is to achieve the highest spiritual state in the cosmos. She told me how Sir Percival was such a well-intended innocent, and this is why he alone among all the knights in King Arthur's court was allowed to grasp the Holy Grail. But the Hanged Man is driven by irrational fears that corrupt and debase him; they turn his virtue on end. This is why the Hanged Man hangs upside down. The Fool lives to laugh deeply and heartily about his own life and the lives of others. The Hanged Man has lost his mirth. The cat abandons the Hanged Man and seeks out some other Fool who has not made himself miserable with his sloth, envy, fear, and pride."

"In my religion, Elegua is like the Fool," Belkis told me. "He's also a trickster."

I thought for a moment. "I don't think Judaism has a Fool, although, like any religion, I suppose there are plenty of fools among us. I can't think of any figure in Christianity who'd be like the Fool, either. The ancient Greek religion did though, Hermes. He was a trickster at least.

"Anyway, I found Natalia's tarot lesson interesting but not very productive. 'What does that have to do with my father?' I asked her.

"'If he is the Hanged Man, he has lost his way. That is why you have difficulty finding him.'

"'Yes. That's why I'm here. What can you do to help?'

"'You must keep a vigil for a week,' Natalia proclaimed. 'During that time you will eat only the foods I prepare for you and drink only water and special teas that I will administer. You will spend your days by the ocean, looking out to sea, for you need not fear death by drowning. I will prepare a spot with shade for you on a secluded stretch of beach nearby. You will return each evening at dusk to dine with me. You will sleep alone in the abandoned house down by the shore. Have no visitors,' she cautioned, as though I knew anyone I might call over to hang out with me. Natalia then added with deliberation, 'Piwacket and Pantherpuss will sleep with you. At the end of that time, you will know how to find your father.'"

"Spooky!" Belkis declared. "But I wouldn't trust her."

"Are you kidding? Neither would I. I had no intention of spending the last week of my summer vacation in an abandoned Texas shanty with some crazy person, much less putting her in charge of what I ate and drank. I was on the verge of standing and leaving, when all of the sudden, the strangest thing happened. My hand was pushing on the armrest, and I was just getting to my feet, when I had a vision. It stopped me dead in my tracks."

"I've had many visions," Belkis stated matter-of-factly. "What was yours?"

"For just a split second I saw myself sitting before the Gulf of Mexico, looking out to sea. Golden light illuminated the scene and made the sea sparkle."

"Yemaya, the powerful female *orisha* who is the spirit of the ocean, was beckoning you," Belkis insisted. "I hope you heeded her call."

"The image passed in an instant. But I knew I had to stay. I couldn't give a reason, but it was obvious that I must remain. So I did."

"Good for you. This was a rare opportunity."

"It just seemed so clearly what I needed to do. I'd never experienced anything like it before, but I just went with it as naturally as a trout who's been released into a stream. There was never any question about whether I'd stay."

"What was your week like?"

"Well, if you've never spent seven days just staring out to sea, you should try it sometime. You'll either come back sane or a madwoman. But you won't be the same. I think I let go of a lot of stress and put some things into perspective. I tried to clear my mind. That was difficult, but it turned into a journey of incredible introspection."

"How so?"

"At first I tried to concentrate on the horizon as sort of a meditation. I'd learned a little about that sort of thing when I was in college. Thoughts about school and friends and my cat Pandora would pop into my mind, but I imagined them floating away in the breeze. Thoughts about Diane, my wife, and Sharon were not as easy to dispel. I had tried to be mature about Diane's decision to place her career over our family. After all, it was her decision to make, and I know how much my career means to me. In the same situation, who knows if I would have chosen differently. So I couldn't very well condemn her. For that matter, I might have resigned my position in Miami and moved to Iowa and gotten some kind of menial work, but I didn't. So I appreciate why Diane did what she did. A life spent grading papers incessantly, without time for creativity, was killing her, just as my brief stint as a substitute teacher had suffocated me. She was struggling to keep her spirit alive.

"But although I acknowledged why she needed to go and I could not condemn her for it, staring out into the ocean all day helped me realize that I nonetheless resented her decision, that I was disappointed and hurt by it. I'd really wanted to act well through all that. For one thing, I didn't want to hurt Sharon, who would undoubtedly be affected by animosity between Diane and me. For another, I think it's in times of disappointment like this when it's most important to emulate the people we most admire. How would Socrates react if someone he loved insisted on leaving? Wouldn't he still love them but let them retain control of their life?"

"Yes, I think he would," Belkis agreed. Then she thought some more. "Obatala might also, but Oshun would tear out his eyes before she'd let him leave, and Chango would stop him dead in his tracks with a bolt of lighting. Different forces of nature respond differently to extreme provocation. It's sometimes difficult to comprehend, but each response is appropriate for each *orisha*. So, there is no one *right* reaction to any given situation. It all depends on whose spirit--which force of nature--resides within you. Would you really want Carmen, the opera gypsy, to behave the same as Shakespeare's Hamlet? Should fire act like the river? The ocean and the wind often ride together as friends beneath a tranquil sky, but when the thunder clouds pass overhead, the wind gathers its strength and sets off in a new direction with force and determination, while the sea churns inwardly upon itself, frothing with rage and roaring with fury. Can you say that one is right and the other wrong?"

Belkis's perspective was totally new to me, and I didn't know what to make of it. It made sense when she explained it, but it contradicted my entire moral foundation. Should we expect different ethics from different personality types? I finally conceded, "I don't know."

Belkis looked closely at me. "Think about it. But in any case, you've always seemed like an Obatala to me. Perhaps Socrates was too. And maybe even Jesus. For all of you, reason tempered by compassion seems best. So, for you, your behavior was appropriate."

"My anger and feelings of abandonment seemed inappropriate to me. Even my frustration and disappointment. What right did I have to be angry at Diane for pursuing not just happiness but, when you come down to it, spiritual fulfillment? So I repressed my resentment."

"That's not a real solution," Belkis insisted.

"No, it's not. It's just a form of denial, and my days by the ocean somehow let me see that. Maybe Diane was acting within her rights to leave me, but I was also in mine to feel hurt by it, and angry and betrayed. And if that's self-contradictory, too bad. I mean, I'm not the one who ripped the family apart and took Sharon away. What's more, Diane's accusations about my careerism were unfair and unfounded. What's wrong, after all, with aspiring to be as good as possible at what you do? That's all I've ever been in this profession for. Plus, I care about my work and I think it's important. If I help dispel the myth of eugenics, I think I will have done humanity some good in my time on earth."

"Plus," Belkis interrupted, "if the creative aspect of Obatala is strong within you, and I suspect it is, then a divine force is driving you to do your work. To deny it is spiritual deprivation, just as it was for Diane when she couldn't write her poems."

"But Diane always talked like I was in it for the recognition. Sure, I like that too. I'd be lying if I said I didn't. But when I pull out some books to follow up a point, or when I sit down at my computer to write, it's not the recognition that I'm thinking about. It's because I'm caught up in an interesting project.

"Well, listen to me ramble. Thinking about Diane can still rile me. Anyway, those were the kind of thoughts I had the first couple or three days, those and thoughts about how much I missed Sharon. How much I enjoyed playing with her when she was a toddler and, as she got older, how much fun it was to watch her mind and imagination develop.

"Anyway, the first few days on the beach I found myself thinking about my marriage a lot. But by the fourth day my thoughts centered more upon my childhood. My mother was an action painter in the '50s. She had a bohemian life style right up until the time she was committed. It made for an interesting childhood. But like everyone else, I guess I had issues. Mom dressed me differently from the other kids; my friends' parents didn't allow them to come to my house because my mother might emerge from her studio half naked and covered with paint to offer my pals milk and cookies, as if this were no stranger than if she wore a house dress and apron. The first time she greeted my ten year-old friend Fred topless, he was so freaked out, he ran crying all the way back to his house.

"Now I know where you get your Obatala traits from," Belkis said. "My Mama was just the opposite." Belkis scowled and fidgeted as she spoke, the first time I'd ever seen her lose her poise. "She tried to make me the same as the other girls. She said she wanted me to be a good Cuban girl. But I think she was mostly afraid of what people would think of her if I was different."

"So, how's she feel about having a daughter who is a priestess in an Afro-Cuban pagan religion?"

"At first she didn't like it. But after I used some of my powders on her behalf and got results, she changed her mind."

"What powders are those?" My interest was suddenly peaked, but Belkis just waved me off.

"Never mind. I don't like to talk about it. Continue with your story."

I pressed her further, but Belkis was clearly uncomfortable discussing her mother and her potions. So I continued.

"Well, I left my week on the beach feeling a lot better about things with Mom. But then, there was the matter of Dad."

"Yes, tell me about that."

"Apart from his books, Thomas Pynchon had always been as much an abstraction to me as he is to the rest of the world. Mom never had much to say about him. She only knew him for a couple months. She said he was brilliant, imaginative, and not as kinky as people thought. Plus, he always had good grass that he purchased from a connection in Greenwich Village. That turned out to be Burnt Umber."

"So your father is a drug dealer?" Belkis raised her eyebrow.

"Not exactly. I think back then he had a connection and was able to pick up a an ounce here and there for Tom. Probably he skimmed some off the top for himself. But he wasn't a dealer, at least not in the conventional sense of what that means."

Belkis didn't seem altogether satisfied, but she told me to continue with my story. I took another sip of coffee and luxuriated in the warmth that passed down my throat and into my stomach. "Maybe we should walk some," I suggested. I'm getting cold, aren't you?"

I stood and helped her up. Then we proceeded farther along the path.

"During my last day on the beach a strange thing happened," I told her. "I'd spent the day thinking about Tom, who I still believed was my dad. My thoughts were murky; he's such a vague figure in my life. Finally, in the late afternoon I was lying on the sand beneath an umbrella, looking out at the sky, and beginning to drift off into a light sleep. I remember listening to the gulls calling and the water crunching against the shore. Then I had another vision. This one lingered a second or two longer than the first. I saw an older man, perhaps in his sixties, dressed in a black trench coat, holding down a coonskin cap that threatened to blow away in the wind. He was pointing down to what I immediately recognized as paw prints of a bear, although I've never seen one in my life. A paw print, that is. I have seen bears. Leaves were swirling behind the man, crashing into and bouncing off of a huge barren boulder. Instinctively, I knew the man was Tom. I thought I heard him say, 'I'm hanging out among the grizzlies. You know where that is.'

"And then the image vanished. Somehow, it was comforting. I had the feeling he wanted to be helpful. But grizzlies hang out in a lot of places, so I don't know how helpful he really was. It did lead me to move my future searches away from the ocean and toward the mountains."

"It took you to Obatala," Belkis observed. "Remember, I told you he is the spirit of the mountains."

I nodded. "The frontiersman's hat reminded me of Davy Crockett, but none of the leads I tried to follow in Tennessee panned out. It wasn't until Martina tracked him down in North Carolina that I realized that the phantom from my vision was Daniel Boone, not Davy Crockett, and the town was Blowing Rock.

"I spent the remaining hour or so before sunset ruminating on this sudden appearance of Thomas Pynchon. Then, as usual, I crossed the street and went inside to talk to Natalia. She ushered me into her office, which reeked with incense, sat down at her desk opposite me, and made me recount everything I could remember. Even in the subdued candlelight I could tell she was greatly impressed. But when she told me that only I could interpret the exact meaning of my vision, I lost my patience.

"'Look, I know Thomas Pynchon was once your client!' I shouted. 'At least you advertise that he was. I've played along with your hocus pocus for a week. And frankly, I admit I'm better for it. But enough is enough. Can you help me find my father or not?'

"Following the strict rules Natalia set at our first meeting, I'd never told her the name of the person I was seeking. Now, when I mentioned Tom's name, her expression turned to ice. Then to fire."

"She sounds like a Chango to me," Belkis interjected. "You'd better watch out around her."

"No kidding! 'Thomas Pynchon!' she screamed. 'Thomas Pynchon! You are the son of Thomas Pynchon!'

"In an instant she sprang across the desk and grabbed for my throat, like a panther going for the kill. Her long fingernails dug into my Adam's apple and almost punctured my jugular. You can still see the scar." I stopped walking and held up my chin for Belkis to look.

She ran her finger along the scar. Her touch was soothing. Then she asked, "What did you do?"

"Somehow I managed to pull away and run out of the house before Natalia could regain her balance and catch me. My neck was bleeding but I didn't even stop to tend to it. I just jumped into my car and hightailed it out of there. I had a change of clothes and a few other odds and ends in my shack, but I wasn't about to go back. She really wanted to kill me."

"But why?"

"At the time, I had no idea why the name of Thomas Pynchon would ignite such a firestorm of rage. But I've since learned, through a fantastic coincidence, that Burnt Umber and Natalia had some dealings prior to my visit, back when he was calling himself Thomas Pynchon. Burnt never explained exactly what their relationship was, but they didn't part as friends. I suspect he might have gotten her pregnant and then abandoned her. That seems to have been a pattern he had with women back then."

"Amazing," Belkis said. "Life can be so convoluted. Imagine the forces that must have been at work to bring you and Burnt Umber to the same gypsy on Padre Island. You know, Tom is the glue that bound you and your father together, as well as you to Martina. And Martina has brought you and me together too."

"Yes," I answered, wondering exactly what she meant by that last statement. "I used to think my life was more or less normal, at least given my presumed parentage. But now I see how things even more unlikely and bizarre happen all the time. You and Burnt Umber being linked to the same W.A.S.T.E. underground, for instance. Can it just be that, given the billions of people and trillions of interactions among them, the laws of probability predict that a certain number of weird coincidences are inevitable?"

"Is that what you think?"

"It used to be. Now I'm not so sure."

As though in response, Belkis turned again to the mountains surrounding us. "It's such a treat follow a stream up towards it source and feel the presence of Oshun. I feel so alive and so in touch with her." Then she turned to me abruptly. "Would you like me to read you now?" she asked. "I feel Oshun has something to say to you."

I was surprised by the offer but after a slight hesitation, I figured why not.

We found a little clearing off the path, beside the stream, folded the blanket for extra insulation, and then sat down beside each other.

"Just give me a minute" Belkis told me. She took a deep breath, closed her eyes, and seemed to meditate. Then she whispered some words I couldn't understand, pulled out her bag of cowrie shells from her coat pocket, and began my reading.

Belkis cast the shells onto the blanket and then handed me one black and one white stone. They felt like river rocks, smooth, cold, and hard. She told me to shake them together and then, without looking, grab one in each hand. After I did, she opened my right hand and gathered the black rock. She threw the shells again and had me shake the stones again. This time she opened my right hand and found the white stone. She nodded silently and cast the shells again. We continued in this way for some time, although sometimes she'd select the rock in my left hand instead of the right.

At last Belkis declared, "Your reading shows blessings from Oshun, but she says that you must do what you know you must do. If you follow through, everything will work out for the best, even if it doesn't look like it at first. Oshun says that you need only to sustain your optimism and to ask Olofi for whatever it is that you truly want. But you must speak your heart to him out loud." Olofi, Belkis explained, is the spirit that animates the sun.

She then stuck her hand through the thin sheet of ice covering the stream, quickly removed it, and sprinkled water on my head and face. "Oshun is the spirit of the river," she reminded as she daubed the cold droplets onto my forehead. She reached down and grabbed a pebble from the brook. "Keep this to remind you of Oshun's blessing."

I accepted the rock and expressed my appreciation. Then we rose and began our trip back to the compound. As we walked Belkis interrogated me about what I truly wanted for myself. I was vague, but she kept pushing me to vocalize my deepest desires. It seemed like a simple request, but I suddenly realized that I hadn't done this for many, many years. Now, stating my most heartfelt wants proved surprisingly difficult. But Belkis encouraged me to do this aloud every day during my walks. She said that if I speak directly to Olofi, it will be easier for me and more effective. "The practice will bring your life into better focus," she assured me.

Chapter 18

Over the next couple weeks, I hiked by myself early each morning in the woods. I had been taking these walks through the silent, snow-covered forest even before Belkis read my shells. They had become my daily meditation. But now I began each stroll with an invocation to Olofi in which I tried to assert what I wanted in my life.

When I started, I thought this would be a simple, straightforward process. But it quickly provoked unexpected self-exploration. My life had changed so much in the past six months, in the last five years. Did I still want the same things I'd longed for before? Or did I need to update my picture of myself? Before I had sought a loving partnership, strong ties with my daughter, and professional success. Now that I was Pie-thrower, absurdist hero, and fugitive from justice, was this what I still desired? Or was it time to imagine an entirely new script for my life?

As I spoke my desires aloud, I found myself listening to assess how much my words rang true to me. Certainly, I still wanted strong bonds with Sharon. Of all the things that had transpired in this half-year of ups and downs, the loving relationship I developed with my daughter felt best; better even than thwarting Martina's pernicious plan to destroy the democracy. Heading my list of requests to the sun was that Sharon and I continue to deepen our love, affection, and appreciation for each other and that we remain active forces in each other's life.

As for a loving partnership? The idea still sounded good, but after Martina I needed to formulate a better notion of what shape I wanted that partnership to take. Of course, there was an energy and excitement to Martina, not to mention a sexual spark that I'd found irresistible, at least at first. But the fire of her intensity had blinded me to a selfish amorality that I'd quickly find unacceptable in any mate, even if Martina hadn't found me unacceptable first.

So, as I beseeched Olofi for love, I found myself thinking back to earlier relationships and asking what I enjoyed and found dissatisfying about each, and what I now wanted in a partnership at this stage of my life. And, for the first time in almost two decades, I seriously questioned what I wanted to do professionally for the rest of my life, or even just for the coming years. Assuming I'd be able to resume my job, did I want to remain a history professor, cultivate my role as cyber-hero, become a political activist, or go off in some entirely new direction? Become a forest ranger and live in the mountains?

All in all, Oshun's strange message that Olofi would grant my wishes sparked a much needed review of who I was and who I wanted to be. Moreover, for the first time in my life, I think, I had some real notion of what it is like to pray. God had always been a vague and abstract notion for me, but the sun was present and real. Consequently, I had more of a definite sense of audience when I expressed my deepest desires on those mountain walks than on those occasions when I attended religious services and prayed to a God I could not apprehend. But mindful of the First Commandment I ended each morning's appeal with thanks both to the sun and its creator.

Finally, my daily address to the sun compelled me to acknowledge the one thing that had most been troubling my soul. I had repressed it out of necessity, but now my morning rituals made it increasingly clear to me that I needed to come to terms with my role in the death of Marion Hines.

In the nights after Oshun spoke to me by the stream, I began having vivid dreams. They were exciting and disturbing, sometimes terrifying, but I could rarely remember them in the morning. I mentioned my dreams one day at breakfast, while Tom was flipping flapjacks for us. He said that he knew some techniques for recalling dreams and for entering into them and semi-consciously reshaping them. He offered to hypnotize me and guide me through a reverie, if I wanted

"Hypnosis can be quite revealing," he told me, "as well as

therapeutic."

I agreed. After we finished breakfast, Martina skulked off to the bedroom and her computer, Belkis returned to her cabin, and Tom and I stepped into the living room. I lay comfortably on a rug by the fireplace, my head on a pillow, eyes closed, and hands crossed against my chest. Tom told me to take a deep breath, slowly exhale, and relax. He described the quiet of the pine forest and had me imagine myself walking farther and farther down a path. As I watched myself proceed into the woods, my eyes became heavy, and I fell into a state of deep relaxation. I tried to lift my eyelids, but it didn't seem worth the effort. Disappearing into the trees, I heard Tom's voice saying that I was now in full communication with my unconscious and ready to learn important and useful things from it.

"You are about to go on a wonderful journey into your mind. It's a self-guided tour. All you have to do now is relax, let go, and let yourself be swept away. Then, at the appropriate time, and you will know when that is, you will consciously enter the scene and participate in it as you desire."

Tom then told me to clear my mind and think of the person from history I most admired. At first I drew a blank, then suddenly a drawing of Socrates from the cover of my old college philosophy text popped into my mind. He was wearing a flowing robe and had long gray hair. Tom encouraged me to converse with Socrates, to ask silently whatever questions I had for him and let the Socrates in my imagination say to me whatever he had to say.

"What do I need to know?" I asked the Socrates in my mind.

"An excellent question," he replied. "What *do* you need to know?"

"What will make me feel happy? What will make me feel complete?"

"And how do you feel now?" Socrates inquired. "Unhappy and incomplete?"

"Yes," I confessed. I hadn't acknowledged this to myself directly before. But I had to admit it was true.

"Even after you thwarted Martina and her radicals and saved the republic? Even though you are a cyber-hero and your daughter loves you?"

"Even so," I confessed.

"What's missing?" Socrates wanted to know.

"I feel I have fulfilled my duty, but apart from Sharon, who has her own life to live, I have no source of joy."

"Have you been actively seeking one out?"

"No, I've been too preoccupied with more immediate demands."

"Yes, saving the nation requires some sacrifices," Socrates acknowledged. "But is that the only reason you've deferred your happiness?"

"No." I surprised was to hear myself say it.

"Why not, then?"

"I don't deserve it."

"If you don't, then who does? You prevented a presidential assassination."

"I killed Marion Hines."

"Yes, you did."

"I can't just let it go, like Martina and Sharon have, and pretend that it didn't happen or that it means nothing or that she was just a casualty of war. She was a narrow-minded, intolerant bitch, but she was a human life and if I hadn't thrown that pie she might still be alive."

"Well, what can you do now?" Socrates smiled kindly at me as he queried.

"I can go to the police and turn myself in."

"And why don't you?"

"I promised Martina and the girls that I wouldn't act unilaterally."

"Is that the only reason?"

"I'm afraid."

There it was, finally, right out in the open. Jail scared the shit out of me. I feared violent harm would come to me there. I feared I'd lose my job and never find another in academia. I was too afraid to do the right thing. But I'd never know joy until I did.

Suddenly Socrates vanished and Franklin D. Roosevelt appeared instead, dressed in a business suit and smoking a cigarette from an elegant holder. "The only thing you have to fear is fear itself," he chuckled and then I awoke. I remembered everything.

Tom was sitting across from me when I opened my eyes,

serene as ever. "Any insights?" he asked.
"I need to come clean."
"About?"
"About Marion Hines."
"I see," Tom nodded.

The next morning I announced at our communal breakfast that I intended to turn myself in for my part in Marion Hines's death. "I need to assume responsibility and accept the consequences of my actions," I declared after Tom finished doling out bowls of oatmeal for all of us.

"YOU'RE A JEW. YOU KILLED THE DARLING OF THE CHRISTIAN RIGHT! THEY'LL CRUCIFY YOU!" Martina screamed.

I hadn't thought about it like that. The prospect that I might fall victim to a one-man pogrom stunned me momentarily. But I refused to give in to my fears. I would be the man of action.

"No. I've got to do this," I insisted. "This is one of those defining moments in a person's life, in my life. And I choose to behave like the people I most admire, so I'll never look back on myself with disappointment. I think that's the one thing I've worked hardest at in my life, to make sure I'll never have good grounds to hate myself. I'd done pretty well until now, but this is something I've got to come to terms with.

"I always intended to make my mark in world through my scholarship and my teaching," I continued while Martina looked on incredulously, as though I were a ranting madman. "Both are valuable and both do make a difference. They're also both pretty safe, and I was never one to go looking for trouble. But trouble's come looking for me. It seems I was meant to make my mark differently than I expected. But I want to make it well. I want it to be legible and say what I want it to say."

"Don't give me all that romantic, liberal *bullshit*!" The bitterness in Martina's voice and her searing blue eyes cut through me. "Surrendering will change nothing. She'll still be dead, but now your life will be wasted too!"

"No. If I turn myself in and stand trial, I'll accomplish several things. First, I'll set in motion a process that might, if I'm lucky, allow me to work my way through this catastrophe and at some point put it behind me. If I don't, I'll wake up every morning wondering if this will be the day the feds show up at the door."

"Until then, at least it will be your door, not some jail cell where you'll rot away." Martina pushed away her half-eaten pancakes in disgust.

"Well, that's the trade-off, isn't it?" I replied. "Peace of mind and spirit, versus freedom and physical well being. It's not an easy choice, believe me, or one that I look forward to making."

Martina just glared.

"Look, I thought I would make my mark on the world through my teaching and scholarship, but perhaps I was meant to speak in a louder voice. 'Destiny seems to have taken a hand,' to quote Rick in *Casablanca*, and I've been elevated from spectator to bit player in the universal fight between right and wrong. Maybe I've become one of Burnt Umber's history-altering little people. Maybe not. I still believe in what we were protesting when we attacked Hines. Her homophobia and her tolerance of, not to say her complicity with, neo-Nazis were despicable. For God's sake, we fought World War II, the Good War, and tens of thousands of Americans died to keep the Nazis from imposing their white supremacist vision upon the world. And this bitch was right there in bed with them. That's disgraceful, and I'm going to tell it to the jury and to the world. And maybe they'll understand why I protested, and maybe my public reminder of how today's neo-Nazis defile the memory of every American casualty from World War II will get through even to America's right-wing patriots. And I'm further going to tell them how I also wanted to thwart an assassination attempt by getting to Hines first with my pie. And maybe you'll cooperate with me and tell the truth to corroborate my story, and maybe you won't."

Martina sat stone-faced and silent.

"But I'm going to tell the truth. I've consistently acted in good faith, and I'm going to accept the consequences of my actions. If for no other reason than I want our enemies to see that at least some liberals have the courage to stand up for their convictions and assume responsibility for their deeds, even when the outcomes deviate from what we planned. In the long run, it is cumulative acts of integrity that will give our side credibility and keep theirs in check. And without integrity, who are we anyway?"

When I finished my speech, I excused myself and went

back to my cabin. I would have liked to gone hiking to relax, but a heavy snow storm had commenced during the night and the blowing snow made it difficult enough just to negotiate my way through the compound.

"Come back, you bastard!" Martina called to me as I walked through the door. She stood to go after me, but Tom subdued her.

Three days later, after making arrangements with a lawyer, I took a bus to Raleigh and turned myself in. Part of the deal was that in accepting my surrender, the government agreed not to pursue charges against any of my accomplices, who would remain unnamed. I had also insisted on provisions for affordable bail. Despite her professional reservations, my lawyer also agreed that when the time came, she would allow me to take the stand in my own defense.

Chapter 19

I surrendered to the authorities in early March. That was seven months ago already. It is early October now. The September 11 terrorist attacks were one month ago, exactly, and everyone is still reeling from the horror. But today, I am celebrating my freedom. I lie back on my blanket and listen to the waves grind against the shore, while the late afternoon sun showers me in yellow light and a balmy breeze caresses my head. This is a blessing from Olofi. And from Jehovah, the God of the Jews who appears as fire and whose voice is the wind. And from the universe itself, which is, after all, a vast ocean of energy, replete with swirling whirlpools, backwaters, and eddies we call matter, time, and life.

But out at sea Chango is stirring up big trouble. A late season storm is approaching the lower Bahamas and drawing a bead on Miami. The forecasters think it might intensify and become a hurricane by the time it arrives, if, in fact, it doesn't change its course and head north for North Carolina's Outer Banks instead. People throughout the city are busy boarding up, buying supplies, and making preparations, but I've already settled my affairs. As often happens before a hurricane strikes, this morning opened under a beautiful blue sky and has remained gorgeous all day, albeit breezy, hot, and sticky. So after lunch I headed for the beach, spread out my blanket, planted my umbrella, and opened myself to whatever the sun and sand and sea and sky have to tell me. Now it's late afternoon already, and I've heard quite a lot.

My trial concluded three weeks ago. It lasted three days. I could have copped a plea and gotten three years for involuntary manslaughter with the likelihood of parole in a year or so. But only a trial would let me publicly acknowledge my responsibility for Marion Hines's death; only a trial would permit me to tell my story as I knew it. And only a trial would give me a platform to hammer home to the world the dangers to our social fabric posed by purveyors of intolerance and ethnic purity.

The pie-throwing angle, alone, brought out the press, especially after my appearance at the inauguration. Hines's stature as a leading voice for a small but vocal constituency from the radical Christian Right further peaked the public interest. CSPN offered complete live coverage of the trial. The major television networks gave me about a minute apiece.

I readily conceded that I had thrown the pie that triggered Ms. Hines's heart attack. Nor did I permit my lawyer to explore the possibility that she might have been in poor health and could have keeled over at any moment, regardless of my unexpected intrusion into her life. It was apparent to me that had I not smacked her in the face with my foul-smelling concoction, Hines would have lived at least a few hours longer. And I had no right to deprive her even of that.

Except that maybe she wouldn't have lasted that long. In my defense I told how a group of radical lesbians was planning to assassinate Hines that very afternoon, how my pie-throwing had been intended to save her life, not terminate it. But Martina remained in hiding and I refused to implicate Sharon and Helena; so I had no way to corroborate this claim, as the prosecutor made painfully clear during cross-examination. Unconvincing as my claims about the HLF's role in Hines's death was, it seemed even more a stretch to implicate it in the thwarted assassination attempt against Bush, so I never mentioned it, even to my lawyer. Instead, I painted Hines as a white-supremacist bigot intent on provoking violence against the gays on Miami Beach and suggested that her early demise may have saved lives. But the prosecutor disdainfully dismissed my speculation as what it was, mere speculation. "Why not praise Lee Harvey Oswald for saving us from the nuclear war that John Kennedy might have led us into had he lived?" he mocked.

So things worked out as my lawyer predicted. I got my platform; I told my story and warned the world of the twin threats from the neo-fascists and the radical lesbians. And I was judged guilty. In recognition of my the fact that I had voluntarily surrendered, I was allowed to remain free until my sentencing, which took place two days ago. I received 3-10 years for involuntary manslaughter, with possibility for probation in a year and a half. It's more or less the same as if I'd plea bargained, so I regard that as some sort of moral victory.

They gave me three additional days to get my affairs in order, and I've done that. Brian Mulligan has agreed to take care of Pandora until I'm released. That was my biggest concern. I've been on unpaid leave at the university since January, but its unlikely that I'll have a job when I get out. The state doesn't take kindly to having felons on the faculty. I spent most of my remaining time emailing Sharon and Helena, who seemed to be doing well together again, and thinking about what I'd learned from my ordeal. I thought about where I was and who I was a year earlier, and the change was astounding. Most importantly, I am feeling happier, stronger, and more self-confident, even though my situation has so deteriorated. I still look over my shoulder from time to time, anticipating the revenge of the HLF, but now that I'm in the spotlight, I guess they figure it would be unwise to invite any further scrutiny of my link to them. So far, they have left me alone. I wanted to spend the final days before my incarceration in the mountains among the bright yellow and deep red autumn leaves. But I'm not permitted to leave Miami-Dade County and must wear an ankle bracelet to identify my location at all times. So instead I'm celebrating my last day of freedom at the beach.

I think that moments like this truly put our personal philosophies to the test. In my case, the trick is somehow to make my time in prison seem worthwhile and well spent. I want to come out a stronger, better, more complete person than when I go in. If I can do that, I'll prevail, and maybe even some unexpected good will come from this imprisonment. Still, I admit I'm scared. The trick is to acknowledge the fear but control it. I can't let it turn to panic or terror.

"When I was in the joint...." I suddenly imagine myself addressing my colleagues at the faculty club. I speak with the self-assurance of a wise guy who's been around the block and seen a few things. And I recognize the newfound respect for me in their eyes. I've already offered to teach reading, writing, and history to the other inmates while I'm in there; you can take the teacher from the classroom, but you can't take the classroom....I hope to use these classes also to teach tolerance and show how prejudice works against those who practice it. I don't have great expectations; I know these are a tough bunch to reach. But who knows, maybe I'll prove to have an unexpected knack. Stranger things have happened, especially if I relate to them as Pie-thrower instead of as Professor of History. If I can turn around a few wayward lives by helping some lost souls find purpose and direction, or just gain a new perspective, I'll be doing them a real service, and society as well. After all, if just one con goes straight because of my efforts, then someone else won't fall victim to his crimes. That won't bring Marion Hines back to life. But it will be something else to add to the positive side of the ledger when and if a Judgment Day arrives. And even if it never comes, or I fail to reach a single inmate, my effort will still make me feel better about myself.

In my spare time, when I'm not teaching or making license plates or working on the chain gang, I hope to learn to meditate better and rekindle the spark that had vanished from my life before my recent adventures began. Oddly enough, my experiences have made me more aware that I am, we all are, spiritual creatures. I realize that a prison cell may not be the ideal place for reigniting the soul. On the other hand, to paraphrase Frank Sinatra, if I can make it there, I can make it anywhere.

All afternoon, I'd been clearing my mind and opening myself to visions, as Natalia taught me on Padre Island. As I stared mindlessly at the horizon, I found myself thinking about jail. I wanted to imagine something positive about it, but it was very hard to do. Suddenly, the drawing of Socrates again flashed into my mind. It made me think about how so many of the figures I respect were willing to go to jail, and even risk death, for what they believed: Socrates, Antigone, Esther from the Bible, America's founding fathers and mothers, the righteous gentile men and women who hid Jews from the Nazis during the Holocaust, the Hollywood Ten, the founders of Israel, Gandhi, Martin Luther King, the Berrigan brothers, Armando Valladares, Irina Ratushinskaya, Vaclav Havel, Nelson Mandela. They made me think that being jailed will be a sort of initiation for me. Without killing me, it will allow me, in my own mind, to join the ranks those who truly possess the courage of their convictions. I can't say that I'm looking forward to being thus initiated, but I am determined to become a better, more fully actualized person for my experience.

In my reverie this afternoon, I realized that I've always questioned whether I am truly strong enough to sacrifice for what I believe in, if push comes to shove. Well, this year push has indeed become shove. Now, I am dispelling those doubts. I am living my values. I am accepting complete responsibility for who I am, what I believe, and what I have done, even though I will suffer for it. This very thought makes my self-esteem swell and my spirit lighten. I'd never recognized before how heavily these doubts hung down on me. But now I shall emerge from prison tested and proven, with my head held high. I will begin to join the ranks of the figures I most admire. If I can retain this perspective and keep a positive attitude, I know I'll survive and flourish.

Now, I'm just basking in these good feelings. I've been paying close attention to my senses, noticing the taste of the salt air and smell of the seaweed, the feel of the sand, hard against my red, white, and blue-striped beach blanket, and the waves of heat that break against my thighs and torso like the sea crashing upon the shore. I feel as though I am the center of a vast field of electromagnetic energy. I am being recharged by the sun, the ocean, and the wind, invigorated for my coming ordeal.

I turn my attention to my breathing as Tom taught me and feel my mind go blank. The ocean still grinds against the beach, the gulls still cry in the air, and the hot, humid breeze still caresses my cheek. But they fade into the background as I draw deep breaths, slowly inhaling, then slowly letting go.

I cease to be me; I merge with the energy that flows easily among the sun, ocean, sand, and sky. I can no longer tell where I end and they begin.

***

PIE-THROWER HOIST BY HIS OWN CUSTARD

Miami Beach, Florida–(AP) Professor Benjamin Branch, better known to the world as the costumed superhero and convicted killer Pie-thrower, received a taste of his own cream pie yesterday as he sunned himself on Miami Beach. Branch was enjoying his last day of freedom before surrendering today to begin a 3-10 year prison sentence for the pie-throwing that caused the death of anti-gay activist Marion Hines. But as Branch was preparing to leave, a group of masked teenagers led by an older man with long gray hair ran up to him, splattered his face with key lime and custard pies, and then scattered down the beach.

A man calling himself by the improbable name of Lift 'n' Separate has since claimed responsibility in a telephone call to the Howard Stern radio show.

Additional details remain sketchy, but when the pies struck him, Branch is reported to have laughed.